soul sisters

catherine robinson

Point

■SCHOLASTIC

Scholastic Children's Books,
Euston House, 24 Eversholt Street,
London, NW1 1DB, UK
A division of Scholastic Ltd
London ~ New York ~ Toronto ~ Sydney ~ Auckland
Mexico City ~ New Delhi ~ Hong Kong

First published in the UK by Scholastic Ltd, 2005

10 digit ISBN 0 439 97358 9
13 digit ISBN 978 0439 97358 8

Printed in the UK by CPI Bookmarque, Croydon, CR0 4TD

6 7 8 9 10

chapter one

Kitty knew it was Bella the moment she saw her, across the crowded college lobby. It was only her back view, surrounded by other people; she was taller, of course, and thinner, and the once-familiar cloud of dark hair was now shorter, and threaded through with multicoloured braids. In reality it could have been anybody, but Kitty knew with a rush of inexplicable inner certainty that it wasn't just anybody, it was Bella. Quite definitely. There was something about the way she was standing; some indefinable aura that emanated from her and wafted alluringly through the air.

"Just a sec," Kitty said to Rhys. "I'm just going to go and say hello to somebody." She gave his hand a quick squeeze, to show she wasn't deserting him, and as she pushed her way through the first-day-of-term crowds she felt a tiny stab of apprehension. What if Bella didn't recognize her, after all this time? What if, given how things had been when they last saw each other, she blanked Kitty? (Unlikely, but possible. Anything was possible with Bella.) Despite these thoughts, she couldn't seem to stop herself. She felt oddly impelled towards Bella, like a magnet towards its pole; apparently powerless to resist the attraction she emitted. Just like before; just as it had been in the beginning.

She tapped her on the shoulder and Bella spun round, mid-sentence, her face animated, her hands busily gesticulating to illustrate the point she was making.

"Hello, stranger," Kitty said, solemnly. She watched the other girl's face register a whole series of emotions – bewilderment, surprise, shock, wide-eyed amazement, all flitted briefly across Bella's face until delight replaced them all and she let out a whoop of pure joy.

"Kitty!" She dropped her bag on the floor and flung her arms around her. "Kitten! Flippin' heck, it really is you! Let me take a look at you!" She hugged her, then held her at arm's length, her face wreathed with smiles. "Wow, you look fantastic! How've you been? What've you been up to? Are you here too – what subjects are you doing? Oh my God, I can't believe it! It's just amazing – it's bloody *brilliant*!"

And she enfolded Kitty again, and Kitty hugged her back, trying to answer all Bella's questions but not able to get a word in edgeways, her uneasiness banished in the face of Bella's disarmingly delighted response. It seemed quite incredible that not only had they bumped into each other again after all these years, but that Bella's reaction at seeing her had been a total reflex, as instinctive as her own.

"So how long is it, exactly?" Rhys asked at lunchtime. They were sitting together in the college canteen; Rhys and Kitty, and Bella, and a lad Bella seemed to have hooked up with called Mal, or Cal, or something.

"Dunno. Must be, what? Four, five years?" Bella took a pack of Marlboro Lights from her bag, shook one out and lit it. "Sorry, does anybody else. . .?" She offered the pack around and Rhys took one, which surprised Kitty as he'd told her he had given up. She caught his eye.

"Ah, Kitty, don't," he groaned. "It's so hard to quit. . ."

"Nah, it isn't. I've done it hundreds of times." Bella flashed him a quick, supportive, fellow-smoker's grin.

Kitty knew exactly how long it had been since she and Bella last saw each other. Five years and three months. She could probably number the days, too, if pushed. The events leading up to that last meeting, things she thought she had forgotten about, came surging into her mind. She squashed them down, not wanting to take them out and examine them just yet.

3

"It must easily be five years," she said. "Easily."

Cal (or Mal) whistled. "Awesome," he said. "And you recognized each other, like, instantly? Totally awesome."

Bella gave a tiny little smile, so tiny that only Kitty could identify it as such. There was a minute pressing-together of the lips, a minuscule flaring of the nostrils. And her eyes. Blue as blue, they twinkled with barely concealed mischief. Kitty knew instantly what was going on in Bella's mind, that she was on the verge of doing one of her impersonations.

"It *was* awesome," Bella agreed gravely, but rather disappointingly in her own voice. "Totally."

"Totally," Kitty repeated, and had to drop her eyes away from Bella's because she knew she'd only start giggling, and Mal (or Cal) would suss that they were taking the piss. On the other hand, he deserved having the piss taken, with his naff surfer-dude speak. Most lads she knew had grown out of talking like that when they were about thirteen.

"Mind you," Bella went on, "she hasn't changed a bit. I'd have recognized her anywhere."

"Neither have you," Kitty told her. "Well, apart from your hair, of course." She stretched her arm across the table and flicked one of the rainbow-coloured braids. "And the pierced nose. You didn't have that when I last saw you. Oh, and the squint. That's new too."

"So's the artificial leg." Bella played along. "And the dentures have done wonders for my smile, don't you think?"

"Oh, absolutely. Call me catty, but the toothless look was never quite you, somehow."

They burst into cackles of laughter, and the two lads looked at each other, baffled.

"I think it'll be all right," Rhys said to Cal (or Mal) behind his hand, in a stage whisper, "if we ignore them. Just walk away slowly, and we'll be fine."

Kitty collected herself. "Sorry, guys. You'll have to excuse us."

"Yeah, sorry. You must think we're barking." Eyes shining, Bella leant over the table towards Kitty suddenly, and caught hold of her hands. "But oh, Kitty, it's so good to see you again."

Kitty felt suddenly slightly uncomfortable. She'd forgotten how touchy-feely Bella was. It had never fazed her before, when they were little. It must be something to do with the lads' presence, the way they were exchanging small but significant glances in that way males do in the face of what they perceive as female over-demonstrativeness. Rhys was looking at Mal – who was positively smirking – with one eyebrow half-raised in a knowing kind of way.

"Er, just how close were you two?" Cal asked now, with a suggestive leer.

Predictably, Bella was neither embarrassed nor fazed. She grasped Kitty's hands even tighter, leant even closer towards her and said, in a low husky voice: "Just about as close as it's possible to be. Isn't that right, babe? Oh, Kitty, hun, I've missed you so much." She gazed adoringly into Kitty's eyes for a full five seconds, then a bubble of mirth escaped from her lips. "Oh God, you two! Your faces!" She flung Kitty's hands aside, grabbed her cigarette from where it rested on the corrugated tin ashtray and took a long drag. "You thought I was serious, didn't you! I really had you going! You want to watch him, Kitten –" She indicated Rhys with her head. "He was getting really excited there for a moment at the thought of some girl-on-girl action."

She exhaled the smoke through her nostrils, still laughing, and Rhys blushed scarlet and grinned and put his head in his hands and denied any such thing. Kitty watched him with astonishment; she'd never seen him like this before, all coy and bashful. It was the Bella factor. She always did have this effect on people, making them do unexpected things. Kitty wasn't sure that she herself would have teased somebody else's boyfriend quite so familiarly only moments after meeting him for the first time, but Bella had never had any such qualms. Kitty had envied Bella her boldness when they were kids, her fearlessness in just coming right out with what she thought, and stuff what anybody else made of her.

Still laughing, Bella mashed out her cigarette in the ashtray. "So what are you doing here, hun? I'd have thought you were a dead cert for staying on at school for A-levels."

"I couldn't do the courses I wanted."

"Which are?"

"English, Drama, History, Philosophy."

"Four? Wow. Clever thing." She looked at the boys, and twisted her lips ruefully. "She always was the smart one. Not like yours truly. Class dunce – that's me."

"Don't be daft. You're here too, aren't you?"

"Yeah, but –" She shrugged. "I'm not doing A-levels. You're not allowed to, when you majorly foul up your GCSEs."

"So what're you doing? Re-sits?" Rhys asked her.

She turned to him. "No way. Far too academic for me. No, I'm doing a Leisure and Tourism diploma." She lit another cigarette. "It keeps me off the streets, at any rate."

There were a million questions thronging Kitty's brain. Such as, why did you foul up your GCSEs, and where did you do them, anyway?

Such as, where did you actually go when you left Penllan five years ago, and did you ever give me another moment's thought, and have you seen Megan yet, and—

"Is Megan here too?" Bella said, suddenly, and a weird tingle passed up Kitty's spine. That was something else she'd forgotten, the way Bella almost appeared to read her mind at times.

"She is, yeah."

"Ah! I might have known. Is that because the old dump didn't do *her* courses, either, or because she couldn't bear to be parted from you?"

Kitty glanced at her, sharply, but Bella was still smiling, grinning wickedly at her through the cloud of smoke she'd just exhaled. "A bit of both, I guess," she confessed.

"You know Megan too?" Rhys asked Bella.

"I did, yeah. Haven't seen her for years, though. I was fostered by her parents when I used to live round here."

"Yeah? You know, Kitty and Megan were joined at the hip when I first knew them," he told her. "Like Siamese twins. I thought I was never going to get Kitty by herself for long enough to have a crack at her – I thought I'd have to give up on the idea, or else invite them both out on a date."

"That's just what we were like." Bella's face took on a pensive, faraway look. "When we were kids. Joined at the hip. That's exactly what your dad always said about us, do you remember?"

"I remember."

She and Kitty looked at each other for a long moment, each lost in her own memories of the past. Then Mal pushed back his chair noisily, and stood up.

"Gotta go," he said. "Time for class. Will I catch you later, babe?"

Bella looked at her watch. "Is that the time already? Hang on – I'm coming too." She stood up and stretched luxuriously, like a cat. Collected her things together, dropped her cigarettes and lighter into her bag. She had this way of dominating the space she occupied, a star-like quality that wasn't lost on three lads sitting together near the door, who were watching her with frank interest. Unaware she had an audience, she put a hand on Kitty's shoulder. "Are you doing anything later? Only we've barely had chance to say hello."

"Erm. . ." Kitty played for time, not sure that hooking up with Bella later was such a good idea. It had been so long; could they really just take up again where they had left off, as Bella seemed to be assuming? Kitty looked at Rhys, half-hoping he would help out by claiming that they had a date that evening, but he just shrugged, leaving her to make her own decision.

"I think I'm free," she told Bella.

"Fantastic! I'll see you outside the main

9

entrance then, shall I? Say, about five?" Bella threw her bag over her shoulder and sashayed off, Mal's arm draped proudly across her shoulders as if she were a prize he'd won. Kitty watched them go, all the way down the length of the canteen and through the door, then turned back to Rhys.

"Don't you mind me seeing her tonight, then?"

"Mind?" He raised a quizzical eyebrow. "Why should I mind? I thought you'd be wanting to see her instead."

"Well, yes, I do, but. . ." Kitty trailed off. It was a complicated situation; far too complicated to explain to Rhys in the few moments remaining before afternoon classes began.

"I just thought – you know. That you were pleased to see her again. It's not every day an old friend comes back into your life after five years, is it?"

"I was pleased to see her again. I *am* pleased." She corrected herself. "It's just –" Back they came again, a whole host of memories flocking through Kitty's brain; things that had been buried and forgotten – her and Bella, Megan, Bruno, Sadie Williams and her gang – all kinds of little half-remembered snippets of things began to run through her head like a video on fast-forward.

"It's just. . .?" Rhys leaned forward and snapped his fingers in front of her face. "Hello? Earth to Kitty? You receiving me?"

10

"Sorry." She smiled, gave herself a little shake. "I was going to say, it's just that we *were* close when we were little, really close, but things weren't brilliant between us at the end. When she moved away."

"Did you have a fight?"

"No, nothing like that. We never fell out, as such. But it all started to change once we started at Brynglas."

"How come?"

"Oh, you know how it is. I suppose –" She dredged her memory, thinking for the first time since it happened about just *how* it had happened, why the glue that had bound them together so closely at primary school had become unstuck once they reached secondary school. "I suppose we just began to grow apart. She started getting into stuff I wasn't interested in. Made some dodgy friends, that kind of thing. And then at the end of the first year she moved away altogether, and that was that."

"Yeah? I'd never have thought you two had parted as anything other than best buddies, seeing you together just now."

"I know." Kitty pressed her lips together wryly. "That's Bella for you. She's so full-on – always was. You just find yourself carried along with her, kind of caught up in the force of her personality."

"So don't see her, then, if you don't want to."

"It's not that I don't want to. Not as such." She sighed. "It's complicated. I'm just not sure it's such a good idea to go back and try to recapture what we had. Fact is, we're not little kids any more. So what did you think of her?" she asked him, suddenly.

"Of Bella?" He considered the question carefully. It was typical Rhys. He was intending to be a lawyer after college and then university, and he never divulged his opinions without considering all angles first. It was what Kitty had first noticed about him, his grave weighing-up of all possible standpoints. She found it very attractive. It made him seem much more mature than most of the other lads at college. Of course, the fact he was a total babe helped, too. "She's very – *theatrical*."

Kitty laughed. "Yup. That's Bella. Don't you think she's beautiful?"

"How do I answer that?" Rhys looked at her, and scratched his head. "I'm dead if I say yes, and dead if I say no."

"When I was little I used to think she was the most beautiful girl I'd ever seen. Like a princess in a fairy tale. Don't you think she has the most amazing eyes?"

"She's not really my type, to be honest. But yeah – she's attractive, I can see that."

"Oh, she's that, all right." The thought passed

through Kitty's mind, briefly, that maybe Bella was a bit too attractive for her own good.

"You'll never guess what," she said to Megan, in History.

"Bella Jones is back," Megan replied.

"Who told you?" Kitty's face fell. She couldn't help feeling crestfallen that her tasty titbit of gossip had been pre-empted.

"Nobody. I saw her this morning, in the lobby. And then sitting with you guys at lunchtime."

"Why didn't you come and say hi?"

Megan gave a small snort. "Are you kidding? After the stunts she pulled?"

"Actually, I meant say hi to me," Kitty said gently. "It was a long time ago. She was just a kid. We all were. She just went off the rails a bit."

"If you say so." Megan's voice was grim. "You didn't have to put up with living with her. So do I take it that, now the prodigal has returned, she's going to be your new best friend?"

"Hardly." Kitty tried to sound reassuring rather than defensive. "But OK, I was pleased to see her. I admit it. We were mates, Megan – when we were little, before all the shit happened. In fact, once upon a time the three of us were all mates together."

"She was always your friend, not mine."

"She did live with you for five years."

"My parents fostered her. That didn't make her my friend. Oh, I don't know." The tutor entered the room, and Megan bent down to her bag and retrieved her History folder. "It's no big deal. It's not an issue any more, is it – what happened when we were kids. Bella moved away, and now she's back again. End of."

Except it wasn't. Kitty could see that by the set of Megan's mouth as she leafed through the folder to find her holiday assignment.

"It's OK," Kitty whispered to her, as the tutor came along the aisle to collect all the assignments. "It's not going to change anything. You and I are still friends too, you know. You and I'll always be mates," and was aware of sounding exactly the way she had when Bella was last around, when they were all twelve years old.

Despite her earlier reservations, Kitty went back after college with Bella to where she was currently living, which turned out to be the top floor of a gracious three-storey Edwardian villa only twenty minutes' walk from college.

"Wow!" Kitty exclaimed, standing on the threshold, as Bella fumbled with the key and then threw open the door with a flourish. "God, this is amazing! How come I'm still shacking up with my parents and the world's worst little brother, and you're living in a place like this?"

"It's wicked, isn't it? Although it's only tiny, really – just this room, and a bedroom and shower room. It's my aunt's house. Well, great-aunt's, really, only she doesn't like me calling her that. Says it makes her feel old."

"I didn't know you had a great-aunt."

"*I* didn't even know I had one until a few months ago." Bella grinned. "Do you know how totally fab it is to see you again? I was going to try and tell you I was back – come round, or ring or something. But I didn't know if you were still living in the same place. And – well, to be honest, I wasn't sure whether you'd want to see me again."

There was a small pause.

"When I saw you at college this morning. I almost didn't come over to say hi," Kitty admitted.

"You're joking!" Bella goggled at her.

"Well, we didn't exactly part on the best of terms, did we."

"That was just circumstances, though, wasn't it? I went through that Killer Pre-Teen From Hell phase." Bella pulled a mad, scowling face, and Kitty couldn't help smiling. "I'm not surprised you didn't want much to do with me then – I didn't like myself much, if you want to know the truth. But before that – we used to be soul sisters, remember?"

"So why didn't you answer my letter?" Kitty was aware of how accusing she sounded, but couldn't help it. She remembered how crushed her twelve-year-old self had felt at the time, how her carefully penned words that had taken her days to get right had been met with a silence that had been as total as it was telling. Or so she'd assumed.

"Letter?" Bella looked baffled. "What letter?"

"I wrote to you in the holidays. The summer holidays after you left."

"Where did you send it?"

"I gave it to Megan's mum, she said she'd pass it on."

"I never got any letter. I'd have answered it if I had."

"Even if it had said good riddance and I hope I never see you again in my life?"

"Did it say that?" Bella stood very still. She looked suddenly vulnerable and fragile, as if she might break into small pieces if she made any sudden movements. Kitty felt a pang of pity for her. As she herself had reminded Megan just a few hours ago, they had only been kids.

"Of course not," she admitted, softly. "I'd never have said that to you. I just said something like, I still want to be your friend, let's keep in touch."

"And we never did," Bella said, mournfully.

"No. We never did."

"But you do believe me, don't you, Kitten? That I never got your letter?"

Kitty looked at her for a long moment. "I believe you," she said, eventually. "But, you know, it's been a long time. Things change – people change. They move on."

"Not us," Bella declared. "I was so pleased to see you earlier, I just can't tell you. It's like we were meant to find each other again. It's like this is a new start for our friendship. Don't you think?"

Her blue eyes looked anxious, despite the positive note her voice held. Kitty felt as if she was being mean and grudging, making Bella plead for them to be friends again.

"Yeah," she said. "It is."

"Cool!" Bella grinned. "So – what would you like? Tea, coffee? Herb tea?" She strode through the sitting room to the galley kitchen at the far end, and stuck her head in the fridge. "I think I might even have a couple of cans in here. Ah, even better!" She withdrew her head triumphantly, a half-full bottle of white wine with the cork shoved back in dangling between her fingers. "Glass of vino?"

"Coffee's fine."

"Coffee it is, then. Coming right up."

Kitty plonked herself down on a cream-coloured sofa with an amethyst velvet throw draped across its back while Bella bustled around in the kitchen. When the coffee was made she carried it across the room and put it down on a table in front of the sofa. "There you go. Half a sugar, right?"

"You remember how I like my coffee, after all this time?" Kitty was touched. "I'm not sure I remember how you take yours."

Bella smiled at Kitty. "I remember when you started cutting down on the sugar."

"So do I," Kitty said, with a laugh. "You used to tease me about having fifteen grains."

"God, did I? I'd forgotten about that. Ah, them were the days," she said, in a mad country-yokel voice, then picked up her mug and held it aloft, in a toast. "Here's to the past! No, on second thoughts, sod the past – let's drink to the future!" They clinked mugs, solemnly.

"To the future."

Their eyes met, and there was a moment of silence. The past seemed so long ago – a different world. Kitty's own life had changed immeasurably since those days – *she* had changed, so much so she was practically a different person.

She reached for the biscuits. "So go on, then. Tell me what you're doing living here."

"I'm, er, going to college." Bella took a sip of coffee, her eyes innocently wide.

"You know what I mean. Where did the great-aunt spring from?"

"And why didn't I live with her when I was little instead of being fostered out with Megan's parents?" Bella added, with an air of finishing the sentence for her.

Kitty blinked. That hadn't occurred to her. "Well, yes. Now you come to mention it. Why didn't you?"

"Because neither of us knew of each other's existence then. My mother and grandmother had fallen out, years ago, and Aunt Susan – she's my grandmother's sister – had totally lost contact with my mother. She didn't even know that my mother had a child, let alone that I was being fostered." Bella took a biscuit and regarded it carefully, as if assessing its quality. "It all happened fairly recently. Through my mother, as it happens. My grandmother had contacted her just before she died – you know, big deathbed reunion kind of thing. I always thought that sort of carry-on only happened in Victorian novels. Anyway, after Grandmother died Aunt Susan was suddenly in the picture, and when she found out I was starting at college she got in touch with me and said I could stay here, if I wanted to." She indicated the room with her head. "It used to be her flat – her parents owned the house originally, and they did it up for her to live in. She never married, apparently; she lived here all her life and then nursed them for years when they were old."

"That was kind of her."

"I suppose there was nobody else to do it."

"No, I mean to let you come and live here."

"Oh yeah, she's all heart." Bella snapped off an oval of her biscuit with strong white teeth and grinned through the crumbs. "Don't be fooled – I reckon she's only doing it for the money."

"Money?"

"Yeah. She gets a whole wad of allowances for having me here."

"Even so." Kitty looked around the flat with approval. "It must be cool to be independent. Not to mention having somewhere you can be alone with the Cals of this world," she added, mischievously, "without parents breathing down your neck."

"Who?" Bella looked blank.

"That lad you were with at lunchtime. Cal, Mal – what was his name?"

"Oh, him! Mel. Actually, I think he could become a bit of a nightmare – he attached himself to me all day and looked majorly put-out when I told him no, he couldn't walk me home because I was meeting you." She shrugged. "Being independent is OK, but I miss company sometimes. A bit of a family life – you know. Aunt Susan's pretty hands-off."

"Lucky you!" Kitty pulled a face. "I wish my parents were. I sometimes think I'll scream if they ask me one more time where I'm going, or what time I'll be back."

"They care about you. Don't knock it," Bella said, and her voice sounded wistful. Kitty could understand it, after years of being fostered. She did wonder how Bella would feel if it was her on the receiving end of the endless parental fussing and questioning, though. A definite case of the grass being greener on the other side.

"So do you see much of your mother these days?" she asked.

"Not much," Bella answered, shortly. She got up from the sofa. "D'you want another coffee?"

"Please." Kitty held out her empty mug. So her mother still wasn't up for discussion. She had wondered, when she'd seen Bella standing in the lobby that morning, whether there might have been some kind of reconcilement now Bella was older, more self-reliant, but that clearly hadn't happened.

"Wait till I tell Bruno you're back," she said. "He's not going to believe it."

Bella turned from the kitchen counter, the corners of her mouth curved up into a smile. "He's not at college too, is he?"

"No, university. Second year. He's doing law. Like Rhys wants to, funnily enough."

"*Second* year?" Bella looked puzzled for a moment. "Oh, right. Of course he is. I'm a year out."

"How come?"

"Because. . ." Bella turned back to the counter, busied herself with the kettle. "Because, like I told you earlier, I messed up my GCSEs."

"So what did you do with yourself last year?"

"Oh, stuff. You know. This and that. Attempted to decide what I wanted to do with my life, mostly. Did a bit of growing up, as I daresay Aunt Susan would put it." She turned round with the fresh mugs of coffee. "I'll tell you something, though – meeting up with you again today has got to be one of the best things that's happened to me recently. It's like an omen; like, my life is going to start getting better from now on. And you know what?"

"What?"

"We've got a hell of a lot of lost time to make up for!" Kitty ignored another slight twinge of misgiving as Bella beamed from ear to ear. She was quite clearly thrilled that they had met up again; surely they could both put the past behind them – or at least the bit leading up to where they parted the last time – and concentrate on building a new, more grown-up relationship? Surely that would be possible.

chapter *two*

It was Bruno Kitty told first, texting him the next day with just two words: *Bella's back*. But as she pressed Send she felt slightly foolish, with a feeling that she was being childishly eager and enthusiastic. She fully expected Bruno to text back in typical smart-arse fashion – *So?*; *Wots up wth Bellas bck?*; or even *Whos Bella?* – but her mobile rang almost as soon as these thoughts passed through her head.

"So where's she been, then?" It was Bruno. Of course.

"Aren't you supposed to be in a lecture, or something?"

"We don't have lectures all the time. It's not like school, you know."

"Of course I know." It was a continual source of annoyance to Kitty that her cousin, who had just eighteen months on her, never ceased to grasp any opportunity to rub in the fact that he was older and therefore, presumably, vastly more sophisticated and experienced. Or something. "I'm not at school either. In case it had escaped your attention."

"A-levels," he said, dismissively. "Not the same."

"Well, no. Of course it isn't. I mean to say, everyone knows you university students are all slogging away the whole time on cures for cancer and saving the planet and stuff. How can mere A-levels possibly compete in importance?"

"Well, they can't, can they? Anyway, aren't you supposed to be, as well?"

"Supposed to be what?"

"In a lesson. Or whatever."

"It's lunchtime."

"So it is. Better take myself off to the chippie, then."

"The *chippie*? You waste your money on going to the chippie? I thought you were in a house this year? Self-catering, your mum said. Why can't you make yourself some beans on toast, or a nice nutritious Pot Noodle?" She clicked her tongue disapprovingly. "Honestly. I thought students were supposed to be poor, now they've—"

"Kitty," he cut across her. "Much as I'd love to have a chat with you about my catering arrangements, this is costing me 50p a minute. Are you going to tell me about Bella, or not?"

"Yes. Right. OK," she said. "Well, what can I say? She's back."

"Ri-ight." He waited for her to continue, and when she didn't he said: "Is that it? She's back? So where's she been – on a world cruise? Discovering

24

herself on a Gujarati ashram? Abducted by aliens?"

"What's a Gujarati ashram?"

He ignored her. "I mean, she's been gone for years. Are you telling me she's strolled back to Penllan without any explanation of where she's been or what she's been doing?"

"Pretty much, yeah." There was a small silence while they both digested this. "You know Bella. She always did work on a needs-to-know basis. Anyway, she's back."

"Don't you think it's a bit odd?"

"What, that she's back?"

"No, that she's not filled you in on what's happened in the meantime."

"Not really."

"Ooh, Catrin Doyle, you big fat liar!" he said, in a silly voice that was presumably intended to sound girly. "I bet you're dying to find out all the goss. And if you're not, I bet Megan is," he added.

"Megan's not that bothered," Kitty told him. "She was dead sniffy about it, actually."

"Well that's hardly surprising, is it? You three weren't exactly all bosom buddies back in the Good Old Days."

"We got on OK," Kitty protested. "We were always hanging out together to start with; it was only later on it went pear-shaped."

"As I recall, it was mainly you and Bella, with Megan tagging along behind. You only ever saw her by herself when Bella wasn't available. I used to feel quite sorry for her."

"Did you?" Kitty started to feel sorry for Megan herself. "Was I that bad? I never realized you took that much notice."

"I didn't. It's just a general observation. Anyway, I guess it'll be interesting to see Bella again. See how she's changed."

"D'you want her number? I've got it here somewhere." She tucked her phone under her chin and began to dig around in her bag, but Bruno was making dissenting noises in her ear.

"No, no. Don't worry. She won't want to be hearing from me – it's not as if we were particularly mates, after all."

"Yes she will. She was asking after you."

"Probably just being polite."

"No she wasn't. When was Bella ever polite?" Kitty sighed. "Bruno, what are you like? You've just said you'd like to see her again."

"Well, yeah. But only out of curiosity. I'm not going to ring her, though."

"OK – send her a text."

"No."

"Why not?"

"Because she'll think I'm cracking on to her."

It was preposterous. Kitty laughed merrily. "No she won't! Why would she?"

"Because," Bruno said darkly, his voice full of

meaning even across the airwaves from Manchester, "it's what girls think when guys contact them out of the blue. Guys trying to pick them up – it's what they expect. Even when they're not," he added, ungrammatically.

"Well now. Isn't that a grand piece of news," Kitty's father said, when she told them of Bella's return at supper that evening. "How is she?"

"She's fine."

"Did I hear what I thought I heard?" Mum came into the room carrying a bowl of pasta. "Bella Jones is back?"

"Yeah. She was at college yesterday."

"I bet that gave you a surprise."

"Sure did. It's funny, though – I knew it was her immediately, even though we hadn't seen each other for years."

Mum put the dish on the table. "So where's she living now? Not back with the Robertses, surely?"

"No – she's staying with some long-lost aunt. Quite near college, as it happens."

"That's handy. Mike, I thought I asked you to call Owen down?" She went to the door to the hallway and yelled up the stairs. "*Owen!* Supper's ready. Oh, where is that boy? *OWEN!*"

Kitty and her father looked at each other, and Dad put his little finger in his ear and waggled it, meaningfully.

"You know where he is." Kitty picked a radish out of the salad bowl on the table, looked at it, shrugged, and put it in her mouth. "Where he always is, when he's not at school or asleep. Upstairs, kicking assorted aliens' butts."

"Such nice Christian pursuits our children follow," Dad murmured, and dug the serving spoon into the pasta. "Well, my darlings, I'm starting, before my stomach thinks my throat's been cut."

"Hey, enough of the children," Kitty complained. "A) I'm not a child, and B) I don't spend all my waking moments playing lame computer games."

"*OWEN! Get off that computer and come downstairs! Now!*" Mum sat down at the table, demurely. "How I love these quiet, intimate little family suppers. Now then. You were telling us about Bella."

"Who's Bella?" Owen came roaring down the stairs and into the dining room. His broad, freckled face was smeared with olive green and khaki paint. Kitty stared at him for a full ten seconds.

"Oh. My. God," she said. She turned to Mum. "Sorry, I was wrong. He wasn't kicking aliens' butts, he was being a commando. All by himself. Sad little person that he is," she added.

"Shut yer face, ho'," Owen growled from the

side of his mouth, in a spectacularly bad American accent. He leant across the table and peered into the dish of pasta. "Bleugh. Macaroni cheese. Cess."

"Don't speak to your sister like that," Mum told him, sternly. "And it's not macaroni cheese, it's spaghetti carbonara."

"You might go and wash your face," Dad said, through a mouthful.

"Oh, for heaven's sake, no. Let's all just eat, shall we? Before it gets any colder." Mum pushed the pasta bowl pointedly towards Owen, who helped himself to a massive plateful.

"Meantime," Kitty said pointedly, "back to Bella. . ."

"So who is this Bella dude?" Owen asked, cheese sauce dripping down his chin and mingling fetchingly with the camo face paint.

"*Dude?* She's not a dude. Girls can't be dudes."

"Whatever. Who is she?"

"A friend of mine. She used to think you were fab when you were little, for some bizarre reason."

Owen shrugged, modestly. "Good taste," he said, and forked another heap of food into his mouth. "I don't remember anyone called Bella."

"She moved away when you were small," Mum told him.

"How small?"

"Oh, I don't know – four or five, I suppose."

"Don't you remember her at all?" Kitty asked him.

"Nope." He shook his head, chewing enthusiastically. "Why did she leave?"

"People do move away from time to time," Kitty told him, peevishly. She certainly wasn't going to go over all the ins-and-outs over the supper table with *him*. "The world doesn't begin and end in Penllan, you know."

"And now she's just started at Kitty's college," Dad said. "Do you know, when you were small, Bella used to push you round in your pushchair and pretend you were her little brother."

"You never know, play your cards right and maybe you could persuade her to do it again," Kitty said drily.

"Shad-*uuuup*," Owen complained, overcome with mortification at the thought of his mature ten-year-old self being pushed around in a pushchair.

"So will you be chumming up again, d'you think?" Mum asked her. "Maybe you've both changed too much for you still to be friends after all this time."

"I think we will." Kitty fiddled with her fork. "I wasn't sure yesterday – I kept thinking about how she left, you know, all the stuff she got into. I wondered whether we could ever be mates again after all that. But then when I got talking to her, it was weird – it was as if all that had never happened. It was just like going back to when we first knew each other."

"That's nice." Dad smiled. "She always did have that irresistible charm. I never knew two friends as close as you when you were small. Joined at the hip, you were. Totally inseparable."

It was true; they had been. Kitty had sensed something special about Bella, something different, from the moment she met her.

The girl has been hanging around for ages. Kitty first saw her through the open French windows when Mummy was cooking lunch – roast lamb with mint sauce, Kitty's absolute favourite Sunday dinner – and she is still there now. Earlier, Kitty kept seeing bits of her through the hedge, disappearing and then reappearing, as she was running up and down the lane. Now, she is crouched down right in front of the garden gate. Cushion is rolling around in a patch of sunshine on the path just inside the gate, and the girl is talking to him.

"May I get down now?" Kitty asks Mummy.

"All right then, *cariad*. Put your sandals on if you're going in the garden," she calls after Kitty.

Kitty goes out of the back door, and creeps stealthily round the side of the house. She stands under the chestnut tree and watches the girl for a few moments, hidden in the shadows cast by the big leafy branches. Heinz bounds after her, barking, and for a moment she thinks he has given the game away and the girl has seen her. She is holding a long twig which she is poking through the bars of the garden gate, trying to get Cushion to play with it, and she suddenly glances up. She is about Kitty's own age, and very pretty, pretty as a princess, with long tangled dark hair and a sort of pointy chin. She reminds Kitty of someone on the telly, but she can't remember her name.

The girl bends her head again and pushes the stick further through the gate, waggling it about. Cushion pounces on it suddenly, taking her by surprise and making her giggle. The sound makes Kitty move out from her hiding place and along the garden path towards the gate, although she doesn't know why. She'd intended to stay where she was, watching this unknown girl.

The girl looks up and smiles as Kitty approaches. Close up, she has dimples, and the bluest eyes Kitty has ever seen. It looks as if her eyes are reflecting the cloudless August sky, just like the sea does on such a day.

"That your cat?" the girl asks, still crouching, and indicates Cushion with the twig.

"Yes," Kitty says. "He's called Cushion."

"That your dog?" Heinz is jumping around Kitty's legs with excitement.

"Yes."

"Can I take him for a walk?"

Kitty frowns. "I don't know." She can hear a clatter from round the side of the house which means Daddy is getting the lawnmower out of the tool shed.

"Go on. He really likes me – look." She stands up and sticks her hand over the gate, and Heinz puts his paws on top of the gate and licks it. Then she puts her face down to his, and his tongue comes out and licks her right across her mouth. Kitty laughs, although she can't help feeling rather shocked too. She is never allowed to let Heinz lick her face. Mummy says she might get germs. "Look – he's kissing me!"

The other girl laughs too, and Daddy comes across the lawn towards them, pushing the lawnmower.

"Hello," he says, and smiles. "Who's this?" he asks Kitty.

The girl doesn't say who she is, but instead says: "Can I take your dog for a walk?"

"Oh, I don't know about that!" Daddy smiles. "He'd pull you over soon as look at you, that one! He's very strong."

"What's he called?"

"His name's Heinz." Hearing his name, Heinz

takes his front paws down from the gate and starts wagging round Daddy's legs. The girl laughs with glee.

"That's a funny name!"

"We call him Heinz because he's a mongrel. A bit of a Heinz, do you see? Fifty-seven varieties?" The girl's face is blank. Kitty thought everybody knew that old joke, from the front of the tins of baked beans. Maybe this girl – whoever she is – doesn't eat baked beans, although Kitty feels pretty sure she's had some very recently, judging by the marks on the front of her T-shirt.

"Wish I had a dog." Her voice sounds wistful, and her face looks sad.

"You like dogs, do you?"

"Not just dogs. All animals. I had a horse once, where I used to live."

A horse! Kitty is filled with envy. She is desperate for a horse; her dreams are full of them, galloping along the beach with ribbons in their manes, and her on their backs.

"Did you, now?" Daddy puts his hand on the latch of the gate, and opens it. "Kitty, dear, where's your manners? Are you going to ask your friend into the garden to play, or is she to stay out here in the lane all afternoon?"

Kitty opens her mouth to say *she's not my friend, I don't know her,* but somehow what comes out is: "D'you want to come and play, then?"

"That your dad?" the girl asks her, once he has gone back to the lawnmower.

"Yes. He's called Michael." She thinks she'll get that one out of the way, before she's asked.

"He talks funny."

Kitty looks hard at her, to see if she is being rude, but she doesn't seem to be. She smiles at Kitty, showing the dimples in her cheeks.

"What do you mean?"

"It's a nice sort of funny. I like it."

"He's Irish."

"What's that?"

"Irish. From Ireland." Kitty can't believe she doesn't know what Irish is. "Haven't you heard of Ireland?"

"Course I have. I've been there." She bends down to rub Heinz's tummy, and as she does so she says: "We call him Heinz because he's a mongrel." Only she doesn't say it in her own voice but in Daddy's. It's odd, but really funny too. Kitty bursts out laughing.

"Say it again!"

But she won't, she just grins at Kitty and says, "What's your name, then?"

"Catrin."

"Your dad called you Kitty."

"Kitty's short for Catrin."

The girl grins again. "I'm Bella."

"Are you on holiday?"

35

"Nope. I've just come to live here. Down there somewhere." She waves a vague hand towards the lane. "S'nice here, isn't it? I like your garden, it's wicked." She turns her head, her eye caught by something in the chestnut tree. "Is that a tree house? *Wicked!*"

Bella is really nice, Kitty decides as they play together in the tree house. She's always wanted a sister to play with; she'd been disappointed when Owen was born and he'd been a boy. She can hear him now, wailing, his cries drifting out through the open window of his room. Bella hears it too; she stops in the middle of what she's doing, which is pouring out make-believe tea from the dolls' teapot and into the dolls' teacups that Kitty keeps in the tree house, and seems to sniff the air exactly like Heinz does when he hears a suspicious sound. Kitty half-expects her to cock her ears, too.

"What's that noise?"

"It's Owen. My baby brother."

"You got a baby? Cool. Can I see him?"

"I'm not sure. He's only just woken up. . ."

But she is talking to thin air, because Bella has shinned down the rope ladder and is gone, running across the lawn to the house. When Kitty catches up with her she is standing by the kitchen door, talking to Daddy.

". . .see him later," he is explaining. "Kitty's

36

mum will be feeding him just now, you see." He looks up as Kitty comes over. "Would your friend like to stay for tea?"

"Oh, yes!" Bella exclaims, her eyes shining. "Can I?"

"Can she?" Kitty says, and then, "I mean, may she?"

Daddy laughs. "Sure she can! Is there somebody you should be ringing, now, just to check it's all right?"

Bella shakes her head, firmly. "No."

"Are you sure? Won't your mammy be wondering where you've got to? You've been here all afternoon."

"She won't be worrying. It's all right, honestly." She lifts her head and looks him right in the eye. "Honestly."

"Oh, please let her stay," Kitty pleads. "Please, Daddy! It'll be –" what was the word Bella had used? – "It'll be wicked!"

He laughs again. "It's only tea, not a five-course banquet! Although I happen to know there were some scones baked this morning."

"I know. I smelt them."

"Go on, the pair of you. Go and see what you can find, and bring it all out here. We'll have tea out here on the patio, just as soon as Mummy comes down with the baby."

"There's some clotted cream in the fridge,"

Kitty tells Bella, confidentially, as Daddy goes to put the lawnmower away. "I saw it earlier. Do you like scones and cream?"

"Mmm," Bella says, smacking her lips. She links her arm through Kitty's as they walk into the house together. "You know something? You're going to be my bestest friend ever."

Kitty and Bella arranged to meet up on Friday evening in a pub close to college. When Kitty arrived Bella was already there, sitting at a window table nursing a bottle of lager. She jumped up when Kitty arrived and hugged her warmly.

"Hi!"

"Hi, Bella. Am I late? Sorry."

"It's OK – I was early. Do you want a drink?"

"Just an orange juice, thanks."

Bella came back from the bar carrying the orange juice and two packets of crisps. She handed the drink to Kitty, then sat down opposite her and tore open the nearest crisp packet. "I'm starving. I'd forgotten how knackering it is, having to concentrate all day."

"So how's the course going?"

"Oh, OK. If you can tell in a week. I'd hoped you and I might be able to see a bit more of each other at college, though. I thought we'd at least be able to have lunch together – I hadn't realized there were different sittings." Bella pulled a face, mock-mournful. "It was the only bright spot about going back to school, when I found out you were there. I thought we'd be hanging out together again."

Somehow, Kitty couldn't buy into the idea of Bella as Billy No-Mates, drooping disconsolately around college with nobody to talk to. It just wasn't her – not unless she'd had a personality transplant since she last saw her. "I'm sure we'll still be able to do that. Cheers!" She picked up her drink and took a sip.

"Cheers. Doesn't your boyfriend mind?"

"Mind what?"

"You seeing me tonight instead of him. I thought he looked a bit – you know. Sniffy. When I suggested we might hook up that first day after college."

"Rhys? Did he?" If he did, Kitty hadn't noticed. "No, he understands we've got a lot to catch up on."

"That's OK, then. So tell me about him." Bella took her cigarettes from her bag and lit one. "How long have you two been together?"

"Nearly a year. We met up at college – he decided to do his A-levels there rather than at his school. Luckily for me." Kitty grinned, and indicated Bella's empty bottle. "Want another?"

"I'd better not, thanks. I've got to be going in a mo."

"Have you?" When they'd arranged to meet, Kitty had assumed they were going to spend the rest of the evening together. "What are you up to, then?"

"Nothing very exciting. Just something that's cropped up, that's all." Bella looked at her watch. "Oh, go on then – I'll have another quick one. Keep you company."

Kitty wondered idly, as she stood waiting to be served, just what Bella had to get back for. Of course, she thought, as she pocketed her change and picked up the drinks, she could always just ask Bella what she was doing. But she dismissed the idea as soon as it occurred to her. *It'd sound as if I was checking up on her. Anyway, we only arranged to meet up for a drink. Why shouldn't she be doing something else afterwards? She's a free agent.*

She took the bottle over to their table. Bella looked up at Kitty and grinned widely, exhaling a cloud of smoke. "Thanks hun. Well, isn't this just so cool. I still can't get over bumping into you the other day."

"I know. You must come over some time and see my parents – they'd really like to see you."

"I'd like to see them too. They were great to me when I was little. I really loved them. D'you know –" She gave a little laugh. "D'you know, I used to have this fantasy, that they adopted me and became my parents, and you became my sister. Daft, isn't it!"

"It's not daft at all. Although we'd have probably been tearing each other's hair out if we'd had to live with each other, if me and Owen are anything to go by!" Kitty leant across and took a crisp. "But then, he's just a pain in the bum."

"Whereas I was all sweetness and light." Something in Bella's tone made Kitty look at her quizzically.

"How d'you mean?"

"I used to be a right cow," she said, unexpectedly.

Kitty was taken aback. "What makes you say that?"

"I've been thinking of how horrible I used to be to Megan. You know – not letting her join in with our little games. Shutting her out. I was *so* jealous of her being your friend first, you wouldn't believe it. I wanted you all to myself, I suppose."

It was pretty much what Bruno had said. Kitty had never really given it much thought at the time, it was just the relationship that had developed between the three of them.

"But you lived with her. If anyone was like your sister, it was her. I was jealous of that."

"Her parents fostered me, that was all. I was never close to Megan. Do you remember how you and me used to have that thing, that we were twins separated at birth? I really wanted it to be true, you know? I wanted to be your sister."

"Where did you go?" Kitty asked Bella suddenly.

Bella pulled a comically exaggerated quizzical face and said, "Sorry?"

"When you left. Where did you go?"

Bella looked down at her lager bottle and moved it an inch to the right, her smile fading. "Away."

"I know away. But where?" Kitty persisted.

"Just away. Does it matter?" Bella said. Her voice was quiet and controlled, but Kitty knew she had touched a nerve.

"No," she conceded; then, "Sorry."

"No look, I'm sorry." Bella moved the bottle back to its original spot, then picked it up and looked at Kitty over the top of it. "It's a fair question. I can't really expect to come swanning back after five years away and not expect to be asked, can I?"

"You don't have to answer though. Not if you don't want to. Not if it's – painful."

"It's not painful." Bella tipped the remainder of the lager down her throat. "I just don't particularly want to drag up stuff from the past. I went to live with a different foster family, that's all. Things got difficult with Megan's family – you must remember."

"But you'd been with them for years!"

Bella shrugged. "Things change. Like I said before, I was a right cow."

"It must have been hard for you to go and live with a different family."

"Not particularly. I couldn't wait to get away, to be honest. I'd had quite enough of bloody Penllan to last me a lifetime. Typical little village, with all the small-minded gossips – I don't know how you've stood it so long." She put the empty bottle back on the table, carefully, and gave Kitty a sudden bright smile that showed her even white teeth. "So anyway. Enough with the past – what's happening in the here and now I should know about?" The whole topic of her moving away was quite clearly closed, just as the one of her mother had been before.

"Well. . ." Kitty thought about it. "Hey, do you remember Nicci Edwards? It's her eighteenth in a couple of weeks – why don't you come?"

Bella looked doubtful. "Are you sure?"

"Yeah – I'll give her a ring tonight, if you like. I'm sure it'll be OK. She's having a big do; I shouldn't think one more will make any difference. There'll be loads of people there you know – you can do all your catching up in one go." Such as Bruno, for example, whom Kitty knew had also been invited. This could be the ideal opportunity for him and Bella to "bump into" each other again, as he'd put it.

"OK. If you're sure." Bella glanced at her watch and dropped her cigarette in the ashtray. "Look, I'm going to have to go. We'll speak soon, yeah?"

Kitty finished up the remainder of the crisps, thinking how much she disliked being in a pub by herself. She always thought some tedious guy was going to come over and start hassling her, assuming she was there solely to be picked up. *I bet Bella never worries about things like that,* she thought. *I bet she goes into pubs whenever she wants, and sits there for as long as she likes, and gives a hard time to any guy who tries to pick her up. In fact, I wouldn't put it past her to do a spot of picking-up herself, if she felt like it.* She smiled to herself, then tipped the rest of her orange juice down her throat and stood up to go.

chapter three

Even though Nicci had said her party was going to be a big do, Kitty hadn't appreciated just how big. The village hall was heaving, wall-to-wall bodies – she must have invited the entire village, not to mention half of college. Or vice versa.

Kitty picked her way through the assembled masses, making for the kitchen which was doing duty as the bar. A small knot of blokes she recognized from college were standing around desultorily, nursing bottles of lager and eying up the talent. Kitty tapped one of them on the shoulder, a tall, well-built lad with dark hair and serious-looking horn-rimmed specs.

"Hey, Bruno," she said, sternly. "I thought you said you'd call round for me? I've been hanging around at home like a lemon, waiting for you."

He turned, raising an eyebrow. "Did I? I can't remember saying that. Sorry. Hi Bruno, how lovely to see you, how are you?" he added, pointedly, and then, spotting the neatly gift-wrapped present his cousin was carrying, put his hand to his throat with a theatrical gesture and said, "Oh, I'm overwhelmed! You really shouldn't have!"

"I really didn't." Kitty curled her lip at him. "It's for Nicci. As well you know. Has anyone seen her?"

She was in the kitchen, getting herself a drink. "Hey, Kitty!" she enthused.

"Hi Nicci. Happy birthday." Kitty gave her a hug, then handed her the present.

"Thanks, babe. I'll just go and put it with the others – I'm going to open them all later."

She went out of the kitchen just as Megan came in, looking for a refill. "Hi, Kitty, you just arrived? Where's Rhys?" she asked.

"He'll be along later. It's his mum's birthday, they've all gone out for a meal." Kitty turned and poured herself a glass of wine, neglecting to tell her friend that actually, she and Rhys had had a bit of a row about it. "You've known for ages it's Nic's party that night," she'd said.

"Well what am I supposed to do," he'd replied, an unfamiliar mulish look sliding across his face. "Tell Mum I can't do her birthday because I'm going to a party for some girl I hardly know?"

"But I was looking forward to going with you," Kitty had said, hearing the complaining note in her voice and hating it.

"Yeah well," Rhys had muttered, "just like I was looking forward to going to the movies with you the other night."

"What other night?" Kitty demanded.

"That night you just had to go and see what'sherface. Bella."

Kitty had stared at him, perplexed. "But you said you didn't mind. You said you understood. You said. . ."

"Yeah, OK, Kitty. Let's just drop it, shall we? You go to the party – I've got to celebrate with my family, or my life won't be worth living. You know what mums are like – all that guilt trip stuff."

And that, it appeared, was that.

"Anything left to drink in here?" Megan's eyes lit upon the mountain of bottles and cans stacked up on the counter by the hatch. "Blimey. Look at all that. No wonder my mum says everyone always ends up in the kitchen at parties. Want one of these?" She picked up two bottles of lager.

"I'm OK, thanks. I didn't know your mum went to parties."

"Oh, yeah." Megan looked around for the opener. "You wouldn't recognize her these days. Some nights she's up till, ooh, at least ten o'clock. She's turned into a right raver."

"Who? Anyone I know? Think she'll fancy a date?" It was Bruno, coming into the kitchen with three empty bottles and a hopeful grin.

"Megan's mum," Kitty told him, briskly. "You could ask her out, I guess, but I don't think Megan's dad would like it much."

Megan gave a girly titter and handed Bruno the bottle she was holding, the one she'd just opened. "Hi Bruno. Want a top-up?"

"Oh, hi Megan. Thanks." He put the empties down and took the fresh one, and Kitty opened her mouth to protest that he'd taken Megan's drink, but shut it again almost immediately. What was the point? She should be used to Megan by now; she really shouldn't be surprised any more by the effect Bruno's presence had on her, given that it'd been happening for so long. But she was surprised. It never ceased to amaze her how Megan could morph from her normal persona of funky, emancipated chick-about-town into a giggling, dribbling, bimbo act-alike, just because Bruno was around. She was at it now, flapping around him with more bottles, offering him packets of crisps and sausage rolls.

"Mmm, terrific," Bruno murmured, cramming two sausage rolls into his mouth at once. "I need regular feeding, or I'm liable to fall over. You know – faint through lack of nourishment."

"Really?" Megan looked at him, wide-eyed. "You'd better have some of these, then." She opened a packet of salt-and-vinegar and held one out to him, like a mother bird feeding its chick. "Does it happen very often? I mean, it could be dangerous."

Kitty raised her eyes to the ceiling and clicked

her tongue. "He's *joking*, Megan." She strode over to the bin and chucked Bruno's empties into it.

Bruno ducked his head and took the crisp Megan was proffering into his mouth, and as he did so one of the bottles he was holding slid from his grasp and on to the kitchen floor, where it smashed. Megan gave a little cry and skipped out of the way as lager splashed up from the tiled floor.

"Oh no!" she gasped. "My new trousers!"

"You great lummox," Kitty scolded her cousin.

He pulled a face, pouting his lips out like Owen in a sulk. "It was an accident. Don't be cross with me, Kitty-witty."

Kitty wondered, not for the first time, why it was that the combination of him and Megan brought out the worst in her. "I know it was an accident, but you still better clear it up. Look, there's broken glass everywhere." She cast around the kitchen and found a dustpan and brush. "Here you go, Laughing Boy. I'll sweep up the glass – you mop up the beer. There's a cloth over there, look."

"God, you're such a slave-driver," Bruno complained, putting the other bottles down and sticking the cloth under the hot tap. He looked at it with distaste. "I need rubber gloves. Cleaning up simply *ruins* my manicure, darling."

Megan fell about laughing, as if it was the funniest thing she'd ever heard. She'd stopped squeaking about her lager-splashed trousers, and instead was leaning against the counter gazing adoringly at Bruno. Oblivious to her cow-eyed expression, he flicked some water at her. She squealed in mock outrage and pushed at him with the flat of her hand. For the life of her, Kitty couldn't understand what she saw in him – he was only *Bruno,* for heaven's sake. She felt a spurt of irritation for the pair of them.

"Just get on with it, Bruno," she growled, crouching down and wielding the dustpan.

"That's right, Kitten – you keep him in order," came a voice from the doorway, and there stood Bella, leaning lazily against the door jamb and holding a vast present wrapped in shiny silver paper and topped with a giant ribbon rosette. She was wearing low-slung black hipsters in a softly draping material, and a silver-grey chiffon spaghetti-strapped top that managed to be both floatily feminine and skimpy enough to show off her smooth cleavage and sickeningly flat stomach.

"Hi – you made it!" Kitty was absurdly pleased to see her. She hadn't been at all sure that she was going to turn up – it took some bottle to arrive at a party by yourself when you didn't know half the people there, and hadn't seen the other half for over five years. Megan and Bruno were standing by the sink, motionless, as if she were some kind of apparition that Kitty had conjured up by sweeping up the glass. The Genie of the Dustpan.

"Sure I made it. Did you think I wasn't coming?" Bella put the present down on the counter, carefully, and produced her cigarettes from somewhere about her person. Megan was immediately galvanized into action.

"I'm not sure you should smoke in the kitchen," she declared, taking a step forward.

Bella looked around her slowly, and Kitty waited for the sarcastic comment, but none came. Instead, Bella put the cigarettes down and gave a slightly sheepish smile.

"You're right. Sorry – didn't think." Then she smiled again. "Hi, Megan. How're you doing?"

"Fine, thanks," Megan muttered, suddenly finding some newly washed glasses on the draining-board hugely interesting. She picked up one of them and a tea towel and began to apply the one to the other.

It wasn't the warmest of greetings Kitty had ever witnessed. Megan must have seen something on Kitty's face, because she said, rather defensively, "It's not the first time I've seen her since she's been back. We've bumped into each other at college a couple of times."

"That's right," Bella agreed. "But you, on the

other hand –" she took a couple of steps towards Bruno, tilting her head appraisingly – "I really haven't seen for years. What's the matter?" she teased him. "Cat got your tongue? Come on – say hello!"

Bruno opened his mouth, and then closed it again. "Wow!" he said at last, weakly. "You look totally – ravishable."

"Don't you mean ravishing?" said Megan sulkily, holding a glass up to the light and examining it closely.

Bruno, who knew exactly what he had meant, didn't answer her, and Bella laughed merrily. "You don't scrub up so badly yourself."

Then they were both crossing the kitchen, towards each other, and Bruno was enfolding Bella in his arms in an immense hug of a kind Kitty was certain he'd never given her before, ever. Come to think of it, she didn't think she'd ever seen him hug *anyone* like that before. Though why should she have, in all fairness? Just because the two of them didn't have what you'd call a huggy relationship didn't mean to say Bruno shouldn't hug anyone else, if he wanted to. And he clearly did want to hug Bella. The hug went on for a very long time, far longer than was usual between two people who'd been barely friends, no matter how many years since they'd last seen each other.

Eventually, they drew apart. Kitty looked at the

pair of them; Bella, her pretty face alight with smiles, looking up at Bruno who was wearing an expression like a kid on Christmas morning, finding that Santa had brought him exactly the present he wanted. It was all very weird and unexpected, considering the relationship they'd had as kids. Kitty thought about the times Bella had been the victim of one of Bruno's silly practical jokes – the frog down her welly sprang to mind, as did the time he threw her homework out of the window of the school bus – and the occasions when Bruno had been on the receiving end of Bella's quick and sarcastic tongue. Yet here they were, long-lost Bella in her sexy party kit and Bruno, all I'm-a-brainy-university-student, beaming at each other like – well, like distinct more-than-just-friends. There was nothing remotely Just Friends about the way they were looking at each other now.

Then Kitty's gaze expanded and took in Megan. She was leaning against the sink and staring at them, the tea towel in her hand going round very slowly inside the glass as if under its own steam and nothing to do with its owner at all. Her face was set, carefully impassive, and not beaming at all. *Oh boy,* thought Kitty, with an inward sinking of the heart. *This is going to be interesting. Very interesting.*

*

Rhys rang Kitty on her mobile at about midnight to say he wished he'd gone to Nicci's party after all. "We went to that new Chinese," he told her. "Crap meal, crap service, and noisy little kids running round everywhere. I'm sorry we rowed. I miss you."

Touched, Kitty went round to see him the next day. They sat on the sofa in his room and made up in the time-honoured way, with a mammoth snogging session.

"I couldn't help feeling sorry for Megan last night," she told him, when they came up for air.

"Hmm?" Rhys picked up the remote and started to channel-surf.

"I said, I felt sorry for Megan."

"For Megan? Why?"

"Well, I suppose because she was hoping she was going to get off with Bruno."

"Was she? Why?"

"Oh, dur. Because she fancies him, of course."

"Does she? You've never told me."

"Well, no. I haven't. Not as such. But you've been around both of them – haven't you ever noticed?"

"Noticed what?"

"The way Megan acts when Bruno's around."

"Nope." Rhys found *The Simpsons,* and settled back on the sofa with a satisfied grunt. "She's just Megan."

For a bright guy, Kitty thought, he could be amazingly rubbish at detecting subtexts and undercurrents between people. This type of chat was definitely more satisfying with another girl – it didn't work nearly so well when you had to translate everything for the other person. *Still*, she thought. *He is very good at other things. Snogging, for example. I can't really complain.*

"So anyway," she continued, snuggling up against him. "There was Megan, alone in the kitchen with Bruno – well, apart from me, and I don't count."

"Don't you? Why not?"

"Because I'm not competition."

"Oh, right."

"So as I was saying, she'd got him alone in the kitchen. And to be fair, I think on this occasion she might even have pulled it off – I mean, she had these new trousers, and her hair was loose for once, instead of all pulled back any-old-how, like it usually is. I have to admit, she did look pretty foxy. And Bruno was flicking water at her."

"Right. And that's good, is it?"

"Course it is! He was *flirting* with her." Did he really not understand? "Anyway, there they both were, and then suddenly there was Bella as well, and the atmosphere just – well, changed. All of a sudden."

"Right."

"It was like someone had turned a light off. Or on, rather – turned on a spotlight, right on Bella. It's hard to explain."

"I see."

"And then poor old Megan may as well not have existed for the rest of the evening, for all the notice Bruno took of her."

"Mm-hmm."

Kitty, sensing she'd lost Rhys, glanced at him. He was absorbed in the cartoon, smiling faintly at Bart and Lisa's antics, and clearly not listening to a word she was saying.

"So then the alien arrived," she went on, "and Megan went off with him instead."

"Right."

"And she phoned me up this morning and told me he wants her to have his babies."

"Great."

"Rhys!" she exclaimed, snatching the remote from his hand and pressing Off. "You're not listening!"

"Sorry." To his credit, he didn't complain at having his precious programme turned off, but instead sat up with a compliant I'm-Paying-Attention-Now expression on his face. "OK, I'm listening. Go ahead."

"I've just told you." She sighed. "Aren't you interested?"

"Yeah, I'm interested. It's just –" He gave a

shrug. "I'm not much good at this relationships stuff. Talking about them, I mean – analysing them. I prefer to just get on with them."

"OK. Fair enough. But I can't help it. I just seem to get so involved."

"That's because they're your mates." He reached for her hand and gave it a squeeze. "And because you're a good friend. But I guess, at the end of the day, you just have to let them get on with their own relationships."

Kitty frowned. "How d'you mean?"

"Well, correct me if I'm wrong, but you're saying Megan fancies Bruno, yeah? But now Bella has come back on the scene – back from the dead, kind of thing – and it looks as if Bruno's taken a shine to her?"

"In a nutshell, yeah. Pretty much."

"So the situation seems to be, Megan's got a choice. She either fights for her man, or accepts the fact that Bruno doesn't fancy her back. Or at least, not as much as he fancies Bella." Pleased with his skilful analysis of the situation, he sat back and folded his arms. "But either way, nothing you say or do is going to make much difference, to any of them. Is it?"

"I guess not."

"Tell you what, though – how the hell does your cousin do it? I mean, two girls to choose from – man!" He gave an appreciative whistle.

"Beats me. It's not even as if he's particularly good-looking."

"I don't suppose Megan would agree with you there. Nor Bella, from what you've said."

"I don't know about Bella." Kitty said, reflectively. "I don't know how she feels about Bruno any more. When we were little she had the same kind of relationship with him as me, but—"

"Which was?" Rhys interrupted.

"Oh, you know. Pesky older cousin, kind of thing. It's not that they didn't get on, but they were always teasing each other and winding each other up. But last night when they saw each other they were like – like once-upon-a-time lovers, or something. Then the rest of the evening, Bella was giving it large with just about every unattached bloke in the room. I mean, don't get me wrong, there's no reason why she shouldn't, she's unattached too, so good luck to her – but every time I caught sight of Bruno, he was looking at her with this dead strange expression on his face. Not leering, I don't mean. Just kind of really wistful."

"Sounds like she's playing hard to get. You know – flirting with other guys, like, look what you could have."

"That was never Bella's style. She was always much more, like, what you see is what you get."

"Perhaps she's changed."

"Possibly." She didn't seem to have, though. She seemed exactly the same as before, down to the last detail; apart from looking more grown-up, of course, and that didn't count. Warm, enthusiastic, exuberant, wicked sense of humour – she even had the same mannerisms and used the same expressions as before.

"So what has she been up to since you last saw each other, then?"

"That's the weird thing. I don't really know."

"Why not? Haven't you asked her?"

"Yeah, I've asked her. But apart from saying she messed up her GCSEs, and the fact she's now living with her long-lost great-aunt, she hasn't really told me anything." Kitty still hadn't found out much about Bella's doings over the past five years. Not that it mattered that much; she just couldn't help wondering. But every time she'd asked Bella a question about the past she'd either skilfully changed the subject or deflected her gently.

"Mystery Woman, then," said Rhys, with a shrug that quite clearly said he didn't see anything odd in it. Kitty wondered whether he'd feel the same way if a friend of *his* came strolling back into his life after so long an absence. Probably, knowing Rhys. Kitty didn't know if it was blokes in general who were satisfied with knowing so little about the other people in their lives, or just her boyfriend. The here and now, that's what Rhys was interested in. It was quite Zen, really, when you came to think of it.

"It's just the way Bella operates," Kitty replied. "She's always been the same."

"So why are you worrying about it?"

"I'm not. I'm just saying, that's all. Doesn't mean I'm worried. Does it?"

chapter four

"You're still living in the Peppermint House!" The smile on Bella's face stretched from ear to ear. It was infectious; Kitty couldn't help smiling back.

"Course we are. Nothing much changes round here."

The sign on the gatepost proclaimed the house's actual name to be Plas Derwen, but Bella had called it the Peppermint House from the first time she'd seen it on account of the colour of its exterior walls. Kitty's mum, rather pretentiously Kitty always thought, maintained it was eau-de-nil, but peppermint was probably closer to the mark; the pale-yet-vivid green of those sweets that come in a tube, with soft centres enclosed in a crunchy outside shell.

She pushed open the gate with a flourish, and made a swooping bow. "Ta da-aa! Welcome back!"

Mum was on nights at the hospital that week and so was at home, in her uniform and making herself sandwiches in the kitchen; but so, unusually for the time of day, was Dad.

"Hi," Kitty greeted him, with some surprise. "What are you doing here?"

"Hi, Dad, how lovely to see you, Dad, let me make you a cuppa, Dad," he said, turning round from the sink with a smile. Then Bella peeped shyly round the door frame and his eyes widened and his smile expanded. "Will you look at who's here!"

"Hello, Mr Doyle," she said, coming in, her hand outstretched formally.

"Mr Doyle be blowed! Uncle Mike not good enough for you any more?" He ignored her hand and went for the hug option.

Mum put down the bread knife and wiped her hands on a tea towel. "Hello, Bella," she said. "How nice to see you again. Mike, do put her down – you'll embarrass the poor girl!"

"Hello, Mrs Doyle," said Bella, liberated from Mr Doyle's grasp and not looking at all embarrassed. "It's so lovely to see you all again, you just can't imagine!" She bent and rummaged in her bag, the huge orange and purple velvet Sixties-looking sack she carried her college books around in. "I brought you this. It's only small, but I wanted to get you something. Sorry it's not wrapped." She held it out uncertainly; it was an onyx egg, smooth and polished and marbled honey-brown and cream. Mum had a teak bowl of them in the sitting room, all different colours

62

and sizes, that she had collected over the years. Touched, she took it from Bella's hand.

"You remembered about my eggs," she murmured. "Ah, Bella; that's very sweet of you. But you don't have to bring us presents, you know."

"Somebody mention presents?" Owen came slouching in to the room, carrying the cat in front of him like a tray. He stared at Bella. "Who are you?"

Kitty clicked her tongue. "Just ignore him, Bella. He was away when they were dishing out social skills."

"No I wasn't." Owen scowled. "So you're the famous Bella, then."

"Well, I'm certainly Bella," she agreed, gravely. "But I'm afraid I'm not famous. Yet." She put out a hand and stroked the cat. "Don't you remember me, Owen? I certainly remember you. You were the loveliest little boy."

"How times have changed," Kitty put in, sweetly.

"Was I?" Owen didn't bother responding to his sister. He looked intrigued. It had been a long time since anyone had referred to him as lovely, if ever, and as a result he was graciously prepared to forget the "little boy" that had come after the lovely bit.

"You most certainly were. I wanted a little

63

brother just like you. And I remember this character too." She gave the cat another stroke, and it struggled from Owen's grasp and jumped to the floor, weaving round Bella's legs like a witch's familiar. "It's Cushion, right?"

"That's right." Owen smiled, and Bella looked around the kitchen.

"So where's Heinz?"

"Ah." Dad pulled a mournful face. "Gone up to that great kennel in the sky."

"Aw, bless." Bella looked sad too. "He was a great dog. He wasn't really ill or anything, was he? That would have been horrible."

"Nope," Owen said cheerfully. "He just got dead old. We had to have him put down last year – he kept peeing and pooing all over the place, it was gross."

"Thanks so much for sharing that with us," said Kitty, pulling a face. "Anyway, there's no need to sound so happy about it. You were the most upset of all of us – you booed your head off for at least a fortnight." She turned to Bella. "Come on – let's go up to my room."

Mum put the lid on her sandwich box. "Are you staying for supper, Bella?"

"Well –" She looked at Kitty for guidance. "Would that be OK? I wouldn't want to put you to any trouble."

Mum put the sandwiches in her bag and slung

64

it over her shoulder. "It's no trouble. If you'd like to, there's plenty to go round."

"It's chicken casserole," Kitty put in, "isn't it, Mum?"

Bella smacked her lips. "Yum! Your mum is such a good cook, Kitty."

"So you're staying?" Dad said, one eyebrow raised enquiringly. "I'll just bung another spud in the Aga, then."

"And I," announced Owen, loftily, "might help peel the carrots."

Kitty muttered, "Don't strain yourself," but Bella gave him a dazzling smile.

"That settles it, then," she told him. "I'm definitely staying now."

After supper, Dad and Owen excused themselves to go and watch the football on TV, leaving Kitty and Bella to chat. They went out of the kitchen and up the stairs, just like they used to. Talking all the while; just like they used to. It was only when they were safely ensconced in Kitty's room, with the door firmly shut against marauding little brothers or inadvertently eavesdropping parental ears, that Kitty was struck by how odd it was. Neither of them had suggested going up to her room, they had just gone. It was as if Bella's presence in the house had somehow transported them back in time, back to what they'd done when they were kids.

Kitty hardly ever had friends in her room these days; it was why Dad had decorated the small room next to it, the room that had originally been the nursery when Owen was a baby, and then the playroom. He had turned it three years ago into a little sitting-room for her, furnished with rattan sofa and chairs and beanbags with corduroy covers in tasteful shades of chocolate and toffee and caramel, and she had inherited the old TV and video from downstairs to put in it. A DVD and mini hi-fi for subsequent Christmases completed the transformation into teenage chill-out zone; or, as Mum put it: "so you have somewhere to entertain your pals". Megan staunchly maintained it was to keep tabs on her when she started taking boyfriends back home ("Damage limitation. There's no bed in here, is there?"). But Kitty didn't care what her parents' motivation had been; it meant the whole of the top floor was hers, and she no longer had to worry about what kind of state her bedroom was in before inviting friends back. Not that any of her friends would have cared, frankly, but the room had its uses. It had impressed Rhys when they began to see each other, for a start.

"You've got your own sitting-room?" he had remarked. "How wicked is that!"

But here she and Bella were now, sitting in her bedroom with Bella in her customary place on the bed, shoes off and legs tucked underneath herself, and Kitty on the small armchair in the corner. It was as if the intervening years had never taken place.

"This is so weird!" Kitty said, with a laugh. "Talk about time warp! We don't have to sit in here, you know – we could go next door if you like."

"Next door?" Bella looked puzzled. "Next door where?"

"Into the other room."

"What, the playroom?"

"It isn't a playroom any more." Kitty explained about the teenage chill-out zone, and Bella insisted on checking it out. She prowled around the small room, minutely examining the furniture and the carpet and the entertainment system (such as it was) before pronouncing it cool.

"It's not that cool," Kitty muttered. "Not any more." She was suddenly aware of how scruffy the room had become; the carpet was stained from months of careless pizza-eating and Coke-drinking accidents, the beanbags saggy and misshapen, the rattan on the arms of the sofa becoming unravelled where it had been picked at during countless scary or emotionally tense video moments. Bella's flat in her great-aunt's house, with its blend of the exotic and the contemporary – that was cool, not this shabby little room with its threadbare carpet and tatty furniture, and walls badly in need of a fresh coat of paint.

By mutual consent, they went back to Kitty's bedroom, closing the door tightly behind themselves again. But Kitty was looking at everything with new eyes; Bella's eyes, as she supposed. The scuffed pine bed with the pink-and-lilac gingham duvet cover, the matching pink-and-lilac gingham curtains, the half-moon rag rug, the dolls and teddies in their mini-hammock suspended from the ceiling – all was pretty much exactly as it had been when Bella had seen it last. Apart from the posters carefully pinned to the large cork board on the wall (which as she recalled had been of some wholesome boy band or other, and were now of the far more phwoar-worthy Orlando Bloom and Sean Bean in semi-undress), it was to all intents and purposes a little girl's room, and Kitty was suddenly, burningly ashamed of it.

"I love this room," Bella said unexpectedly, demonstrating her mind-reading skills again.

Kitty blinked, taken aback. "Do you? I was just thinking how babyish it looks."

"Babyish? I don't think it's babyish. It's you –

it's exactly how I remember it. Tell the truth, I'd have been dead disappointed if you'd feng shui'd it, or whatever!" She laughed, and leant back against the pine bedhead, comfortably. "The number of times I imagined myself back here with you, closeted away against all-comers; us against the rest of the world, with our packets of Smarties and bottles of 7-Up."

"Not to mention our Barbies," Kitty put in, laughing too.

"Yeah, that's right! God, we so had fun, didn't we?"

"Didn't we just. Do you remember that time –"

Her words were cut off by the abrupt opening of the door; and there, all of a sudden, stood Megan, her look of surprise mirrored on the faces of Kitty and Bella. But there was another emotion on Megan's face, other than surprise; something sour and unpleasant.

"Hi," she said, awkwardly. "Sorry; I did knock but I didn't think you heard. Your dad said it would be OK just to come up," she added.

"Course it is," Kitty said, getting up from the chair. "Here – sit down."

"Where are you going to sit?" Megan was appropriately solicitous, concerned at taking her hostess's seat, and Kitty in turn politely reassured her that it was fine, she would fetch a beanbag from the other room.

"Don't be daft," Bella declared, swinging her legs sideways on the bed so they hung over the edge. "I'll just move. There you go, plenty of room now." She patted the space she had created, invitingly.

Megan, not looking at her, sat down in the chair Kitty had vacated and crossed her ankles, neatly. Kitty and Bella exchanged glances, and then Kitty, with a shrug, sat down on the end of the bed next to Bella. Bella raised one eyebrow expressively at her, and then smiled at Megan.

"Hello Megan," she said, gravely. "How are you?"

"I'm fine thanks," Megan replied, equally gravely. "How are you?"

"I'm fine too."

"Well, that's all right then," Kitty said. "Now you two have ascertained you're both fine. I'm fine too, in case either of you were wondering." She folded her arms and looked at her two friends in turn. Was it her imagination, or was there a distinctly chilly atmosphere? She turned her head to Megan. "Did you come round for anything specific, or just to say hi?"

Megan looked slightly wounded. "Just to say hi. I didn't know there had to be something specific, or I'd have invented some pretext."

"I didn't mean that." *Boy! Touchy or what! What was her problem?* She tried again. "I just meant, you know, was there anything in particular you wanted me for?"

Megan got to her feet, huffily. "Nothing in particular, no. Sorry – if I'd known you were otherwise engaged I'd have rung first. Perhaps I'd better come back when you're not so busy."

"No, no." Bella stood up too, with an almost imperceptible sigh. "Look, it's time I was going anyway." She gave Kitty a brief hug, brushing aside her protestations. "See you soon, hun. See you, Megan." Then she was gone, picking up her velvet sack and slipping from the room.

Kitty turned to Megan. "What was all that about?"

"What?"

"You, just now."

"I don't know what you mean."

"Yes you do." The look on Megan's face as she had entered the room and seen Bella sitting there had taken Kitty right back, back to early primary school days and things she thought she'd forgotten all about.

Kitty has been looking forward to going back to school, mainly because she is going to be in the Juniors. Being in the Infants was good at first, but things like the sandpit and the dressing-up corner are far too babyish for her now. She is looking forward to seeing Megan again, too. She hardly saw her at all in the summer holidays.

But now Kitty is standing in the doorway of her new classroom. She is in Miss Wright's class this year. Miss Wright has dark hair pulled back into a neat little knot on the back of her head, and a severe expression. She wears straight black skirts and little pearl earrings in her earlobes. She is not a bit like Kitty's teacher last year, Mrs Budd, who had a long blonde plait that always had bits of hair escaping from it, and wore big woolly cardigans and patchwork skirts. If anyone in the class did an especially good bit of work, or was upset about something, Mrs Budd would put a gentle arm around them and reach down into the capacious pockets of her skirt and bring out a toffee or a fruit bonbon. Somehow, Kitty doesn't think Miss Wright keeps sweets in her pockets.

"Hiya, Kitty!" Megan has just come in to the classroom, her ginger plaits bouncing. She looks very pleased to see Kitty. "Did your mummy have her baby?"

Owen seems to have been around for ever, and Kitty had forgotten that Megan doesn't know about him yet. He is cute and she loves him, but for a small baby he takes up an awful lot of space, not to mention time. Mummy's time, mostly.

"Yes," she tells her friend.

"So what have you got?" she asks, impatiently. "A little brother or a little sister?"

"A little brother," says a voice behind Megan, and there, unbelievably, is Bella, the girl from Kitty's back garden.

"Hello," says Kitty, in surprise. Bella says hello back, a big wide smile all over her face.

"Do you know Bella?" Megan looks puzzled.

"Yes," Kitty replies, equally puzzled. "Do you?"

Megan explains that Bella is staying with them, and Kitty suddenly understands. When Bella had said that she lives here now, Kitty thought she had just moved to Penllan with her family. But she hadn't. She has come to stay with the Robertses. Megan's family are foster-carers, which means there are often other children living in Megan's house with her and her mum and dad, often for months on end, but they are usually quite a lot younger than Megan. This is the first time she has brought one of them to school with her.

"So how do you know each other, then?" Megan is asking, and Kitty is just about to explain, that Bella turned up in her garden the Sunday before last and they played together all afternoon, when she catches Bella's eye. Something on Bella's face tells Kitty not to tell Megan all this, for reasons Kitty doesn't wholly understand but may have something to do with Mr and Mrs Roberts probably not having known where Bella had been. She has no idea how she can possibly know this; she just does. So instead of explaining to Megan what had really happened she just says, "I can't remember," in an uncertain kind of way, and then starts saying how nice it is to be in the Juniors, and then Bella says she's been practising joined-up writing all holidays. Then Miss Wright claps her hands for silence and the whole topic of how the two of them know each other has been passed over.

Miss Wright begins to organize the class into groups to sit at the tables, and seeing Kitty and Bella and Megan standing talking together puts them at a table along with Nicole Edwards and two boys. So that's where they sit, with Bella and Megan on either side of Kitty, and Kitty feels a big rush of happiness that the three of them have been put together, she and her two best friends, her old one and her new one.

Sometime during the morning, Miss Wright asks Megan to go up to her desk about something. Kitty and Bella and Nicole and the two boys are getting on with the work Miss Wright has set the whole class, which isn't really proper work at all but just writing a story called What I Did In The Holidays. ("In silence.")

Kitty glances at Bella's piece of paper, which she is shielding with her hand. She is frowning with concentration as she writes, the side of her bottom lip caught on her top teeth. At the top of the page, not hidden by Bella's hand, Kitty can just make out three words in large untidy capitals: *I MET KITTY.* Kitty's own work begins with almost the same thing: *In the holidays I met Bella.* At that moment Bella looks up from her paper and catches Kitty's eye. She looks down at Kitty's piece of paper and, seeing her own name written there, she grins, and Kitty grins back. It's funny that both of them are writing about the same thing.

Then Megan is coming back from Miss Wright's desk, and Kitty glances up at her. She is staring at Kitty and Bella with such a peculiar look on her face that for a moment Kitty thinks Miss Wright called her up to her desk to tell her off, but almost immediately she knows that can't be right because Megan is always such a good girl, just like Kitty herself. They are never in trouble in class, not like some people Kitty could mention – such as Craig Griffiths and Ben Flower, for example.

"Are you all right?" she says to Megan as she sits down, but quietly, because she doesn't want to be told off for talking in class, especially not on the first day of Juniors.

"Course I am," says Megan, but she still looks odd so Kitty says, "Are you sure?"

"Yes," Megan replies, and then she smiles at Kitty and picks up her pen and carries on with her writing, and Kitty is left thinking maybe she imagined the peculiar look.

But Kitty knew she hadn't imagined the look, neither then nor now. It was one of frank jealousy.

"Yes you do," she repeated.

"You mean, why didn't I jump for joy when I came in and saw Bella sitting on your bed?" Megan exclaimed. "Why didn't I fall on her neck and say, oh goodie, Bella's here, well never mind that I wanted a private chat with Kitty, let's all do girly things together instead? Is that what you mean?"

Kitty blinked. "Jesus, Meg," she said, mildly. "Don't hold back, will you."

"Well, what did you expect?"

"I don't know. But not this."

"This what?"

"This *attack*."

"I'm not attacking you." She sighed, and sat down again. "Look, I'm sorry, OK. But when I came up and heard you both laughing in here. . ."

Suddenly Kitty saw it from her point of view. *In the inner sanctum. With the door closed. Shutting her out. . .* "We weren't laughing at *you*," Kitty assured her.

"I didn't think *you* were."

The emphasis wasn't lost on Kitty. "Neither of us were," she assured her.

Megan pulled a doubtful face. "Hm-mm. . ."

"We weren't, Meg. I promise. I know Bella's not your favourite person, but she wouldn't slag you off behind your back." She took a wild guess. "Look, I know why you're pissed off with her. I know how you felt at Nicci's party when she turned up and Bruno started drooling over her, but she didn't do it on purpose."

"Didn't she?"

"No. I'm sure she didn't. She doesn't even know you like him. They were just pleased to see each other again, after all this time – she hardly looked at him for the rest of the evening, did she?"

"Well he sure looked at her," Megan observed, drily.

"She couldn't help that though, could she? I mean, it's a free country. A cat can look at a king, as they say."

"I guess." Another sigh. "So you don't reckon she fancies Bruno, then?"

"No, I don't. The way is clear for you."

Megan flushed, the ginger freckles that matched her hair standing out as if in 3-D against the crimson of her face. "What makes you think I want the way clear?" she declared, with a careless toss of her head.

It didn't fool Kitty. "Oh, just the way you mention his name at every opportunity. The way you live round here in the holidays, and want to know if he's got a girlfriend at uni yet, and quiz me about every detail of his life from the first moment he arrived on the planet. Little things like that." She didn't say, *The way you turn into a dribbling inarticulate fool whenever he's around.* Somehow, she thought that might be going a bit far.

"Oh. So you've guessed I like him, then." Suddenly, unexpectedly, she grinned. "Thank Christ for that. It means I don't have to keep it a secret any more."

If that had been Megan's idea of keeping her interest in Bruno secret, Kitty hated to think what she was going to be like now she'd been rumbled. She didn't say that either, though.

"So how long have you –?" she asked instead, waggling a hand meaningfully.

"Oh, ages." This time the sigh was of the lovelorn variety, deep and expressive. "Years."

"So how come you never told me before?"

"I don't know. I guess I just felt awkward, with you two being cousins and everything. I mean, you're always on each other's case, aren't you – I didn't think you'd understand what I saw in him. But I think he was probably the first guy I noticed – as a guy, I mean. He just gets lusher and lusher as he gets older. Other guys just don't measure up, somehow." She gestured towards Orlando Bloom, peering down from Kitty's cork board. "Don't you think he looks like Bruno, a bit? Minus the specs, of course."

"No way!" Kitty, startled at the novel idea of her cousin as sex symbol, was even more alarmed at the thought that she had his apparent lookalike pinned on her bedroom wall to lust over. "Well, maybe just a tiny bit," she amended, seeing Megan's adamant look slide over her face, and not feeling up to the inevitable lengthy comparison of Orlando's eyes versus Bruno's eyes, Orlando's smile versus Bruno's smile, etc. etc. She knew just how obsessive her friend was capable of being when in this mood. She changed the subject, hastily. "So am I forgiven, then?"

"What for?"

"For having Bella round when you wanted to talk to me."

"Course you are. It's not you I was annoyed with, like I said."

"And you don't mind if she carries on coming round?" Kitty wanted reassurance from Megan. She could understand that Bella's return had stirred up old grievances, but they were Megan's grievances now, not hers. She didn't want to feel guilty every time she happened to see Bella; or worse, be forced into choosing between her and Megan.

But Megan just shrugged. "Like you said, it's a free country. She's out of my hair now, isn't she. You can be friends with whoever you like – you don't need my permission, do you?"

chapter five

Even though Kitty had realized she wasn't going to see much of Bella at college – it was a big place, they were doing different courses – it still felt odd. As if they could only be friends outside college hours. In many ways they had dropped back into their old friendship as if the time in between had never happened. But in other ways, Kitty was only too well aware that Bella had other interests, was forming other relationships that didn't involve her at all. She kept seeing her around college; catching glimpses of her in corridors, or on staircases, or walking across the car park with her orange and purple sack of books hefted over one shoulder, always talking animatedly, always smiling, and always – *always* – surrounded by other people. Chief among whom appeared to be Nicci Edwards, she couldn't help noticing – only natural, she supposed, as they knew each other from school, and were doing the same course, albeit with Bella a year behind Nicci.

Don't be so pathetic, she kept chiding herself on these occasions. *You're acting like she chucked you,*

or something. You're old friends – not old flames!
She is allowed to have other friends too.

But she couldn't seem to help it. Every time she saw Bella amidst the laughing group of her new friends (which, bizarrely, appeared to include Mel Thing, the guy who was hanging round her on the first day and whom she'd seemed majorly keen to shed – hadn't she told Kitty she thought he was a nightmare, or had Kitty imagined it?) she felt a peculiar stab of something unpleasant in that bit of her between the belly-button and the breastbone. She knew exactly what it was. It was jealousy, pure and simple. Or perhaps impure and extremely complicated might be a more accurate way of putting it. She supposed it brought uncomfortable echoes of the past, when Bella making other friends (in particular the dreaded Sadie Williams) had meant she drifted away from Kitty's sphere and then her life.

Totally pathetic, really. Bella never had been a shrinking violet; she had always been perfectly capable of looking after herself as well as choosing her own friends. The only time Kitty could remember any different was long ago, when Bella as the new girl at school knew only herself and Megan. Once – just once – she had required saving from the inevitable teasing about her newness and, by definition, her strangeness. But ever afterwards the dynamic of their joint relationship established itself with Bella as the undisputed leader, and never altered.

Bella is standing in the far corner of the playground. Kitty sees her when she and Megan come out of the classroom at playtime, a little after everybody else because they are classroom monitors and have been helping Miss Wright to tidy away the art things. Bella usually waits for them right by the entrance so as soon as they come out they can go off and play together. Kitty is a little surprised to see her about as far away from the entrance as it's possible to be and for a moment she thinks perhaps it's not Bella at all but somebody else. She looks around, half-expecting her to leap out from around the corner, saying, "Boo!" and laughing at making them jump. But even as she is looking around Kitty knows that it is Bella. She recognizes her slightly-too-big navy coat, bought at the beginning of term by Megan's mum to allow for growing. She can also see the scarlet hairband holding back Bella's long dark hair, the one Kitty herself gave her for her birthday with her name on it, picked out in fancy embroidered letters.

She is just about to call out to her when she notices the boys for the first time, a small group of them with Bella in their midst. She hurries across the playground without really thinking about what she is doing and with Megan trailing reluctantly behind her. The boys are older, a year or two above them, and she doesn't know any of them although she recognizes Ben Flower's older brother, Brad.

"Hasn't got a fa-ther! Hasn't got a mo-ther!" Brad Flower is saying, in a nasty low jeering voice, and Kitty realizes with a kind of horrid jolt that the jeers are directed at Bella. The other boys join in and Bella seems to shrink into herself, her head goes down, lower and lower, until Kitty can't see her face at all but only the top of her glossy dark head and the scarlet hairband proclaiming her name. Kitty turns and looks agonizingly at Megan, who nibbles nervously at her thumbnail and does a kind of hop from foot to foot, then dashes back off across the playground, leaving Kitty alone with the jeering boys and poor shrunken Bella.

"Bella Smeller! Bella Smeller!" another boy begins to chant, and Kitty has a sudden fervent wish that she hadn't given Bella that name hairband, that somehow it is all her fault. She wants to shout at the boys to stop, to leave her friend alone and go away, but she can't, she is too scared that they may then turn their tormenting on to her. Then suddenly Megan is coming back with the teacher on duty beside her, Mr Bevan with his loud PE-teacher voice, who tells the boys to push off and not be any more stupid than they can help or their parents will be hearing from him, and then they'll be sorry.

"You all right?" he says in a quieter voice to Bella, who by some miracle isn't shrunken any more but quite restored to her normal self.

"Yes, Sir," she says, and smiles at him.

"They been bullying you?"

"No, Sir. They're just stupid, like you said. They don't bother me."

Kitty is left with an ashamed feeling that she should have done more to help her friend but that she wasn't brave enough. But Bella doesn't seem to think so.

"Don't be silly," she declares afterwards, when Kitty says sorry. "What are you sorry about? You couldn't have done anything. They wouldn't have taken any notice of you. Anyway, I was all right."

But you weren't all right, Kitty wants to say, you looked all little and scared, but something tells her that Bella doesn't want to hear this.

"What did they mean," she says instead, "that you haven't got a father or a mother? They really *must* be stupid, if they think that!" She knows all about how babies are made – Megan has a book which she showed Kitty once, full of rather scary pictures of ladies' insides and couples hugging each other.

"It's because I live with Megan," Bella says,

with a shrug. "Auntie Enid says not to take any notice if people say things like that, they're just igger – igger-something."

"Ignorant?"

"Yeah. That's it – ignorant."

"So where are your parents, then?" Kitty doesn't intend to ask the question, it just comes out, but as she says the words she realizes that she has been wanting to ask Bella this for ages, since Bella first told her about living with Megan's family, in fact.

"Away." Bella waves a vague hand. "Not here."

"No," Kitty agrees. "But where?"

Bella goes all secretive, and looks around herself as if checking that she won't be overheard. "If I tell you," she says, quietly, "you must promise not to tell anyone else."

"All right," Kitty says, eagerly.

"Not even Megan."

"Doesn't Megan know?" She is surprised.

"No. Nobody knows."

"Not even Megan's mum and dad?"

Bella calls them auntie and uncle now, even though they aren't really. "No. Not even them."

"All right. I promise."

"OK. Well, my mum was rich and my dad was poor. He was a gypsy, you see," Bella tells her.

"What's a gypsy?"

86

"Don't you know? I thought *everybody* knows what a gypsy is!"

Chastened by the implication that she is somehow silly not to know something so vital, Kitty droops slightly as Bella explains how her mum's rich family didn't want them to be together on account of her dad being a gypsy, but they couldn't help falling in love. Kitty doesn't really understand, especially not why this should mean that Bella doesn't live with either of them now, but she can hear a kind of proud excitement in Bella's voice as she goes on to say how they loved each other so much that her mum would sneak out on to the moors near where they lived so they could meet in secret, even though her family didn't approve; and she understands that, whatever those boys might say or think, their teasing can't touch Bella because even though she doesn't live with her parents she is not a bit ashamed of them. Not a bit.

Bella had just got out of the shower when she heard Aunt Susan's voice calling up the stairs. She wrapped a towel round herself and opened the door.

"Isabella!"

"Hello?" She peered over the high mahogany bannister. Below, on the half-landing, was the upturned face of her great-aunt. "Sorry, Auntie. I was in the bathroom."

"It's all right, dear. It's just that you've got a visitor."

Bella shrank back slightly, hoisting the slipping towel up under her armpits. "A visitor? Oh. Let me just –" Catching sight of another face behind Aunt Susan's shoulder, she stopped. "Oh, hi Kitty! Come on up – that's if you don't mind me getting myself ready round you."

Kitty duly followed Bella's towelled back view up the stairs. Her bare shoulders were speckled with drops of water and her feet left damp marks on the pale carpet.

"Sorry," Kitty said, slightly breathless at climbing all the stairs. Especially the last steep and narrow flight that led to Bella's top floor eyrie. "I didn't mean to disturb you. Your aunt didn't know whether you were in."

"No worries. Just make yourself at home while I get dressed." Bella waved an encompassing arm at the room in general and went into the bedroom, leaving the door ajar.

Kitty felt slightly discomfited at having caught Bella unawares, even though nothing at all in Bella's manner suggested she minded. Kitty could hear vague getting-ready noises coming from the bedroom; drawers being opened and closed, the faint whoosh of an aerosol spray.

"Your aunt seems nice," she remarked.

"Does she?" Bella's voice sounded muffled, as

if through some item of clothing being pulled on over her head.

"Yeah. Friendly. She offered to make me a cup of tea while she went to fetch you."

"Wow." Bella appeared in the doorway, barefoot and dressed in tracksuit bottoms and a T-shirt. "You are honoured. She usually grills anyone who comes to see me to within an inch of their lives – like she suspects them of coming round to sell me drugs, or something."

"Bet that goes down well with your visitors. Why did she call you Isabella?"

"Dur – because it's my name?" Bella grinned as Kitty's eyes opened wide with surprise.

"I never knew that."

"Why should you? Nobody ever calls me anything other than Bella any more. Apart from Aunt Susan, that is – I hate it."

"Do you? I think it's a nice name. Pretty." It was odd that she had known her for however many years it was, and had no idea that she was called anything other than just Bella.

Bella pulled a face. "Not exactly me, then, is it. Hey, look, don't take this the wrong way, but did you come round for anything in particular? Only I'm off out in a tick."

Kitty took in Bella's bare feet, her jogging bottoms and T-shirt, which was big and baggy and had a faded picture of Bagpuss on the front.

She had rarely seen anyone look less ready for a Friday evening out.

Bella followed her glance. "Self-defence class," she explained, pulling out the bottom of the T-shirt and regarding Bagpuss solemnly, upside-down. "I look shit, don't I? Not much chance of pulling anyone dressed like this, let alone Mr Buff."

"Who's Mr Buff?"

"Rather tasty instructor. He's not really called Mr Buff, it's just what I. . ." She tailed off, and peered into Kitty's face. "Are you OK? You look a bit –"

"A bit what?" Kitty crossed her arms, defensively, and went and sat down on the sofa.

"Not sure. Morose just about covers it. Are you pissed off with me?"

"No." *Yes. When I saw you were in, I thought we were going to be able to spend some time with each other. And how come I've known you all these years but never knew your name was Isabella? And I never knew you went to self-defence classes, either. Saying it would be too lame for words, though.* "*No*," she repeated, firmly. "I've just had one of those days. Look, I won't keep you as you're going out, but Nicci asked me to give you this." She stood up and handed Bella the folder she was carrying, and Bella looked at it askance.

"What is it?"

90

"Notes from the classes you missed on Tuesday. You left college today before she had a chance to dig them out and give them to you, apparently."

"Oh, right. I was at the dentist," she said. "Thanks for bringing them round," she added.

Her eyes slid away from Kitty, towards the window. Kitty knew immediately what she was looking at: the clock on the kitchen wall. She had the unpleasant sensation that she was holding Bella up, preventing her from doing what she wanted to do. It made her uncomfortable.

She got up from the sofa. "I'm sorry. I should have rung you first. I just assumed—"

"It's OK," Bella said, cutting across Kitty, which was probably just as well as she didn't know how she could have finished the sentence in a way that didn't sound presumptuous or, worse, patronizing. *I just assumed you'd be in. I just assumed you'd be pleased to see me. I just assumed you'd have nothing better to do of a Friday night than be sitting at home, waiting for me to call round on spec.* She never used to have to think about how she said things to Bella, when they were kids. Maybe it was called growing up – engaging your brain before opening your mouth, rather than after. If at all.

"It's OK," Bella said again. "It's nice to see you, even if it is only a flying visit. Sorry I can't offer you a coffee or anything, but—"

"It doesn't matter." Now it was Kitty's turn to interrupt. She was probably being over-sensitive – Bella certainly didn't look inconvenienced, or even as if she especially wanted Kitty to go. She was just smiling rather ruefully. "I ought to be going, anyway."

"Are you seeing Rhys?"

"No. I kind of told him I was seeing you this evening."

"Megan, then?"

"No. She's not well – tonsillitis. She's been off college since Wednesday."

"So you're going to be at a loose end?" As usual, Bella had sussed her.

Kitty shrugged, an attempt at nonchalance. "It's cool – like I said, I should have rung you first."

Bella looked hard at her then, what Kitty always used to think of as her X-ray stare; her eyes – always the brightest shade of blue – seeming to see right through Kitty's skull and into the thoughts that lay beneath.

"I am sorry, Kitten. Honestly. Please don't be pissed off with me – I can't bear it."

"I'm not pissed off with you," Kitty protested, feeling guilty as she did so for the undisputed pissed-offness she had indeed felt.

"Promise?"

"Promise." She goofed her teeth at Bella,

comically, and sketched an X across her chest with a forefinger. "Cross my heart and hope to die."

"That's all right then." Bella hugged her warmly. "I wouldn't want us to fall out. Not over something so unimportant."

All the way home on the bus, Kitty fought down a silly childish feeling of unfairness. She had been so certain that Bella would be in, pleased to see her and free for the evening.

It's no good feeling like that, she thought, cross with herself. *You just assumed, didn't you? Look, it's fine that Bella's life is no longer entirely bound up with yours. You wouldn't want her hanging round your neck the whole time, would you, being clingy and possessive?* But all the time these thoughts were going through her mind she had the sneaking suspicion that that, in fact, was exactly what she had wanted, almost from the moment Bella had first reappeared on the scene. Maybe she had seen it as a way of redressing the balance of their friendship – Bella had always called the tune when they were kids. Not that she'd minded; Bella always had the best ideas, which Kitty had invariably been perfectly happy to go along with. She supposed she'd been a pretty boring child by comparison, easily led.

By the time she got home Kitty had decided to ring Bella. She thought she might arrange another time for them to meet up properly, and at the same time just kind of drop in an apology for having called round unannounced. She had a nasty feeling that she had come across as sulky and petulant, annoyed with Bella for not dropping everything for her, and while she didn't want to turn it into a big issue she equally didn't want Bella to think that was what she was expecting of her now. To cancel all her plans because Kitty happened to come round. Who wanted a friend like that, after all?

Bella didn't have a mobile phone – she tossed her head with scorn at the very idea of owning something so commonplace and, as she saw it, unnecessary, although Kitty privately suspected Bella's lack of mobile had more to do with not being able to afford one and too much pride to admit to it than a wish to avoid following the crowd. So Kitty waited until just after ten, when she judged Bella would probably be back home, and then dialled the number Bella had given her.

"Hello?" The answering voice, when it came, was cool and firm and quite obviously not Bella's.

"Oh, hello, er –" How should she address her? She could hardly call her Aunt Susan. She went into polite mode. "Hello there. This is Kitty Doyle – I called round earlier to see Bella?"

A moment's pause, then, "Oh yes, I remember. Hello, my dear."

"May I speak to her, please?"

"I'm afraid she's not in."

"Oh, is she still at her class?"

This time the pause was longer. "Class?" the older woman said.

"Yes. Her evening class – self-defence?"

The longest pause yet. "I don't think she's gone to any self-defence class, dear. A young man called round to see her at about seven, and they went out together. I'm afraid I've no idea when she might be back. I'll tell her you called, shall I?"

chapter Six

Kitty pushed back the sleeve of her overall and looked at her watch. Still only half-past ten. Two hours to go until her lunch break. Six hours until going-home time. A hundred and twenty minutes to lunch – three hundred and sixty minutes until she could go home. So that meant – um –

Her mental arithmetic failed her at that point. She'd only been at work since nine o'clock, but was already so bored she was reduced to trying to calculate the seconds until she could go home. How sad was that?

When she and Megan had got Saturday jobs at Boots in town, she'd been thrilled at the prospect of being able to spend the whole day with her mate with the odd bit of customer relations as light relief, not to mention all that wonga after having to cope with a miserly five quid a week pocket money. The reality, however, didn't work out quite like that. Four pounds thirty an hour didn't go nearly as far as she'd imagined, especially when constantly surrounded by temptation in the shape of all that make-up, all the latest hair products, perfumes, body lotions, blah blah blah, not to mention the staff discount which increased the allure – it was a wonder she ever had any of her wages left over at all. Added to which, Sharon, the Saturday staff supervisor, was a total cow who seemed to take it personally if any of the girls weren't busy doing something every second of the day. She could only be in her mid-twenties but she acted as if she was fifty, and what's more had reached that age by totally bypassing her own teenage years. The sight of, for example, Kitty and Megan just innocently passing the time of day talking when customers were thin on the ground sent her into a total frenzy.

"Come along, girls!" she'd shriek, her over-plucked eyebrows disappearing into her over-lacquered hairline. "Don't stand there gassing, there's things need doing! There's shelves need tidying, and counters dusting, and if you're at that much of a loose end you can check the stock room!"

Nightmare. And today Kitty was left by herself to Sharon's tender mercies, as Megan still had tonsillitis and was off work. She looked at her watch again, marvelling not for the first time how it was that time could gallop when you were doing something interesting or exciting, yet when you were bored the clock's hands could appear to go backwards.

She was just musing on this when she felt a hand on her shoulder and a deep voice said in her ear, "Excuse me, miss. Where can I find the extra-large condoms?" She turned, startled, the acid put-down borne of many such comments from so-called college wits dying on her lips as she found herself looking into the grinning face of Bella.

"Oh, hi," she said, brightening.

"Do you work here, then?" Bella was saying. "I never knew."

Kitty, who didn't think it worth pointing out that she had told Bella about her Saturday job some time ago, regarded her deeply horrid navy-blue nylon regulation-issue overall and looked around herself in an exaggeratedly furtive manner. "No," she whispered, "but see that miserable-looking old bag over there? She kidnapped me and brought me here, and forced me to wear this. She's demanding ten quid ransom money."

"Oh my God!" Bella gasped. "Do you think your parents will cough up?"

"Not a chance. Where are they going to find that kind of dosh?"

"Looks like you're stuck here for the duration, then."

"Looks like it. Eh up, she's heading this way." Kitty grasped Bella's upper arm and steered her into the Haircare aisle. She picked up a packet of hair dye and shoved it under Bella's nose. "Pretend you're asking me about this. She won't bother us if she thinks you're a customer."

"Only one problem."

"What?"

Bella lifted a strand of her hair. "You don't dye your hair if you've got dreads. You can't. Not this kind of dye, at any rate. Not all over."

Tutting, Kitty replaced the dye and picked up a bottle of conditioner instead. "This, then. Ask me about this."

"Same problem," Bella told her.

"What, you don't use conditioner?"

"I don't use shampoo."

There was a moment's silence as Kitty digested this. "You mean you don't wash your hair?"

"Nope," Bella replied, cheerfully.

"What, never?"

"Not since I had this done."

"Eurgh! That's mingin'. It's not conditioner you need, it's nit lotion. Over there, madam – the prescriptions counter. The pharmacist will sort you out."

Giggling, Bella gave her a shove. "That how you talk to all your customers? Nice! Here, watch out, your kidnapper's coming over. So do you recommend this?" she asked Kitty, in an overly loud, poshed-up voice.

"Oh yes. Definitely. It, er, it reduces static and gives loads of added body," Kitty read off the back of the conditioner bottle. She could see Sharon watching them, her suspicious face peering through the display of hair bobbles and scrunchies at the end of the aisle. "And it gives your hair a wonderfully fresh citrus scent," she added.

"But will it get rid of my nits?" Bella demanded loudly, taking the bottle and scrutinizing it with feigned interest. Kitty pulled an urgent shut-up face at her, but Sharon had been approached by a woman with an opened pack of tights and a cross expression who clearly wanted her full attention, and the two of them walked off together in the direction of the tills.

"Actually, I've been thinking of getting it all cut off," Bella was saying.

"It's OK, she's gone. You don't have to pretend any more."

"I'm not. I *have* been thinking of having it cut. What do you think?"

"Yeah, why not? Get a Number One," she joked.

"I was thinking more of having it all totally shaved off. You know – the total slaphead look. The nits wouldn't stand a chance then."

"Kitty!" Sharon's strident tones cut through their laughter. "As you're obviously not busy you can relieve Sarah on till one while she goes for her break."

Bella, her back to Sharon, crossed her eyes at Kitty. Then she turned round. "Your assistant was just recommending some hair products," she said, her voice at its most sincere and charming. "I must say, she's extremely knowledgeable. I must congratulate you on your staff training."

Sharon's eyes narrowed. She knew when she was being taken for a ride. She gave a loud "hmph", turned on her heel and walked off.

Crossing her eyes behind Sharon's departing back, Bella said, "So if it's Sarah-on-till-one's break now, when's it yours?"

"Not till half twelve." Kitty pulled a face. "Don't suppose you feel like hanging round that long, do you? We could go and grab some lunch."

"No worries. I've got other stuff to do. I'll be back," she said, in Arnold Schwarzenegger's voice, as she pushed the bottle of conditioner on to the shelf, gave Kitty a wink and left.

Of all her friends, only Bella would have had the nerve to front it out with Sharon, Kitty reflected, removing the conditioner from where Bella had shoved it amongst the hairsprays and returning it to its correct position. Everybody else would have felt intimidated in the face of the supervisor's bossy yet unarguable rank-pulling.

Apart from Bruno, possibly – he had it too, that poised self-confidence which meant never being at a loss in any social situation. Kitty envied it of both of them, although she'd never admit that to Bruno. She'd never live down confessing to envying anything of her cousin's.

By the time Kitty arrived at the sandwich bar in town Bella was already there, sitting at one of the shiny fake leather banquettes with a large, laminated menu in front of her.

"Hiya. D'you know what you want? We should order pretty quickly if you've got to report back to the Queen of Mean – these places always take ages when they're busy."

Kitty plonked herself down opposite Bella and took the menu from her. "Erm – OK, I'll have the toasted ham and cheese ciabatta with a side salad, and a cappuccino. Oh, and a portion of chips. I'm so hungry I could eat a scabby dog. How about you?"

"I'll have a green salad and a fizzy water."

"Is that all? You won't get fat on that!" Kitty laughed, waiting for Bella's punchline (*Oh, and a double cheeseburger with fries on the side*, or some such), but none came. She just shrugged.

"I'm not very hungry. I only had breakfast an hour or so ago."

She took her cigarettes from her bag and lit up,

and Kitty regarded her with some dismay. It had just occurred to her that, unlike her, Bella didn't have a Saturday job and so wasn't earning.

"Is it the cash? Let me pay – it'll be my treat. I've still got most of my wages from last week, look." Kitty opened her wallet and showed Bella the contents, two crisp new ten-pound notes.

"It's not the cash." Bella took a determined drag on her cigarette and let the smoke trickle slowly through her nostrils. "Honestly. I'm just not hungry. These things suppress your appetite, anyway."

"Is that why you do it?"

"What, smoke?" Bella looked slightly startled, as if she'd never given the reason for her smoking any thought before. "No. I just enjoy it. I like the taste."

Kitty recalled when she'd briefly dated Simon Kershaw, back at school. He'd smoked, and when they kissed he had both smelt and tasted like an old ashtray. The words to tell Bella about this rose in her mouth, but she swallowed them hastily. It would sound really preachy. Let Bella smoke if she wanted to – after all, Kitty was hardly going to be snogging her, was she?

"I'll go and order then, shall I?" Bella got up and went to the counter. Kitty picked up both menus and stacked them neatly together behind the pepper and salt pots and a flower in a little white china bud vase. She knew she ought to mention to Bella what her aunt had said on the phone last night about her not having gone to a class at all, get it sorted. It had been bothering her ever since but it would have been impossible to get it straight in the shop earlier, with Stroppy Sharon jackbooting around in the background.

"Bella," she said, when she got back.

"Mm-hm?" Bella sat down, and picked up her cigarette from the ashtray where she'd left it smouldering. "Hey, look at that guy sitting over there – see his jacket? How cool is that! I wonder where he got it – not round here, I'll bet."

"Bell," Kitty said, firmly. "Shut up a minute. There's something I want to ask you."

"That sounds serious." She leant across the table with her free hand and touched Kitty's arm, gazing gravely into her eyes. "Yes darling, I will marry you," she said, and then went off in soft peals of merriment as the couple at the next table stopped their animated conversation and stared at them curiously. "Sorry. What is it?"

Kitty didn't quite know how to put it. "Don't take this the wrong way," she began, and then stopped.

Bella squinted at her through a cloud of smoke and frowned slightly. "C'mon Kitten, cut to the chase will you? You're getting me worried."

Kitty started to fiddle with the flower in the

bud vase, a pink-and-white spray carnation. "I rang you last night," she said, slowly.

"Oh yeah, Aunt Susan did say, now you come to mention it. Was it about something important?"

"No."

"Sorry hun, but you've lost me."

A bored-looking waitress arrived with their food, and Kitty was glad of the few moments of delay.

"Enjoy your meals," she told them, in an indifferent automatic voice, and left them to it.

Kitty took a deep breath. "I don't want you to think I'm checking up on you," she said, uncomfortably aware that she was doing exactly that, "but when I spoke to your aunt last night she told me you'd gone out with some lad." Not wanting to look directly at Bella, she picked up her fork, speared a chip and put it in her mouth. Only when she had chewed it thoroughly and swallowed it did she look up. Bella was regarding her salad with a slightly baffled smile.

"Gone out with some lad?" she repeated slowly; then, as if the penny had suddenly dropped, "Oh, you mean Mel!"

"Mel?"

"Yeah, Mel. You know – Mel."

"I know who he is, I just didn't know you were seeing him."

"I'm not seeing him!" Bella smiled broadly, as if the idea was preposterous. She stubbed out her cigarette and picked up her own fork. "He just called round to see if I wanted a lift to the class, that's all."

"The self-defence class?"

"That's right, yeah."

"You mean he goes too?"

"Yeah. It was him who told me about it, actually. Then last night he called round, and offered me a lift."

"But I thought you said you didn't like him?"

"Did I?" Bella looked mystified. "When?"

"Ages ago." *I think he could become a bit of a nightmare.* Kitty could hear her saying it. "At college. The first day of term."

"Oh." Bella shrugged, offhand. "He's OK. We're not *together* or anything – we just have an occasional drink, and he gives me a lift from time to time."

"To your classes."

"That's right."

"That's another thing – your aunt didn't seem to think you'd gone to any class."

For a moment Bella just looked at Kitty, her fork suspended halfway to her mouth, a drooping bit of watercress hanging from one of its tines. Then she laughed.

"Flippin' heck! What is this, the Spanish

Inquisition?" She put the fork back down. "You don't think Aunt Susan knows what I'm doing and where I'm going, do you? I don't have to tell her anything – she's not my parent. Anyway, she's not remotely interested. She has her life, and I have mine. It suits both of us." She stabbed a piece of cucumber with some force and lifted it to her mouth, and Kitty was left with the troubled feeling that she shouldn't have said anything.

"Sorry," she said, humbly.

"What are you sorry for?" Despite her savagery towards the hapless cucumber, Bella's face was scrupulously impassive as she chewed on it.

"She just surprised me when she said she didn't think you'd gone to a class. I didn't mean to turn it into an issue."

"You haven't." Bella swallowed, and then looked up and gave a slightly tight smile. "It's not an issue. Honestly. I've just got a bit of a thing about being – *monitored*, or whatever the word is. Years of foster parents on my case, I guess. It's not your fault."

"As long as you're sure." Kitty didn't want Bella thinking she believed her aunt rather than her. They were friends – friends trusted each other, they accepted the other's word about things.

"Course I'm sure. Let's just forget it, shall we?"

After lunch Bella went back to Boots with Kitty and gave her a warm hug before leaving, so Kitty was pretty certain that the misunderstanding was now firmly in the past. She was glad. She hated confrontation, even though she knew that it was sometimes necessary, and always loathed the feeling that she might have inadvertently upset somebody she cared about. She took her coat off in the staffroom and scurried back on to the shop floor, hoping to avoid the attention of Stroppy Sharon.

"Hello, Catrin." Today was obviously the day for seeing people she knew. This time it was Megan's mum, clutching a giant-sized bottle of pearly pink bubble bath and a bumper pack of soap.

"Oh, hi, Mrs Roberts. How are you?"

"I'm fine, thanks. Doing a bit of early Christmas shopping."

Kitty wondered who was going to be the lucky recipient of the soap. "Oh, right. How's Megan?"

"Not too great, *cariad*, thanks for asking all the same. She's drooping around the house feeling all sorry for herself."

"Aw, poor thing. Shall I call round after work to say hi?"

"You could do. She'd be pleased to see you, I'm sure." Mrs Roberts looked towards the exit. "Was that Bella Jones I saw you with just now?"

"It was, yes."

"I thought I recognized her. Megan said she was back in the area. She well, is she?"

"Very well, yes. She's at college, doing Leisure and Tourism."

"So where's she living?"

"With an aunt. A great-aunt," she corrected herself. "Didn't Megan tell you?"

"No."

"Oh." Kitty didn't know what to say next. Given that Megan hadn't exactly been thrilled at Bella's return, she could understand that her mum wasn't going to be jumping for joy either. Nonetheless, Kitty thought Megan might have filled her mum in on what Bella was up to by now; after all, she had looked after Bella for five years – to say she'd been her surrogate mum wasn't putting it too strongly. Surely she'd want to be kept up to date with Bella's doings, no matter how difficult things had become at the end?

"You must have missed her when she went away," Kitty said, impulsively.

"I felt bad about it. She was a good kid. When she was little." Mrs Roberts looked at Kitty suddenly, straight in the eye. "I was fond of her, you know. I always am – of all the children who pass through. Some are naturally loveable, the majority grow on you in time, but there was something special about Bella, when she was small."

"But things changed when she got bigger?" Kitty laughed, making a bit of a joke of it, but Mrs Roberts pursed her lips regretfully.

"They did. I daresay it was hormones, and all that. Adolescence. They don't stay little for ever, kids, wanting cuddles and suchlike. More's the pity," she added, briskly. "We eventually decided a change would be the best thing all round, and she went to live with other foster parents. And that was that."

It suddenly struck Kitty how odd it must be for Mrs Roberts to know absolutely nothing about Bella's life now. Kitty didn't know whether this was usual or not – maybe all foster parents lost touch with their charges once they moved on, maybe they had to, even, maybe it was all part of the fostering agreement, to let go and move on to the next, because how else could they cope with the dozens of kids in their care over the years? How otherwise could they manage to look after them and provide them with stability and care and affection, if not actually love them, and then not miss them like crazy once they'd gone?

Kitty had no idea. It wasn't anything she'd given even an atom of thought to before now. "Would you like to see her again?" she suggested, rather rashly but prompted by the heartwarming mental image of a doorstep reunion brought about by her, Kitty. "Would you like her to call round sometime; shall I suggest it to her?"

Mrs Roberts looked startled for a moment. "Well, yes, if she'd like to; that would be –" Then she seemed to give herself a tiny shake, as if her mind had dashed off somewhere by itself and she was fetching it back. "No," she said, decisively. "If she's been back since September, as Megan says, and she hasn't felt the need to call round off her own bat, I don't want her to feel she ought to start now." Kitty started to demur, to say, "But I'm sure she'd love to see you again," but Mrs Roberts shook her head firmly. "It's not how it works, *cariad*. They stay in touch because they want to, or not at all. Best to leave the past in the past, where it belongs."

chapter seven

Megan was over her tonsillitis and back at college the following week.

"I bumped into your mum at work on Saturday," Kitty told her.

"Yeah, she mentioned she'd seen you."

"Did she say she saw Bella, too?"

"No – where?"

"In the shop."

"She never told me that." Megan frowned slightly. "What did she say to her?"

"Oh, your mum just saw her in passing, kind of thing. They didn't talk to each other."

"Right." Megan nodded. There was something smug about that nod, something annoyingly self-satisfied – as if she was pleased that her mother and Bella hadn't spoken.

"Why didn't you tell your mum about Bella?" Kitty asked her.

"I did. I told her she was back."

"But nothing about what she's doing now, where she's living. . .?"

Megan lifted a shoulder. "Didn't think she'd be bothered."

"Well, you were wrong!" Kitty couldn't help sounding sharp. "She was interested – she wanted to know where she's living, and stuff like that."

"Really." A calculatedly bored expression slid over Megan's face.

"Yes, really." Megan's almost perverse non-interest in Bella was beginning to seriously wind Kitty up. "Look, I know it all ended in tears but the way you tell it, it's like once she left it was out of sight, out of mind. I can't believe your mum felt like that, not after she'd taken the place of Bella's own mum for so long."

"She never took anyone's place. You know, some foster-mothers like the kids to call them Mum, but she never does. She's always Auntie. She's really hot on that. Anyway, out of sight out of mind is exactly what happens once they've moved on, loads of times. From them, not Mum – she's used to it by now. You don't actually know anything about how fostering works, do you?"

She was pulling rank, something she was prone to doing on occasions. Kitty felt a spurt of exasperation with her. "Well, I do know your mum was fond of her. She told me."

"When?"

"When I spoke to her on Saturday."

"Oh." Megan looked surprised, although Kitty didn't know whether this was because her mother had told Kitty she had been fond of Bella, or because Megan had been unaware of the fondness.

"In fact –" Kitty stopped, wondered whether to press home her advantage, then thought better of it. Probably best not mention to Megan that her mum had been on the verge of having Bella round to catch up. Something told her that wouldn't go down very well.

"In fact?" Megan prompted.

"No, nothing. Meg –"

"What?"

"Did we gang up on you?"

"Gang up on me?" Megan wrinkled her nose. "How d'you mean?"

"When we were kids. Bella and me – did we, I don't know, deliberately exclude you?"

She looked startled. "Why are you asking after all this time?"

"It's just something Bruno said. He maintains we shut you out. And Bella said the other day that she used to be a cow to you."

Megan pressed her lips together wryly. "Well, how about that. The truth finally comes out."

"No, but really. Is that how you remember it?"

"Well, yeah. I suppose so. Since you're asking." She sighed. "It was years ago, Kitty – does it really matter any more?"

"I suppose not."

Megan sighed again, patiently. "It was years ago," she repeated. "Like you said, we were kids. You know what kids are like, they can be really mean to each other. Besides, someone always gets left out when there's three. My mum always used to say three's a crowd."

"Did she? My dad always called us the Gang of Three."

"I know. I remember that, too. They were probably both right – sometimes we all got on, sometimes we didn't. But it was so long ago. I don't see any point in going over it, raking up what may or may not have happened in the past."

It was more or less what Megan's mother had said to Kitty, on Saturday.

"Perhaps you're right. I guess it's now that matters, isn't it?"

"I suppose so. Just don't forget life has moved on for everybody – don't expect us all to slot back into the places we occupied before Bella went away. Life's not like that."

Kitty creeps across the lawn towards the rhododendrons as quietly as she can. She is holding her breath and biting her top lip with the effort of not giggling, because she is almost certain she can see Bella hidden inside. The bushes are laden with flowers, beautiful vivid pink blooms the size of a dinner plate, but here and there between the glossy green oval leaves Kitty can see little glimpses of Bella's turquoise-blue T-shirt.

She reaches the edge of the lawn, and glances quickly around before stepping on to the bark chippings spread carefully on all the flowerbeds in the garden to stop the weeds from growing. Ducking down, she slips through a gap in the lowest branches of the rhododendrons. From the lawn the bushes look dense and solid and enormous, taller than Daddy, but there is a hollow in their centre that is floored with bare trodden-down earth and large enough to stand upright in, and there in its very centre is Bella, smiling broadly. She gives a little jiggle of pleasure at seeing Kitty, and holds a finger to her lips.

"Sshh!" she hisses, and smiles again, her blue eyes dancing. She doesn't seem very upset at being found. Kitty looks about her in wonderment. The hollow in which they are standing is even bigger than she first thought, laced about with bare rhododendron branches and with stray fingers of sunlight creeping in through the leaves and forming intricate patterns upon the earth floor.

"I didn't know you could get in here," she whispers. "I always stay on the grass."

"Do you?" Bella whispers back. "It's wicked. A

secret hidey-hole. If it was in *my* garden, I'd come in here the whole time."

"It's like a cave."

Bella nods her agreement. "I used to live in a cave, once."

"*Did* you?" Kitty is, all at once, intrigued and not entirely believing. She didn't think people lived in caves – not really lived in them. "Why? When?"

"A long time ago. It was only for a little while. We were escaping from someone." She nudges Kitty with her foot. "Look."

Kitty looks. There, perched on a branch at about shoulder height, sits Cushion, his eyes black and wild and his tail twitching with excitement, alert and ready to pounce.

"What's he doing?"

"He followed me in."

Kitty lets out a snort of amusement, then claps a hand over her mouth.

"*Sshh!*" Bella says again, urgently, and grabs Kitty's arm. "She's coming!"

The two girls clutch at each other frantically as Megan appears in vision through the leaves, standing on tiptoe to peer over and around bushes, and as she draws closer Kitty can see an expression of perplexed anxiety on her face.

"Kitty?" she calls. "Bella? Are you in there?"

Almost too late, Kitty remembers how Bella's

T-shirt could be seen through the leaves, and she drops to the ground, taking Bella with her. Megan comes even closer, and Kitty stuffs her fist in her mouth to stop the laughter from bursting out. It is very warm inside the rhododendron bushes, warm and quiet, apart from the roaring of blood inside Kitty's head and the sound of a blackbird singing in the still air. From far away, Kitty can hear a dog barking – Heinz, somewhere in the house.

Suddenly there is a loud rustling sound, and Cushion leaps off his branch and through the cover of leaves, landing on the grass almost by Megan's feet. She gives a start and a little cry of surprise, and Kitty and Bella almost explode with the effort of keeping quiet, but then Megan starts to walk away, following Cushion who is stalking back towards the house with his tail raised in the air like a flagpole. Kitty and Bella stand up cautiously, still clutching each other.

"Come on!" Bella commands, in a whisper, and they creep out of the back of the rhododendron cave and along the perimeter of the lawn, hidden by the bushes.

As they reach the garden gate they can hear Megan. She is calling: "Kitty! Bella! Where are you? Come out! I don't want to play this game any more!"

They grin at each other as Bella opens the gate,

silently, carefully, and they slip through it and along the lane, where at last they can laugh out loud with the relief of giving Megan the slip.

When they go back, half an hour or so later, Megan is sitting at the kitchen table with a glass of orange squash and an untouched piece of Auntie Carys's home-made *bara brith* on a plate in front of her. Her face is pale, the freckles standing out as if stuck on. Her eyes are rimmed with red as if she has been crying. She looks up at them as they come in, full of reproach. Even her plaits look reproachful. Mummy turns round from the sink.

"There you are!" she says, in a cheerful voice. Kitty recognizes the voice as the one Mummy uses when she's annoyed about something but doesn't want to make a fuss, at least not yet, while there are other people around. "We've been wondering where you'd got to, haven't we, Megan?"

Megan doesn't answer, but instead picks up her *bara brith* and takes a careful, reproachful bite. Her front teeth leave squarish marks in the butter.

"Well, we're here now," says Kitty, boldly. "Can we have a drink?"

"May we," Mummy corrects, automatically.

"May we," Kitty repeats. Bella crosses her eyes

behind Mummy's back, which almost makes Kitty laugh again. Mummy opens the fridge door and takes out a big blue-and-white striped china jug of orange squash, which she pours into two glasses. She turns to hand the drinks to the girls.

"*Duw!*" she exclaims, noticing Kitty and Bella's clothes for the first time, which are all earthy from lying on the floor of the rhododendron cave. Bella's hair is tangled, and she has a twig stuck in it. "The state of you both! What have you been doing?"

"Playing hide-and-seek," Bella tells her, innocently, and smiles.

"Whatever is your Auntie Enid going to say when she sees you?"

Just then there is the sound of a key in the front door, and Daddy comes in, home from work. He smiles when he sees Kitty, Bella and Megan all sitting at the kitchen table, drinking their orange squash together.

"Ah," he says. "The Gang of Three. Have you been having a good time, now, girls?"

"Yes thank you, Mr Doyle," says Megan, politely, and Kitty doesn't dare catch Bella's eye because she knows she will want to laugh out loud if she does.

"Why don't we all have a drink sometime?" Kitty suggested. "In fact, why don't we get some tinnies in and have a bit of a get-together round my place."

"What d'you mean?" Megan looked suspiciously at her.

"OK. Let me explain. A drink – it's like liquid refreshment, served in a glass. Sometimes – and I don't want you to be shocked by this – sometimes it's even alcoholic."

"Ho ho. The drink bit I got – it was the 'we all' bit I didn't understand."

"Oh, you, me, Rhys. Bruno. In the Christmas holidays, perhaps. He breaks up soon."

Annoyingly, Megan wasn't distracted by the mention of Bruno. "And would Bella feature in this cunning plan, by any chance?"

"She might do." Kitty shrugged. "Depends if she can find a window. She's always dead busy these days."

"I've noticed. With Nicci, mainly."

"Nicci?"

"Yeah. Every time I've rung Nic recently to suggest doing something, it seems like she can't make it because she's seeing Bella. She's her new best friend, apparently – didn't you know?"

"I've seen them together around college a bit. Well, Nicci could come too, couldn't she – the more the merrier, far as I'm concerned."

"She could, yeah." Megan looked at her friend beadily. "So what's your motivation, then?"

"Excuse me? My motivation? It's Christmas." Kitty waved her hands around animatedly. "You know – 'tis the season to be trollied."

"Kitty. It's barely December – it's not Christmas for *weeks*. This is all for mine and Bella's benefit, isn't it? You want to engineer it for us to be all friends together again. The Gang of Three rides again."

"Yeah, OK then." Kitty let her hands drop and looked sheepish. "Guilty as charged. I can't help it – you're both my friends, and I'd really like us all to get together from time to time. Don't be arsey about it, Megan."

"I'm not being arsey. I'm up for a drink any time. You should know me by now. Just one condition – no, two. No, make that three."

"That'll be just the three conditions, then? Before you agree to coming round and drinking my drink?"

Megan ignored her and began ticking off on her fingers. "One, you definitely invite Bruno. This might be the ideal opportunity to convince him that what he really needs to make his life complete is, well, me, basically. Two, you invite a spare man along for Bella – I'm not having her nabbing him again, not like at Nicci's party."

"I think I can manage that. What's the third condition?"

"That you don't expect miracles. I know you

want me and you and Bella to be jolly chums again, but this isn't Enid Blyton, it's real life. We're not the Gang of Three any more, and to be honest –" she stopped, suddenly serious – "to be honest, I don't believe we ever were."

Kitty's bright idea of organizing a seasonal get-together with some of her friends had made her start to wonder what plans Bella had for Christmas. Presumably she was going to be spending it at her great-aunt's. Christmas in the Doyle household was always a big, overblown occasion, the whole works – tree, tinsel, turkey, tons of presents for everyone, open house on Christmas Eve for all Dad's important clients and the family round for lunch on Boxing Day. The thought of Bella spending it alone in her top-floor garret, or making artificial merry with her uninterested Aunt Susan, was too tragic for words.

"Would you mind if I invited Bella to mine for Christmas?" she asked Rhys.

He wrinkled his nose. "Shouldn't you be asking your folks, rather than me?"

"I will do. I just wanted to check with you first – that you don't mind sharing me with Bella."

"I expect I'll cope for one day." He put an arm round her. "Even if it is Christmas Day. We'll just have to make up for it on Boxing Day."

"Well actually. . ." Kitty tailed off, guiltily.

"Uh oh. This sounds ominous. Well actually. . .?"

"I thought I might see if she can come and stay for a few days. You know what it's like at that time of year – I don't like the thought of her all by herself in that little flat while everyone else is out partying."

"I thought you said her flat was cool."

"It *is* cool. Just a bit . . . well. You know. Lonely. You don't mind, do you?" She pulled away and peered at his face, looking for confirmation and finding something else instead – petulance, grumpiness. "You do mind," she stated, positively.

"No I don't," Rhys protested. "Did I say I minded?"

"Your face did."

"I can't help my face."

"It's a lovely face." She tucked her arm through his and snuggled into his shoulder persuasively. "Ah, go on, Rhys. She's one of my oldest friends." He sat very still, not responding, and she looked up at him. "What's wrong?"

He shrugged. "Nothing."

"I know it's not nothing." She nuzzled his neck in the way he normally couldn't resist. "Come on. It's Christmas. She hasn't got anywhere else to go."

"Really?" He raised an eyebrow. "Are you telling me she doesn't have any other friends? Every time I see her at college she seems to be in the middle of a whole crowd. Mainly of lads, as it happens."

"Well, she's not likely to be spending Christmas with them, is she?" Kitty pointed out, reasonably. Somewhere at the back of her consciousness she was dimly aware of a little voice telling her not to push it, that Rhys clearly wasn't keen on the thought of her devoting several days over Christmas to Bella, but she tried to ignore it. Perhaps she could make him come round to the idea.

"No?" he was saying. He gave a cynical little laugh. "It looked like she was about to elope with Mel Thomas the other day, never mind just spend Christmas with him."

"What? What d'you mean?"

"Tonsil tennis in the corridor," he elaborated.

"Mel Thomas? You mean, *Mel*? The guy she was with in the canteen the first day of term?"

"That's him."

"Are you sure?"

"Positive. They were all over each other."

We're not together or anything; he gives me a lift from time to time. . .

"That's odd," she said, slowly. "She told me there was nothing going on between them."

"It was definitely him. She wasn't exactly fending him off, either."

"I'm sure there's some logical explanation." Just one that, for the moment, she couldn't think of.

"Yeah, right," he scoffed. "And we all know what that is, don't we?"

"Don't you like her?" The thought had never occurred to her before – he had always been perfectly polite to her when they had met, which come to think of it hadn't actually been that often. Bella and Kitty tended to do their socializing with just the two of them.

He lifted a shoulder. "I don't really know her, do I? To like or dislike."

"What's that supposed to mean?" She stared at him but he wouldn't respond. "Look, if you'd rather I didn't invite Bella for Christmas, that's fine. Just say."

"No, no." He held up his hands as if warding off unfair accusations. "Go ahead, invite her. She's your long-lost mate, after all. Far be it from me to get in the way. I'll just stay away."

"Oh, no!" Kitty was dismayed. "There's no need for that. Can't you both come round?"

Rhys sighed hugely, as if trying to explain something to somebody dim-witted. "If you really want to know the truth, I don't want to. Not if Bella's going to be here."

"But you said you didn't dislike her." Kitty was beginning to feel baffled. Was all this mind games? If so, she didn't think she could be bothered to play.

"I don't *dislike* her. It's just –" He sighed again. "Ever since she reappeared on the scene, it seems she's the only one who matters. The only person you ever want to spend any time with."

"You're not *jealous*?" Kitty almost laughed out loud with incredulity, but the look on his face made her stop in her tracks. "Oh, Rhys. Don't be like that. There's no need. You know how I feel about you – you know I love being with you."

She spent the next ten minutes trying to mollify him, and he eventually softened. By the time he left he seemed appeased, and told her that he understood why she wanted to invite Bella for Christmas, and didn't mind. But try as she might, she couldn't persuade him to come round too, and they agreed to meet up the day after Boxing Day to exchange presents. It was odd – she hadn't had him down as the proprietorial type, not at all. On the other hand, if that's how he was feeling maybe it was just as well they weren't meeting up until after Bella had gone. At least Kitty wouldn't have to worry about the possibility of him going off on a moody because of her presence. Nonetheless, she had to fight down guilty feelings of having chosen Bella over him, despite common sense telling her that it was Rhys who had made that choice, not her.

She sighed. Why were her relationships getting so complicated?

"Really? For the whole of Christmas? That's so kind of you." Bella was clearly touched by the invitation. "Aunt Susan's going up to Scotland to stay with friends. She did ask me if I wanted to go too, but I knew she was only being polite. I was planning to get in a whole pile of the most un-Christmassy videos I could find, and open a tin of beans."

"Well, don't let me stop you."

"Are you kidding? Beans on toast versus turkey with all the trimmings? No contest!" She laughed. "Aw, thanks Kitten – I can't think of anything I'd rather do for Christmas than spend it with you lot." She enfolded Kitty in an affectionate hug, her eyes suspiciously bright. Kitty thought she might actually be going to cry.

"Steady on! I'm only inviting you for Christmas, not to share my life with me!" she joked. "Which reminds me – what's all this I hear about you and Mel?"

"Mel?" Bella's brow creased in concentration, as if trying to remember who Mel was. "Oh, Mel! What about him?"

"Oh, Mel? Don't give me that! My spies tell me you were spotted at college getting frisky with each other."

Bella flapped a dismissive hand. "He's been getting a bit persistent. Nothing I can't handle." She changed the subject swiftly. "Hey, why don't you 'n' me go to Chester at the weekend and do some Christmas shopping?"

Kitty blinked. "Blimey. Is everyone doing their Christmas shopping early except me?"

"We can beat the crowds. I want to get your parents something really nice to say thanks for having me."

"OK then," Kitty said. "Let's hit Chester. It'll have to be Sunday, though. I'm working on Saturday. God, Bell – when was the last time we went Christmas shopping together?"

Bella grinned. "Must be years ago. Do you remember that trolley thing we did?"

"Oh my God, yes, I'd forgotten all about that! How on earth did we get away with that one? It was begging, really. It's just as well my parents never found out about it – my mum would have gone totally ballistic. I'd have been grounded for, like, ever."

Bella grinned. "But it was good, wasn't it? I thought it was a fab idea."

"So did I. You always thought of fab ideas."

*

At first, Kitty thinks it a dreadful idea. It is cold and raining, and December, so it will be dark by about half-past three. Kitty would much rather stay indoors, but Bella is adamant. So they catch a bus to Llandudno from the bus stop outside the library (an adventure in itself as Kitty has never been on a bus without her parents before). This in itself makes her extremely nervous, but Bella brushes her concerns aside.

"It's OK – don't worry. Nobody's going to find out what you're doing. Where did you tell them we were going?"

"Back to your house."

"Well, there you go. They're not going to check up, are they."

"They might. What if Megan goes round to call for us?"

"She won't."

"She might."

"She *won't*. She wanted to come along too, but I told her she couldn't, it was just you 'n' me."

"Oh." That would be Megan in a bad mood the next time she saw her, then. She tried another tack. "But what if my parents decide to go out, and drive past and see me?"

"Were they going to go out?"

"Well, no. But what if they change their minds?"

"They won't change their minds," Bella declares, positively.

"Or what if someone else sees me? Mrs Thomas from next door, or – or Auntie Carys, or Bruno? They're going to wonder what I'm doing standing at the bus stop."

"They'll probably think you're waiting for a bus."

"But I don't catch buses by myself."

"You're not by yourself, are you? You're with me. *And* –" Bella puts out a hand and rustles the sleeve of Kitty's long and voluminous cagoule – "you're all wrapped up in this. Nobody's going to even recognize you with your hood up. *I* wouldn't recognize you, if I wasn't with you."

Just at that moment the bus comes sailing along through the rain, and stops at the bus shelter with a swish and a hiss of airbrakes. Bella jumps on to the step.

"Come on, Kitten – don't be a wuss! It'll be great, you'll see!" she says over her shoulder, with a grin.

The girls get off the bus opposite the supermarket, and walk through the car park. It is busier than Kitty has ever seen it, with cars driving slowly round and round, trying to find a spare space.

"Why's it so busy?" she asks Bella, who shrugs.

"It's always busy on Saturday. *And* it's Christmas."

"Not for three weeks." It seems like a lifetime away, even though the shops have had Christmas cards and decorations in since September, some of them.

"Hey, I got a joke." Bella turns to Kitty, her hair sodden rats' tails, rain dripping down her face. "What d'you do if you see a spaceman?"

Kitty frowns. "*I* don't know. What?"

"Park in it, man!" Shrieking with laughter, Bella grabs Kitty's hand and they splash through the puddles to the entrance, where the trolleys stand corralled in a little roofed enclosure. They are kept tethered together on short metal chains which require a pound coin in a slot to release them, which is returned when the trolley is put back. Bella's idea is simple, but brilliant: stand near the entrance and offer to take people's shopping trolleys to their cars for them, help them unpack their shopping, and then take the trolley back to the trolley park.

"Then when we put them back, we get to keep the pounds!" Bella explains, with glee.

Kitty is more doubtful. "Won't people want to take them back themselves? To get their money back?"

"Not if it's raining!" Bella says, triumphantly. "Well, OK, some of them might," she amends. "But I bet you loads of them can't be bothered. Specially if we've helped them unpack, and everything. A pound's nothing to them."

And she is right. Bella and Kitty watch as people emerge from the warm dry cocoon of the shop with their plastic bags of shopping piled high before them, their faces changing when they see the rain beating relentlessly down outside. Some of them brush the girls' offer of help away, impatiently, but plenty more accept. A couple of hours later they are cold and damp, but nearly twenty pounds apiece better off.

"Twenty quid!" Bella exclaims, with glee. "What are you going to do with yours?"

Kitty has never had so much money at one time before, especially not in pound coins. They are weighing down the pockets of her cagoule. She thinks about all the things she could buy – that cute furry pink pencil case she's seen in WHSmith's, the glittery nail varnish and matching lipgloss in Boots, that special magazine with all the *Pop Idol* stickers, a month's supply of Curly-Wurlys. . .

"Dunno," she says. "How about you?"

"I'm going to buy all my Christmas presents," Bella says, her eyes shining. "I can get Auntie Enid and Uncle Phil something really cool now."

Kitty feels slightly guilty at planning to spend all her money on herself. Perhaps Bella might like the furry pink pencil case. She is her best friend, after all, and deserves a nice present.

When they got to Chester on Sunday the girls split up for an hour to do their own personal shopping. Within half an hour after meeting up again, Kitty realized that any concerns she may previously have had about Bella's funds, or lack of them, had been seriously misplaced. She was flashing cash about like there was no tomorrow.

"You're not going to buy all of those, are you? You come into a fortune or something?" Kitty teased her in Accessorize. Having flitted from one beautifully arranged colour scheme to another with little cries of delight Bella was now in front of the mirror, one arm draped about with long filmy scarves of black, cream and gold organza, her hand clutching four pairs of earrings which she held up to the side of her face in turn as she tried to decide which ones suited her best.

She grinned at Kitty's reflection. "I love this shop, don't you? I try to convince myself I'm only coming in to get prezzies for my mates, but I always end up buying more for myself than anybody else."

Kitty caught a glimpse of the price ticket on one of the three scarves. Nineteen ninety-nine. That was sixty quid's worth of scarves Bella had over her arm.

"Where do you get all your money from?" The words were out before Kitty could stop them, tumbling off her tongue as if they had a life of their own. "I mean, you explained about your aunt getting allowances and stuff – do you get one as well?" She tried to rephrase her question but now she sounded clumsy as well as prying. She hoped Bella wasn't offended – friends or not, her financial set-up was really nothing to do with Kitty.

Bella looked thoughtfully down at the earrings in her hand and selected another pair, lifting them to her lobes and turning her head slightly to get the full effect. *What makes you think it's any of your bloody business?* Kitty could sense the question forming in Bella's mind, but when her friend opened her mouth to reply she said nothing of the kind.

"Something like that," she said instead. Their eyes met in the mirror. After a tiny, uncomfortable moment, Bella said solemnly, "Actually, my mother's a rich heiress. Didn't I ever tell you?" Then her eye was caught by something wonderful at the back of the shop. "Hey," she exclaimed, grabbing Kitty's hand and darting over. "Isn't this hat just fab?" It was a velvet beanie, panelled in black and amber. She took it from the display and pulled it on to Kitty's head, tucking her hair underneath so just a few curly

135

blonde strands escaped, and adjusting the angle. "There. It's so you, hun. You must have it."

Kitty regarded herself gravely. "It is lovely," she agreed. "It makes me look –" She waved her hands, unable to find an adjective that wasn't too immodest.

"Foxy as hell," Bella finished for her.

Kitty took it from her head and looked at the price. "Bloody hell!" she exclaimed. "Nearly thirty quid! I don't think so."

"Let me buy it for you, then," Bella said. "As your Christmas present."

Kitty shook her head, reluctantly. "You can't. It's way too much." She was severely tempted but knew there was no way she could afford a similar amount for Bella's present, and anything else just wouldn't be fair. It was one of the unwritten rules of friendship, wasn't it – as you receive, so shall you give, or something similarly biblical-sounding.

"Ah, go on, Kitten – let me treat you," Bella wheedled; but Kitty wouldn't be swayed, and after a few more unsuccessful attempts at coaxing her, Bella returned the hat to its hook, pulling a face of mock rebuke at Kitty as she did so.

"You know what you said about your mum earlier on?" They were sitting opposite each other on the train, homeward bound. Bella never

136

spoke of her mother, never; that she had done so had struck Kitty as unusual at the time, but then they had become distracted by the business with the hat.

"What about her?" Bella held on to her bags on the seat next to her as they rattled over a bumpy set of points.

"About her being a rich heiress."

"Oh that!" Bella made an amused noise down her nose. "Maybe I was exaggerating a touch. Maybe not rich, exactly. Not *rich* rich."

"But still an heiress."

"Yeah. Well, when my grandmother died she left her everything. That's being an heiress, isn't it?" There was a moment's silence while Kitty digested all of this. Then Bella said, quite casually, "Maybe it made up for the other stuff."

"What other stuff?"

"She had a rough deal when she was pregnant with me. My mother, I mean. Not my grandmother. Obviously."

"How d'you mean?"

"My father beat her up."

"While she was pregnant? What a bastard!"

"All the time. Before she was pregnant, too. But that was the last straw. He broke her nose, and three ribs. She left him after that – went to a women's refuge."

Kitty was horrified. "Christ, Bell," she said,

leaning forward, "that's awful. Your poor mother. What did she do?"

"Stayed there until I was born."

"You were born in a women's refuge?"

"No, in hospital. But while she was still living there."

"Did she ever see him again?"

"Don't know. Don't think so. She always found me hard work, I know that much. Perhaps I reminded her of all of it, or him, or something. I've always kind of felt that's why she wanted shot of me."

"That's awful," Kitty repeated. She took hold of her friend's hands in a unconsciously Bella-like gesture. "Why didn't you tell me all this before?"

Bella's eyes – blue as blue, speedwell blue, and apparently unclouded by any distress at all – looked back into Kitty's own. Then she shrugged. "It's no biggie."

How could she say that? It was awful, not just for Bella's mother but for Bella herself. What a terrible start in life. It explained so much – Bella's being fostered, how she never mentioned her mother or indeed any family of any kind (apart from Aunt Susan, of course, whose function seemed to be more that of landlady than actual family). "Bella, I—"

"It's OK," she said, squeezing Kitty's hands as if to cut off her words. "Really. I shouldn't have told you – you've got such a nice family it's probably hard for you to get your head round other people's domestic arrangements being – what's the word? – dysfunctional. But I've always known about it – before I was fostered, my mother used to crack on about what bastards men are and how you should never trust them. Even though I was only a little kid and didn't have the faintest idea what she was on about."

"But –"

"Honestly." She removed her hands. "It's not a problem. Women get beaten up and kids get fostered all the time."

"Yes, I know, but –"

"Honestly," she said again, firmly. "Don't worry about it." She leant back in her seat. "C'mon, hun. No gloomy face allowed – think of all those wicked Christmas goodies we've got!"

Another example of her fobbing-off tactics. When she didn't want to talk about something, nothing Kitty or anybody else could say would make her change her mind. It was pointless even to try.

The train swayed and clattered over more uneven points, and two of Bella's carrier bags slid off the seat and on to the floor, half-disgorging their contents as they did so. They both reached to retrieve them, laughing as they narrowly avoided crashing heads, and as Bella lifted them on to the seat, shoving their contents back inside, Kitty caught sight of a sudden flash of something familiar. It was the amber-and-black velvet hat from Accessorize, the one she had quite clearly seen Bella return to its place on the display.

chapter eight

"Are you saying she stole it?" Kitty could quite clearly hear the disbelief in Bruno's voice, even down the line or across the airwaves, or however the hell mobiles work. "In front of a shop full of people?"

"Of course I'm not saying that." Hearing him saying it, out loud like that, made her realize just how ridiculous a notion it was. A free spirit Bella might be – a loose cannon, even, at times – but she wasn't a thief. Kitty was pretty sure of that.

"So what are you saying? She offers to buy you a scarf—"

"It wasn't a scarf, it was a hat," Kitty muttered, Bruno's argumentative tone bizarrely making her feel as if she was somehow in the wrong.

"Whatever. She offers to buy it for you, you say no, she puts it back – and then later on, bugger me, out it falls from her bag. Is that what you're saying happened?" he demanded.

"Pretty much, yeah. Don't *hector* me, Bruno," she complained. "I'm only telling you what I saw."

"Or thought you saw. Are you sure you didn't

have one too many alcopops at lunchtime? I know what you girlies get up to when you're out doing your retail therapy."

"Look, I know what I saw, OK? There's nothing wrong with my eyesight. Stop bloody patronizing me. I'm not suggesting she stole it – I just wondered what it was doing in her bag, that's all."

"You could always ask her."

"What?"

"Ask her. Tell her you saw it in her bag, and couldn't help wondering how it got there."

Kitty said with heavy sarcasm, "Oh yeah. Fab idea. That's so what I'm going to do."

"Well, why not? It's perfectly logical."

"Oh, logical, schmogical. You're such a –"

"Such a what?" She could hear him frowning at the other end, ready to take offence at whatever she said. But how could she possibly ask Bella? It was tantamount to accusing her of pinching it. Besides, what if it was all perfectly legit – if Bella had somehow bought it without her seeing, and was intending after all to give it to her for Christmas?

"Such a lawyer," she finished. Odd how both he and Rhys were set on that path, when they were so unalike.

"Aw, thanks, cuz," he said cheerfully. "That's the nicest thing anyone's ever said to me."

If nothing else, mentioning it to Bruno had

clarified in Kitty's mind the impossibility of actually doing anything about it. In which case, the only sensible thing to do was to try and forget it.

"I expect there's some perfectly rational reason for it," she declared, firmly.

"What, me being a lawyer?"

"Of course not you being a lawyer." She clicked her tongue impatiently. "I meant about the hat being in Bella's bag."

"I know what you meant. I was just being smart, as we lawyers like to do."

"Something tells me you're not taking this entirely seriously."

"Sorry, Kitty. I just can't see Bella as a shoplifter. I mean, tell me honestly – can you?"

"Not really, no." A sudden vision passed through her mind, of Bella's bulging wallet and all the money she had spent that day. "Apart from anything else, she doesn't actually need to nick things. She seems to be loaded these days."

"Really?" Bruno's voice perked up. "Perhaps I ought to get to know her a bit better over the holidays. I always fancied hooking up with a rich chick."

"In your dreams," Kitty said with scorn. "Bella knew you in your Acne Stadium days, remember. She's seen you in those mingin' swimming trunks you used to wear. The ones that were age seven to eight, that you wouldn't let Aunt Carys throw away."

Bruno's voice took on a dreamy quality. "I remember those. They were top trunks."

"They were mingin'! They had Winnie the Pooh on them!"

"There's nothing wrong with Winnie the Pooh," he said indignantly.

"Not for an eight-year-old, granted. You were twelve. Face it – Bella thinks of you like a brother. There's no way she's ever going to fancy you." Even as she said it another vivid image came into her head, this time of Bella and Bruno embracing at Nicci's party, and Megan's freckled face bobbing around behind them, her features stamped with unmistakable jealousy.

Since Bella came back, life seemed to be getting rather complicated. Before, all Kitty's relationships were simple and easy to handle. She knew where she was with them – Boyfriend Rhys, Best Friend Megan (who fancied Cousin Bruno, in a harmless yearning-from-afar kind of way), Lesser Friend Nicci, Irritating Little Brother Owen – everybody occupying their rightful slots, fulfilling their respective roles. But Bella's return seemed to have changed all that. Rhys quite plainly had some kind of problem with her (despite his assurances to Kitty that he was cool about the Christmas plans, he had taken to pulling a kind of long-suffering face every time she mentioned Bella's name); the dynamic between Bella and Bruno seemed to have changed to the extent that Megan was now viewing her as a serious love rival; Nicci's affections appeared to have switched from Megan to Bella; even Owen had morphed from being your archetypal pain-in-the-bum, girl-hating kid brother to a slavish devotee of Bella's, hanging on her every word when she was round and constantly asking Kitty for little snippets of information about her when she wasn't as an excuse for mentioning her name: "Does Bella like pepperoni pizza?"; "What's Bella's favourite TV programme?" It was like in Chemistry, where introducing another element into the equation upsets the whole formula, changes the entire balance so that the end result becomes utterly different and unrecognizable from the original. Still, you could hardly blame Bella for people's reactions to her. She was just being herself.

"Just no way," she repeated, but slightly less emphatically than before. *At least, I hope not, else the shit really is going to hit the fan with her and Megan.*

"No?" Bruno retaliated. "Sounds like a challenge to me." Somewhere in the background there was a sudden hubbub of raised leery voices, then a muffled sound as Bruno covered the mouthpiece to reply. "Look, gonna have to go." His voice was suddenly loud in her ear.

"Lecture?" Kitty sympathized.

"No, down the pub."

"God, it's a hard life. Still, somebody's got to do it."

"Too true. Look, I'm back for the holidays at the weekend – I'll see you then, yeah? And don't worry – I'll be sure to pack my pulling pants. The ones without Winnie the Pooh on."

Then he was gone. Kitty was almost certain he was joking about trying to pull Bella, but you could never be sure with Bruno, who much of the time appeared to do things just to be perverse. She wondered whether she ought to warn somebody – Megan, or Bella. Or even Bruno himself – tell him about Megan's long-term crush on him, how upset she would be if he even pretended to try and cop off with Bella just to prove a point to Kitty. . .

She gave herself a little shake. *For God's sake! It's not up to me to tell people who to fancy or what to do. I'm not personally responsible for other people's happiness – I must let them just do what they want. They always do, anyway – with or without my intervention.*

Bella arrived at the Peppermint House on Christmas Eve afternoon. Kitty spotted her from her bedroom window, trudging up the lane in the gathering gloom and enveloped in what appeared to be some hooded garment, like a monk's. She sprinted down the stairs and opened the door just before Bella had a chance to ring the bell.

"Oh hi," she said, looking up in surprise. "You beat me to it."

"Amazing coat," Kitty told her. It was full-length, dark brown and lustrous and surely not real fur. "Where did you get it?"

"Oxfam." Bella pushed the hood back with one hand. "I love charity shops, you can pick up some fab stuff. It's amazing what people chuck out. Flippin' heck, it's cold out here. Aren't you going to ask me in?"

Kitty was staring at her. "My God! You've had your hair cut!"

"No, I've had my ears lowered." She ran a be-ringed hand over her short spiky glossy crop and grinned. "What d'you reckon, then? Does it suit me?"

"You look amazing," Kitty said slowly. She'd thought Bella's dreads had suited her but this was something else, the severe shortness of the cut flattering the sharp angles of her jawline and cheekbones. "Like a model."

Bella sucked in her cheeks and struck a pose. "Naomi Campbell, eat your heart out. Well, am I coming in, or what? I'm freezing my butt off out here."

"Oh yeah, sure. Sorry." Kitty bent to pick up two supermarket carrier bags from the doorstep. "Is this all you've got?"

"And this." Bella indicated her velvet hippy sack, swinging from her shoulder. "I don't need much. Careful with those!" The carrier bags chinked as Kitty picked them up.

"Blimey! What's in here, secret booze supplies?"

Bella lifted her chin and narrowed her eyes – what Kitty called her inscrutable face. "Presents for your folks," she said, tapping the side of her nose with a finger. "You'll see soon enough." She followed Kitty up the stairs and into the guest bedroom.

"Here you go – you're in here." Kitty turned the bedspread down, drew the curtains and switched on the bedside light. "Towels, hangers in wardrobe, blah blah blah. Just shout if you need anything. D'you want me to leave you to get unpacked?"

For answer, Bella slithered out of her coat and laid it across the end of the bed, then opened the wardrobe door and threw her velvet sack inside. "Sorted," she said. "Let's go and put those presents under the tree, shall we?" She regarded Kitty with a suddenly serious expression. "I've

148

really been looking forward to this, you know? It's so kind of you to invite me. Really thoughtful." She held out her arms and gave her a hug.

"It's OK." Kitty returned Bella's hug, slightly awkwardly. "I've been looking forward to it, too."

Bella hugged her back with characteristic warmth and enthusiasm. Kitty could feel the thinness of her beneath her sweater, the slightness of her bones. It was like hugging a child.

"It's going to be such a great Christmas," Bella said. "The best."

They all gathered around the tree on Christmas morning, with a glass of champagne apiece and Dad in his habitual role of chief present-distributor.

"This is so cool," Bella kept saying, as if she was from a different culture and had never experienced this particular tradition.

"Haven't you ever had Christmas before? What does your family do?" Owen wanted to know, with typical lack of tact, or sensitivity, or whatever it was.

Kitty cringed inwardly. "Shut up, Owen."

"What?" All wounded innocence.

"Bella was fostered for years," Mum reminded him.

"So? I thought you said she used to live with Moaning Megan – didn't they do Christmas?"

"Not like this." Bella looked round at the four of them, beaming.

"So what did they used to do?" Owen persisted.

Kitty tutted, and raised her eyes heavenwards. "For God's sake, Owe, give it a rest will you."

"They did do Christmas," Bella told him, "but it wasn't as classy as this. They didn't have champagne, for a start, and Megan's mum was always rushing round seeing to the turkey and basting the spuds and—"

"Whatting the spuds?"

"Basting them. I never knew what it meant, either. And Megan was usually feeling sick from eating her Cadbury's selection box from Mrs Thing Next Door before breakfast, and Uncle Phil – Megan's dad – would always nick off down the pub to get away from all the hassle. We didn't all sit around opening presents together like this – it's so *civilized*." She took a sip, her eyes sparkling at Kitty over the top of her champagne flute.

"OK." Dad picked up another parcel, beautifully wrapped in gold tissue paper and hung about with a cascade of gold and cream ribbon. "Who's is this? Oh, it's for you, Catrin."

"You make a great MC," Bella said. "MC Mike.

Is dere a Santa in da house," she added, being Ali G. Owen fell about laughing as if this was the funniest thing he had heard all year, and Kitty and Bella exchanged knowing glances.

"Too much fizzy," Kitty declared. "Don't give him any more."

"Leave him alone. It's Christmas," Dad said firmly, picking up the bottle and topping everybody up. "Oh, not enough for you as well, Owe. What a shame. Aren't you going to open that, Kitty-Cat?"

"It's almost too pretty to open," Mum said. "Who's it from, *cariad*?"

"Bella." Kitty knew what was in it without having to open it. Slowly, with a feeling of dread, she pulled the paper from around it and exposed the panels of black-and-amber velvet.

"What is it?" Mum and Dad craned to have a look, and Kitty discarded the remaining paper and smoothed out the hat.

Feeling slightly sick, she pulled it on to her head, her blonde curls escaping around the brim. She had a sudden sharp memory of another Christmas, years ago, and another present from Bella.

The doorbell goes just as Kitty is looking at the pile of brightly wrapped presents underneath the tree and thinking how she can't wait for tomorrow to come so she can see what is in all of them. Daddy comes in to the sitting room with Bella, who is holding a plastic carrier bag.

"Look who it is." He beams down at her. "Would you like something, now? Glass of pop? Mince pie?"

"No thanks, Uncle Mike. I've just called by to see Kitty."

"I'll leave you to it, then."

They go upstairs to Kitty's room and close the door firmly behind them.

"Where's your mum?"

"At work."

"On Christmas Eve?" Bella pulls a sympathetic face. "Pants."

"I know. But she always says people don't stop being sick just because it's Christmas. She finishes at four. It's OK really."

"Where's Owen?"

"Having a nap." She frowns slightly. "I thought you'd come to see me?"

"I have. I've brought Owe's present, that's all. I wanted to give it to him." She roots around in the carrier bag and produces a model car, a bright red Mini mounted on cardboard and covered by rigid plastic with a hollow bubble in the middle in the car's exact shape. "I know he's into cars at the moment. D'you think he'll like it?" she asks.

"He'll love it," Kitty replies.

152

"Sorry I didn't wrap it. I didn't have any paper – I thought maybe you could do it for me?"

There are bagfuls of wrapping paper in the guest bedroom, much of it matching the presents neatly stacked downstairs under the Christmas tree. Kitty doesn't think she is supposed to have noticed that, or even to know the paper is there – she is sure her parents think she still believes in Santa Claus and she plays along because she doesn't want to disappoint them – but it is not exactly hidden away, just dumped on top of the bed. Even though she is not much good at wrapping presents, always getting in a mess with the Sellotape, she is sure she will be able to manage this one.

"OK." She gets off her bed and goes over to her CD player. "What shall we do – shall I put some music on? Spice Girls?"

"Bleurgh!" Bella pulls a comical face and pretends to be sick over the side of the bed, and Kitty laughs.

"What's the matter? I thought you liked the Spice Girls."

"I did, but Megan's been playing that CD over and over. I'm fed up with it. We're *all* fed up with it." She imitates Mrs Roberts, frowning and tilting her head as if calling up the stairs. "'Megan Louise, turn that flaming racket down! We'll have the neighbours banging on the walls, complaining!' I caught her looking at herself in the mirror the other day, singing into her hairbrush and pretending to be Ginger Spice. Lame."

Kitty laughs again, feeling a tiny bit guilty as she does so. Megan, after all, is her friend as well. But Bella is right, she *does* want to be Ginger Spice. She told Kitty so herself, only the other day.

"So what shall I put on, then?"

"Don't worry. I can't stay long. Aunt Enid wants me and Megan to go to some church thing later." She pulls a disgusted face. "Who wants to go to church at Christmas!" She bends, and rummages in her Tesco bag again. "Anyway, look, here's your present."

She has something small and shiny enclosed in her fist. She passes it to Kitty, and Kitty opens her own hand to discover a silver locket on a chain lying there. It looks vaguely familiar, and is so beautiful and so unexpected that she doesn't know what to say.

"What's wrong?" Bella asks her anxiously. "Don't you like it? It's real silver, it said so on the label."

Suddenly Kitty remembers where she has seen it before – at the market in town, weeks ago, on a stall along with other jewellery, bangles and bracelets and earrings. *Sterling silver*, the sign above it all had said. She remembers now. Bella had asked the stallholder what sterling meant. She can't remember what the price had been, but she knows it must have been a lot.

"It's lovely." Kitty sighs with bliss. "It's – it's wicked."

"You know what?" Bella sits up on the bed, looking pleased. "It opens – look." She leans across and fiddles with a small catch at the top, and the locket obligingly falls open. "You can put pictures in, one on each side. One of you and one of your boyfriend."

"Don't be daft! I haven't got a boyfriend."

"Well, when you do."

"Or of my mum and dad?"

"If you want. Or me and you." Bella looks closely at her. "That would be cool, wouldn't it? One of me and one of you. Soul sisters."

"Soul sisters?" Kitty smiles. It sounds good, it has a nice ring to it. "Is that what we are?"

"Yeah. Didn't you know?" Suddenly Bella isn't smiling, her kingfisher-blue eyes not sparkling with mirth as usual but grave and serious. "We're twins, separated at birth. That's why we're so alike. We're sisters, only nobody knows but us."

For just a moment, Kitty half-believes her. Then Bella throws back her head and laughs delightedly, showing her pearly-white teeth.

"Oh, that would be so cool! If you were my sister, instead of Megan."

"She's only your foster sister. Not your real one."

"No. Thank God. Talking of God –" she looks at her watch – "I'd better go before Aunt Enid sends out the search party. Have a lovely Christmas, Kitten."

She gives her a sudden hug and is gone. Kitty sits on her bed with the locket in her hand, listening to her soul sister clumping down the stairs, loudly singing the disdained Spice Girls song and calling goodbye to Daddy.

"What's up?" Bella was looking at her with some anxiety. "Is it OK?"

"It's beautiful," Mum said. "It really suits you, Kitty."

"I've never seen you in a hat before." Dad looked at her approvingly. "You should wear them more often."

"Is it OK?" Bella asked again. Still with the hat on her head, Kitty looked at them – her parents, both smiling encouragingly, and Bella cross-legged on the floor, her hands folded meekly in her lap and her face clouded with disquiet and disappointment. "I've kept the receipt, so you can take it back if you want," she said, quietly.

Kitty leant across and put her arm round her friend. "It's fab," she said. "I just love it. Thanks, Bell."

*

When Kitty rang Rhys later that afternoon, to wish him Merry Christmas, she got his voicemail. Fighting down a stab of disappointment and renewed guilt she left a falsely cheery message, which Bella, coming into the room, caught the tail end of.

"I was wondering where Rhys was," she said. She offered Kitty an open box of Quality Street – her present from Owen, carefully wrapped in paper featuring Mickey Mice in Santa hats. "Want one of these? He's coming round later, is he?"

Kitty rummaged round in the box, making a big thing of trying to find a purple one and wondering if she could avoid answering directly. "Er, not exactly." She looked up, straight into Bella's gimlet-sharp blue gaze.

"What does 'not exactly' mean?"

"Um. No, he isn't." She unwrapped the sweet and put it in her mouth.

Bella frowned. "Why not? It's not because of me being here, is it?"

Her directness made Kitty redden, uncomfortably. "No, no, of course not," she mumbled, through the chocolate and caramel. But her crimson face told a different story.

Bella plunked down on the sofa, her eyes clouded with dismay. "I knew it. I knew he didn't like me," she declared.

"He does like you!" Kitty protested, swallowing the chocolate with effort.

"So how come he avoids my eye whenever I see him?" Bella asked, softly. "How come he never talks to me? How come you're not seeing him today – Christmas Day?"

Kitty didn't know how to answer. "It's not because he doesn't like you," she said, staunchly. "I promise you."

"What, then?"

"To tell you the truth. . ." Kitty sighed, sat on the chair next to Bella and put a hand on her arm. It felt important to reassure her that, whatever Rhys's reasons for staying away (and Kitty didn't fully understand them herself), it wasn't through dislike. "To tell you the truth, I think he's a bit jealous."

"*Jealous?*" Bella wrinkled her nose. "What on earth of?"

"You. Well, no, not you," she amended. "It's nothing personal. More like, the time I'm spending with you. I think that's how it goes."

"Rather than him?" Kitty nodded, and Bella exhaled through half-closed lips, expressively. "Phew. That's a bit heavy, isn't it? I couldn't cope with a possessive boyfriend."

"Oh, he's not possessive," Kitty assured her, quickly. Perhaps a bit too quickly. "Not really. It's no big deal, honestly. I think it's more like, you've come back on the scene after all this time, and suddenly I'm seeing so much of you, and. . ." She tailed off.

Bella twisted round and caught hold of her friend's hands. "Kitty," she said, earnestly. "Don't fall out with Rhys because of me. Please don't do that. I mean it. I don't want to be the cause of any trouble between anybody. I mean it, Kitty – don't fall out with him."

She sounded so urgent that Kitty found herself clutching her hands back. "I won't," she said, seriously. "Don't worry – I won't."

According to tradition, the family came round on Boxing Day – Aunt Carys and Uncle Martin, Bruno and, on a rare visit home, Kitty's eldest cousin Ged, bringing up the rear. She hadn't seen him for some time, two or three years at least, and she scarcely recognized him now as he came in the front door and stood in the hall amid all the loud and enthusiastic seasonal greetings.

"Who's *he*?" Bella whispered to Kitty, standing on the last-but-one stair with an appreciative little smile hovering around her mouth.

"Ged," Kitty told her.

"Cousin Gerald? No *way*! He always used to be a total minger."

At around ten years older than them, they had seen little or nothing of Ged when they were small; he would have been doing A-levels, Kitty supposed, when Bella was first on the scene, and then shortly afterwards gone off to uni and thence work (something in computers in London). He had been utterly outside their sphere, and as such Kitty was mildly surprised that Bella remembered him at all. But he was still her cousin, when all was said and done; she couldn't let Bella's belittlement go totally unchallenged.

"No he wasn't," she objected, *sotto voce*. "Not a total one. A bit zitty, maybe, but hardly a minger."

"And a bit speccy," Bella added. "And a bit swotty."

"And here's Catrin," her dad was saying, yuletide bonhomie and his first pre-lunch glass of whiskey making his voice even more Irish than usual, "and do you remember her friend Bella, from way-back-when? She's with us for Christmas."

"Is she now." Ged's eyes gleamed as he gave his cousin the most perfunctory of embraces before making for Bella, who had come down the remaining two stairs and was now standing slap-bang in the middle of the hallway, her face raised like a flower to the sun for the kiss that she was totally confident was coming her way. And she was right: Ged homed in on her like a Scud missile fixing on its target.

*

Kitty had a go at her about it later, when the two of them plus Bruno were ensconced up in the Zone. Bella and Bruno were both in their preferred location with a beanbag apiece on the floor but Kitty, due to a new-for-Christmas, slightly too-tight pair of trousers, was sitting comparatively primly on the sofa. If she sat on the floor, she doubted she'd ever get up again. Not without serious damage to the trousers, at any rate.

"You were a bit obvious, standing right under the mistletoe like that," she complained. "You were like, hey babe, gissa snog."

"I so was not!" Bella laughed.

"You so were. You were blatant."

Bella shook her head and laughed all the more, and Bruno said, "I shouldn't worry about it, Kitbag. Bella's not my bro's type. I like your hair, by the way," he added to Bella.

"Do you?" She ran a casual hand over it. "Honestly? I wasn't sure. I wondered if it was a bit too short."

"No. It's cool – suits you."

"Suits you, sir." She inclined towards him and they both laughed again, although whether at Bella's camp tones or something else entirely, Kitty wasn't sure. She felt a sudden prickle of irritation with the pair of them, tittering together as if at some private joke that she was excluded from.

"So what is Ged's type, then?" she enquired, disliking the sulky edge to her tone but seemingly incapable of doing anything about it.

"Oh, you know. Blonde. Bosomy. More like you, actually."

"There you go then, Kitten. Your big chance."

They laughed some more, and Kitty's irritation grew.

"For your information," she began, loftily, "I'm not in the slightest bit interested in Ged." Bella and Bruno looked at each other, Bella biting on her bottom lip to stop herself laughing, then Bruno pulled a mad face and set them both off again.

"He's my cousin," Kitty added.

Bella howled with laughter, rolling on the floor and clutching her stomach, while Bruno removed his specs and wiped his eyes with a tissue, speechless with mirth. For the life of her, Kitty couldn't see what was so funny. She picked up a cushion and threw it at Bruno.

"For God's sake, act your age," she snapped.

It caught him on the side of his head. Still chuckling, although not quite so manically, he picked it up and threw it right back.

"Oh, get off your high horse. We're only having a laff."

Yeah, at my expense. The only thing that stopped her saying it out loud was that she

162

wasn't altogether certain that it *was* at her expense. She had no real evidence. It just felt like it, that was all. She picked moodily at a loose bit of rattan on the arm of the sofa.

"That's you all over, isn't it, Bruno? Always having a laugh." Even she was taken aback by the sourness in her voice.

Bruno lumbered to his feet, his face sombre. He put his glasses back on, pushing them up the bridge of his nose with his forefinger, something he had done since childhood and a gesture that was so familiar to Kitty that it seemed to define him. He could almost have it on his passport under Distinguishing Features: *scar on chin from childhood bike-riding accident, weird specs-straightening thing*.

"Uh-oh. PMT, is it, Catrin?"

"Oh, piss off," she muttered. The piece of rattan came away in her hand, leaving a medium-sized hole in the sofa arm.

"If you're going to go off on one, that's exactly what I'm going to do. Piss off downstairs and see if there's any of that red wine left."

He shot Bella a look that was half-rueful, half-apologetic, and was gone, shutting the door surprisingly quietly behind himself. Kitty thought he was going to bang it, or maybe that was just the way she herself was feeling – like slamming a door, hard.

163

Bella was sat very upright on the beanbag, hugging her knees and looking at her with an expression of concern.

"Are you OK? What's up?"

Kitty looked back at her; her new elfin haircut, her skintight jeans that emphasized the fact that she had not an ounce of fat on her thighs, her oversized chunky chenille sweater that would have turned Kitty into a barrel but just made Bella look waif-like and vulnerable inside its voluminous folds. What could she say? *Why do all the men in my life make a beeline for you?* How sad would that make her sound? It was true, nonetheless. Ged, Bruno, Uncle Mart, Owen, even Dad – Bella had them all eating out of her hand. The only person who didn't seem to think she was the dog's bollocks at present was Rhys, and look how he'd been behaving about her. Kitty couldn't say all that, though. As well as sad, it would make her sound awful: insecure, needy, jealous – take your pick. Why would Bella be making her feel like that? It was ridiculous. She was her friend.

She sighed. "Nothing," she said instead.

"Are you sure? It didn't sound like nothing."

"It's just Bruno. He always knows how to wind me up." She stuck her finger through the hole she'd created in the arm of the sofa. "You don't really fancy Ged, do you?"

"Behave! He's far too old for me." Bella sat up even straighter and looked more closely at her. "Is that what this is about? You don't really think I was seriously hitting on your cousin, do you?"

No, it's because I'm afraid my other cousin is about to start hitting on you. She couldn't say that either, though. "I don't know. It did look a bit like that. But you say you don't fancy him, so –" She shrugged.

"I don't. Honestly. Even though, admit it, he is pretty fit."

"And how about Bruno?"

"Bruno?" Bella wrinkled her nose, puzzled. "He's just Bruno. You know, there's lads you like and lads you fancy, and Bruno's in the first category. Always has been. Although come to think of it, he does scrub up pretty well these days. Not bad at all." She flashed Kitty a sudden, wicked grin.

"But you don't want to, like – you know, get it on with him?"

"Look, what is this? Are you trying to matchmake me with your cousins, or something?"

"No, no – the opposite," Kitty said hurriedly.

"What – warn me off?"

"Not exactly. It's just –" How could she tell her without breaking Megan's confidence? "It's just that somebody else really likes him, that's all.

Someone who'd be dead upset if you and he got together."

"Ah. Megan."

"How did you guess?" Kitty pulled a face. "Look, I didn't tell you, OK?"

"You didn't have to. Short of going round wearing one of those sandwich board things with *I Love Bruno* written on it in big letters, she couldn't really make it more obvious. Her tongue practically hangs out when she's looking at him."

"I don't think Bruno's noticed."

"Well, he's a guy. What can I say? They never get it, not unless a girl actually jumps them. Either that, or they swan round thinking they're God's gift. There never seems to be a happy medium, does there?" She gave a little shrug. "Look, tell Megan she needn't worry about me and Bruno; we're just mates. But she should get in there if she wants him, before somebody else does."

"That's what I think, but I can't see her doing it somehow."

"Why not?"

"It's just not her. She never hits on guys."

"Maybe she should start. You never get anywhere by hanging around waiting for people to take notice of you. And I'm talking life in general – it doesn't just apply to lads."

"Are we speaking from experience here?" Kitty grinned.

"Sure. You've got to grab life with both hands, or things slip away. You don't often get offered a second crack at stuff."

She spoke with passion, and Kitty wondered just what she was referring to. "I guess."

"It's true." Bella subsided against the back of the sofa. "This has been so nice, you know – Christmas? I love your family – they couldn't have made me feel more welcome if I'd been part of it."

"Well, you are practically, aren't you? We go back a long way."

"We sure do. Soul sisters, remember?"

Kitty smiled. "I remember. A lot of time's passed since then, though. A lot of water under the bridge, as they say."

"Yeah, but –" Bella screwed round to look at Kitty at the exact moment she looked down at her, so their eyes met. "We always had a special friendship, didn't we? We'll be best mates for ever, no matter how much time goes by. Won't we?"

They regarded each other solemnly for a moment, then Kitty smiled. "Sure we will. Best mates for ever."

chapter nine

Up in the Doyles' guest room later that night, Bella reflected on just how perfect Christmas had been. Kitty would probably never know just how much she had appreciated it, how much being invited to share it with them had meant to her.

She'd had some crap Christmases in her life, that was for sure. The ones spent with the Robertses hadn't exactly been crap, to be fair, but she'd never really felt as if she belonged there, was properly part of the family. At Christmas or any other time. Not that that was their fault, though; they'd been decent enough foster-parents. It was just that the Peppermint House had always felt so much more like home to her as a kid, from the very first time she'd set foot in the place. And what was so brilliant was, it felt like home still.

Kitty was so lucky to have such a fantastic family life, but she probably didn't appreciate it. Bella could understand that, though. It was only when you didn't have that kind of stability and security to warm your existence that you began to realize how fortunate people were who did.

Bella rooted round in the bottom of her psychedelic velvet bag and took out a quarter-bottle of vodka. She unscrewed the lid and looked at herself in the mirror on the dressing table, which was stripped pine, stained a deep honey brown and lovingly hand-polished. The furniture and soft furnishings were in impeccable good taste and the room smelled the way the Peppermint House always did and always had, a familiar comforting mix of lavender furniture polish and home cooking and something else she couldn't identify. Privilege, probably. However that smelled.

Cheers! She raised the bottle in a toast to her reflection and took a deep, satisfying swig. *Here's to the end of crap Christmases for ever!*

"Bella!"

Someone is calling her name, and shaking her.

"*Bella!* Come on, baby – wake up!"

She doesn't want to wake up; it is night-time, time for being asleep, and she is all warm and cosy, and having *such* a lovely dream.

"Come *on!*" The covers are being taken off her now, and she is not warm any more. "There's something you've just got to see!"

She feels herself being lifted out of her nice warm cosy bed and carried out, past the drooping rubber plant that Sylvie has put a bit of tinsel on in lieu of a proper Christmas tree, and out on to the balcony. The cold, windy balcony. She can hear dead leaves being blown along it. They hurl themselves against the kitchen wall and get trapped there, tumbling around with a dry scratchy sound like paper being scrunched up.

"Now look up."

She shakes her head, buries it in a shoulder, squeezes her eyes tight shut, but a hand takes hold of her chin and lifts it, gently. Bella opens her eyes, cautiously, half excited, half scared, not sure what to expect. There is nothing to see – just the street below, and the dark night sky above. She turns her head back, puzzled.

"Look!" Sylvie says, and points with the hand that's not holding Bella. "The stars! Look at the stars! They're like – like diamonds on velvet! Aren't they the most beautiful thing you've ever seen?" Her voice is full of wonder. Bella looks at the pointing hand, the silver bangles on the wrist and the silver rings on the long white fingers, and thinks they are much more beautiful. She grabs hold of the hand and pulls it and the attached arm round herself, whimpering.

"Are you cold, baby? Not to worry. I'll warm you up." She jiggles Bella up and down and starts to sing, loudly, happily. "Twinkle, twinkle little star, how I wonder what you are!"

There is suddenly another voice, just as loud,

but it is not singing and it doesn't sound at all happy.

"For Christ's sake, put a bloody sock in it! Have you got any bloody idea what the bloody time is?"

Sylvie takes no notice, just carries on jiggling Bella and singing even louder. "Like a diamond in the sky. . ."

Bella listens to the two voices for a few moments, the loud happy singing one in her ear and the equally loud cross shouting one on next-door's balcony, until the jiggling and the cold and the noisy voices become too uncomfortable to bear any longer. She wriggles and slides her way out of Sylvie's arms and down on to the concrete floor of the balcony, which is wet and freezing on her bare feet. She goes through the open door into the dark lounge, but is too tired to go any further. She climbs on to the couch and pulls down the throw that lives over its back. It is old and faded, and smells comfortingly of Sylvie – mingled cigarette smoke and a sweet perfumy smell. She can hear Sylvie still singing outside on the balcony, although the shouting has stopped. There is a moment's silence as Sylvie lights another cigarette – Bella hears the click of her lighter and there is a brief flare of light – and then she starts singing again, but it is not "Twinkle, Twinkle Little Star" any more. It is a song Bella doesn't know, something about rainbows and flying bluebirds. The words are nice, but the tune is sad. Bella can see the glowing red eye of the cigarette twirling around through the lounge window. Sylvie is dancing out there, all alone on the balcony, and that makes Bella feel sad. So she pulls the throw over her head and curls up tightly, as tightly as she can, into a tight little ball, and puts her thumb in her mouth and closes her eyes and goes back to sleep.

"So did you have a good Christmas, then?" Rhys leant back on the sofa, comfortably, and put his feet up on a beanbag and his arm round Kitty's shoulders. He seemed fine now about the Bella business, which was the main thing.

"It was fab. Really good."

"Cool." He leant sideways, to his jacket which he'd slung over the arm of the sofa, and retrieved something from its pocket. "I almost forgot – here's your present. Merry Christmas, babe."

He handed her a package which, although undeniably beautifully wrapped, was square and flattish and quite clearly not shaped like the chased silver bangle she'd been dropping heavy hints about for weeks. Or even an unchased one, for that matter. Opened, it revealed itself to be a two-set CD of dance music hits. Kitty pushed down a lurch of disappointment. She had actually been intending to buy it for some time. A CD was fine, even if it possibly wasn't the most personal Christmas gift for a girl to get from her boyfriend. At least it showed he'd been thinking of her. He hated dance music – it must have taken a lot for him even to have gone into the shop and picked it up, let alone bought it.

She hid her feeling of let-down under a bright appreciative smile, and gave him a big fat kiss. "Aw, thanks, Rhys." She reached behind the sofa and produced his present. It was a book of case studies by a famous barrister that she'd heard Rhys talking about and had managed to track down on Amazon; hardback, and horribly expensive, it had taken her weeks of saving up her earnings from Boots.

"Hey!" His face lit up as he tore off the paper, and she knew she'd got it absolutely right. "You clever thing! How did you know I wanted this?"

She shrugged, modestly. "Like you say. I'm clever."

"A mind-reader, more like. I didn't think I'd mentioned this book to you."

As he kissed her, Kitty reflected smugly on what a top snogger he was. And all hers. She was well aware of the way other girls looked at him in the street, or in the cafeteria at college. What a catch – a love magnet, and smart to boot. And really, so what that he had given her a CD for

Christmas? It was a cool CD; and after all, she'd given him a book in return, which some might say was just as impersonal. And at the end of the day, when the chips were down, she could forgive him anything when he kissed her like that. . .

"Mmm," she said, appreciatively, pulling away slightly. "Hey, I know what I was going to tell you. You know I was going to arrange that party?"

"What party? You didn't tell me about any party." He reached for her again, and she giggled and flapped at him, fending him off.

"Behave! I'm sure I did tell you. It's not a party, exactly – more of a little do. A bijou do-ette. For Christmas."

"But Christmas is over."

"Exactly. That's what I'm trying to tell you. The parents have said I can have it here on New Year's Eve – they're going out on the razz with some of Mum's nursing cronies, apparently. And Owen's been invited to some kids' overnight do at one of his mates, so the way is clear. What d'you reckon?"

"Sounds cool. Who're you inviting?"

"Oh, just a select few. Bruno, Megan, Bella – people like that."

He frowned slightly. "Is that a good idea? I thought those two hated each other. Aren't they both after Bruno?"

"No way! Well, Megan might be, but Bella isn't."

"Hmm." He sounded doubtful. "That's not what Megan seems to think."

"How do you know what Megan thinks?"

"Oh, I bumped into her in town the other day. She insisted on dragging me off for a coffee and bent my ear about it all for hours."

"I see." Kitty felt slightly uneasy, but she didn't know if it was because of her boyfriend having coffee with one of her mates without telling her, or hearing him speak so dismissively about said mate's feelings. "You never said."

"I didn't think it was that important. The thing is, she doesn't seem to have a very high opinion of Bella. That's the impression I got, anyway."

"Why, what did she say?"

"I can't remember exactly. To be honest, I wasn't really listening that much. You know what Megan's like – she could natter for Britain. I don't think it was anything specific, though – just a general impression that she disapproves of her."

"*Disapproves?*" Kitty gave a laugh. "You make her sound like a teacher!"

"It just seemed odd, that's all. According to you, the three of you lived in each others' pockets when you were kids; but Megan seems to see her as some kind of bad influence on you."

"Is that what she said?"

"Pretty much, yeah."

"Oh well – Megan's obviously got her own axe to grind," Kitty said, thinking Rhys had probably misinterpreted what she had said. "Anyway, I'm still going to invite both of them. It'll be a chance for them to get to know each other all over again."

"'S'up to you." Rhys shrugged. "It's your party. Sorry; I mean bijou do-ette."

"Hi Megan."

"Kitty! Heyyy! Wassup?" She sounded very chirpy.

"Are you doing anything on New Year's Eve?"

"Dunno yet. Why?"

"Thought I might have that get-together I was talking about before Christmas."

"The one you're going to invite Bruno to?"

"Amongst others, yeah. You up for it, then?"

"You bet. Just as long as you keep Bella away from him."

Kitty sighed. "I keep telling you, she's not interested in him." *Which reminded her. . .* "Meg, did you tell Rhys she was a bad influence on me?"

"Sorry?" Down the line, Megan laughed. "When am I supposed to have said this?"

"The other day. When you went for a coffee together, apparently."

"Coffee together? Oh, *that*. We didn't exactly go for a coffee together. I was sitting in Mason's waiting for Nic, and Rhys came in and saw me by myself and bought me a cappuccino while I was waiting."

That wasn't how Rhys had told it, but Kitty wasn't in the mood for splitting hairs. She wanted to know what had been said about herself and Bella.

"Whatever," she said. "So what's this bad influence thing?"

"Search me."

"You didn't tell Rhys that Bella was a bad influence on me?"

"No." Megan's voice took on an air of mock patience. "I know you'll find it hard to believe, but I don't spend my entire life talking about Bella. Unlike you, I don't find her that fascinating. Although actually, now you come to mention it –"

"Ye-es?"

"I did tell him about that time you and she did that secret initiation rite thing, or whatever it was; you know, when my mum went into my bedroom to change the beds and found you two had nearly set fire to the curtains, and you both had blood all over you."

Blood sisters. How long was it since Kitty had thought about that?

*

Bella lights the candle and draws the curtains. Kitty shifts her position on the bed, wriggling a little with excitement.

"What're you going to do now?"

"Sssh!" Bella, frowning with concentration, opens the drawer in the chest beside her bed. She takes out a small kitchen knife, the kind you use to prepare vegetables, and Kitty's eyes widen.

"What're you going to *do*?"

"Sssh! Megan'll hear you. It's OK, Kitten; just do as I say."

She lays the knife on top of the bedside table and takes hold of Kitty's hands, tugging her to her feet. The curtains are thick and it is quite dark in the room, even though it is the middle of the afternoon. The light from the candle flickers on Bella's face, illuminating it with a ghostly Hallowe'en glow and adding to Kitty's sense of slight unreality mixed with thrill.

"Right, repeat after me: I do solemnly promise."

"I do solemnly promise."

"To be a faithful friend."

"To be a faithful friend."

"Right to my life's end."

"Right to my life's end."

"Because I know."

"Because I know."

"I will never have a friend as good as what

Kitty is. Only you say Bella," she adds in an undertone.

Kitty repeats it obediently even though she thinks it would probably be more correct to say "a friend as good as Bella".

"OK then." Bella lifts the knife and Kitty shrinks back a little with alarm. "It's all *right*, Kitty. Trust me." She nicks the pad of her own thumb with the pointed end of the knife, quickly, and a bright bead of blood appears. "Your turn. It doesn't hurt, honestly."

Kitty holds out her thumb, a little reluctantly. Bella wields the knife, and Kitty flinches, rather needlessly as it happens because Bella is right, it doesn't hurt. A matching red blob blossoms on her thumb, and Bella holds her own up in the air like a Roman emperor giving the signal that the Christian gladiators should live.

"Press it together with mine; look."

As Kitty presses her thumb against Bella's, her friend produces the cord of Megan's dressing gown, pink and silky and plaited, and winds it around their wrists with her free hand, joining them together.

"I belong to you and you belong to me," she intones. "You're supposed to repeat it," she instructs Kitty.

Kitty does so, and Bella pushes her thumb against Kitty's, hard, and wiggles it about before removing the dressing-gown cord. She holds her hand up, the thumb raised triumphantly.

"Our blood's mixed now."

"Our blood's mixed now," Kitty repeats gravely, and Bella starts to laugh.

"You don't have to repeat that bit. I was just saying, our blood's mixed now."

"Oh." Kitty starts to laugh as well, and Bella throws herself down on her bed with delight.

"Our blood's mixed now," she says, in a deep, serious, low voice and then, "Our blood's mixed now," in a comical, high, squeaky one, for good measure.

"Stop it!" Kitty objects, but still laughing. "I didn't know you'd finished, did I!"

Bella sits upright, suddenly solemn again. "You know what this means, don't you."

"What?"

"We're blood sisters now. Wherever we go and whatever we do, we have a bond that will never be broken."

Her voice is filled with a kind of hushed earnestness. Kitty looks at her thumb, smeared with her own blood and that of Bella's, her best friend in all the world, and she has a sudden deep conviction that Bella is right, they will always be together. Not just soul sisters now. *Blood sisters*.

*

"Your mum really went off on one about that, didn't she!"

"Are you joking – it took us all evening to get her off the ceiling." Megan chuckled. "But I don't think I told Rhys that Bella was a bad influence on you. Maybe he just took it that way."

"Maybe. He can be a bit – what's the word?" *Judgemental?* "A bit serious."

"Perhaps he was just being protective of you. You know – didn't like the thought of you getting into trouble."

"It was years ago!"

"I know." Megan glanced at her. "Has he got a problem with Bella, or something? Only he seemed very keen for me to dish the dirt."

"No, no," Kitty said, with an airiness she didn't quite feel. "No problem. Nothing I can't handle, anyway. I think he's just a bit fed-up with me seeing so much of her recently."

"Like at Christmas?"

"He mentioned that?"

"He did, yeah."

But he told me it was OK, he didn't mind! Kitty pulled a rueful face. She would have to talk to him again about it, make sure he understood once and for all that she couldn't just drop Bella now she was back, and reassure him that there was plenty of room in her life (not to mention affections) for both of them.

"I think he was bit jealous. But it's fine now. It's sorted."

Or at least, it would be once she got the chance to have that chat with him. She was sure it would.

"Hi, this is Nicci. Give me one good reason why I should phone you back, after the tone."

Beep.

"Hi Nic. It's Kitty. Is a party a good enough reason for you? New Year's Eve, round at mine. Bring a bottle. Oh, and any spare guys you can round up. Well-behaved ones, mind – I don't want any pissheads. Call me back and let me know if you're coming. See ya."

"Bruno. Hi."

"Yay, cuz! *Bon soir!*" He was in Expansive French Speaker mode. He got like this from time to time.

"What're you doing for New Year's Eve?"

"Down the pub, probably. As per. Why?"

"I'm having a bit of a party."

"Yeah? Cool! Am I invited, then?"

"Why d'you think I'm ringing, doughnut? To show off about it?" Kitty tutted good-naturedly. "Oh, and by the way –"

"*Oui, mon petit chou?*"

"I wanted to say sorry."

"What?" Bruno gasped in mock astonishment.

182

"Is this a first? Hold the front page – Catrin Doyle apologizes to cousin! What for, or do I have to guess?"

"For being arsey on Boxing Day."

"You weren't being arsey. Well, no more so than usual," he added.

Kitty ignored that bit. "Yes I was. It was just –" Just what? To be honest, she wasn't sure what it had been. "It just felt like you and Bella were having a pop at me."

"Yeah, I did gather that. We weren't, though."

"I know. I'm just saying, it's how it felt."

"You don't fancy Ged yourself, do you?"

"What? No way! I thought we'd had this conversation at the time. Anyway, he's my cousin!"

"Doesn't mean you can't fancy him. Only it was after Bella was doing her Little Miss Foxy thing under the mistletoe with him that you got your knickers in a twist. It did seem a bit of a coincidence."

"Well, that's all it was," she responded tartly. "I really don't fancy your brother. I mean, I'm sure he has his admirers, but I'm not one of them." She hesitated for a moment. "Do you really think Bella's Little Miss Foxy?"

"Are you kidding? She's sex on legs!"

Oh God, poor Megan. . . "You're not going to try and cop off with her at my party, are you?" she demanded.

He matched his tone to hers. "And why shouldn't I, pray?"

"Because –" She couldn't come right out with it and tell him about Megan, could she? She somehow didn't think Megan would be exactly thrilled about it. *My friend fancies you. . .* It was so – so *juvenile*. "Because somebody else really likes you," she managed instead.

"Yeah?" Bruno's voice perked up noticeably. "Who?"

"I'm not saying."

"Aw, Kitty! Don't be a tease! You can't tell me somebody fancies me and then not say who it is!"

"Yes I can. She'd kill me if I told you."

"Why?"

"Just – just *because*." Did he really not know? God, guys were dim at times!

Down the line, Bruno gave a gusty sigh. "Jesus; women! I'll never understand them. Why can't you just tell me, and save time?"

"Whaddya mean, save time?"

"Well, if I fancy her back we can cut to the chase, can't we? Spare her all the meaningful looks and subtle nuances of expression that you chicks all seem to go in for instead of just asking us for a date."

"Bruno! I didn't realize you knew what the word subtle meant."

"Sure I know. I just prefer the direct approach, myself. Like I said, it saves time."

"Yeah, well, I'm still not going to tell you. Anyway, you're missing my point."

"And your point is. . .?"

"My point, dear thing, is don't bother hitting on Bella, because I happen to know she's not interested."

"Ouch!" Bruno sucked in his breath, mock-offended. "You certainly know how to wound a guy."

"They say the truth hurts. So look, are you coming?"

"Pardon me?" He gave a dirty chortle.

"You know what I mean. To the shindig. On New Year's Eve."

"Oh, well, if it's a shindig, how can I refuse. Can I bring some mates?"

"Sure. The more the merrier. And Bruno –"

"Yeah, yeah, I know. Hands off Bella."

"You got it. Later, then."

"*Au revoir, mon petit chou.*"

"Oh, and Bruno?"

"*Oui?*"

"Don't keep calling me a shoe."

"Hiya Kitten. It's me."

"Bella! Hi! I don't believe this – I was just about to ring you! Like, I've got the phone right here in my hand! That is just so spooky."

"Nah. I got the psychic vibes. We're soul sisters, remember?"

"And blood sisters. Megan and I were talking about that time we did that blood-mixing thing, do you remember that?"

"God, yeah. I'd forgotten all about it." A pause. "Why were you talking about it with Megan? She wasn't part of it."

"Dunno. She just reminded me about it, that's all."

"Right. Listen, I was just ringing to say thanks; you know, for Christmas and everything."

"No worries. It was really great to have you – Owen keeps asking when you're going to come and stay again."

Bella chuckled. "Tell you what, why don't I move in to your spare room permanently."

"God, he'd love that! You'd never get any peace though. He's got a serious crush on you, just in case you hadn't noticed."

"Aw, bless!" She laughed again. "So why were you just about to ring me?"

"You know I said I was going to ask Mum and Dad if I could have a party on New Year's Eve? Well, they said yes."

"Wicked! So who's coming?"

"Oh, you know. All the usual suspects. Bring someone if you want."

"Thanks, hun. Although I expect you've already invited everyone I know." There was the sound of voices in the background, and Bella's muffled response as she put her hand over the receiver to reply. Then she was back. "Sorry, Kitten – I'm going to have to go. I'll see you at your party, yeah?"

chapter ten

By ten o'clock on New Year's Eve, Kitty was beginning to regret having so blithely told everyone to bring their mates. The downstairs rooms were packed, wall-to-wall fun and frolics, and she was beginning to lose track of who was there and who she was still expecting. Apart from Bella, whom she was almost certain hadn't arrived yet. *It's just as well Mum and Dad have gone out*, she thought grimly. She just hoped things weren't going to get out of hand. Maybe she could get rid of some of the, er, partygoers – she could scarcely call most of them *guests* – before they got back. They thought Kitty was having an intimate little soirée with just a few of her closest friends. *Hmm. Well, none of them had better throw up, that's all I can say.* Cleaning up other people's vomit was definitely not on her list of must-dos for the new year, although the way the booze was disappearing it was looking almost as inevitable as a James Bond movie being on the telly tomorrow afternoon.

"Why is James Bond always on TV on New Year's Day?" she shouted at Rhys.

"Sorry?"

"I said, why is – oh, never mind. God, this music's a bit loud, isn't it?" she yelled, and waded through the throng towards the stereo, where Bruno was holding court with some of his ex-schoolmates.

"Rocking party," someone she didn't know remarked, passing her with two bottles of Pils in each hand and another couple tucked precariously between elbow and ribs.

"Oh, er, cheers. Sure you've got enough to drink there?" She manoeuvred her way through the heaving mass of bodies and mouthed at Bruno. "Have you seen Bella?" He just raised his eyebrows at her and shrugged, smiling in a way that suggested he couldn't understand her. As she turned she nearly bumped into Megan.

"Hiya," Megan yelled. She beamed. "Happy new year!"

"It's not the new year yet," Kitty yelled back.

"What?"

"I said –" Kitty gave up trying to make herself heard over the din and steered her friend into the kitchen. At least the music was only loud in there, rather than at ear-bleeding volume. She poured two glasses of wine and handed one to Megan. "Have you seen Bella at all?"

Megan frowned slightly. "So she's coming, is she?"

"Yeah. I told you, remember?" She looked more closely at her. "Problem?"

"No, no. You did tell me, I remember now." Megan took a careful sip from her glass, at which point the door opened and Bella herself came into the kitchen.

"Hey guys!" She was swathed in her charity shop fur coat, her eyes sparkling and her cheeks glowing from the cold. "Sorry I'm late, hun." She enfolded first Kitty and then Megan in a typical Bella bear-hug. Kitty hugged her back enthusiastically, but Megan stood stiffly, still holding her glass, a faintly awkward look on her face. It was as if, Kitty thought, she was permitting herself to be embraced.

"Hello," she said once Bella had released her, but her voice was perfectly normal, if on the small side. She even smiled. Kitty let out her breath in an inaudible sigh. Perhaps everything was going to work out OK after all. Then she noticed a familiar tall skinny figure behind Bella, leaning against the door jamb and wearing a slightly goofy expression.

"Oh hi, Mel," she said, in some surprise.

He lifted a languid hand. "Yo."

"You said it was OK to bring someone," Bella said removing her coat and throwing it across the back of a chair. "You know Mel, don't you? Oh, fab – food. I'm starving." She took a piece of quiche off the plate on the kitchen table and popped it in her mouth. "Everything going OK?" she enquired, through the pastry crumbs.

"Yeah, it's cool. I'm just going to get Bruno to turn the music down a bit; if he pumps up the volume any more, Mum and Dad are going to hear it."

"Where are they? Next door?"

"No." Kitty grinned. "Ten miles away, with some friends."

In the sitting room, Bruno was nowhere to be seen. Kitty turned the music down herself by several notches and then went to check out the rest of the house to see exactly what was going on. Despite the multitudes, to her relief everybody appeared to be pretty much behaving themselves. The scenes of debauched mayhem upstairs she'd been fearing weren't happening, and, besides, Rhys and Bruno were around to keep an eye on things. For the first time that evening, she began to relax and enjoy herself. All she wanted now was for everyone to stop leaning against the walls, and start dancing.

An old Blondie hit was playing when she went back into the sitting room; old or not it was doing the trick as the room was full of cavorting bodies. As she scanned the faces she noticed Mel and Bella were dancing along together with Nicci. Then Bruno appeared in the doorway, a bottle of lager in his hand. Bella turned and saw him, her face lighting up. She grabbed him by his free arm and included him in the dancing, inclining her body towards him. She lifted her arms above her head and swung her slim jeans-clad hips in time with the music, her eyes locked on his, a smile of pure pleasure on her face. Her crop top had ridden up slightly, exposing her Hallé Berry-esque belly, flat as an ironing board. Debbie Harry belted out the lyrics, and everyone in the room sang along with her. *I'm gonna getcha getcha getcha getcha. . .* Kitty could see Bella's lips moving along with the words as she undulated around Bruno, lithe as a belly dancer. She watched them both, fascinated and apprehensive at the same time.

Then someone went "Eurgh!", loudly. Extremely loudly. Right in Kitty's ear, in fact. "Eurgh! Someone's thrown up!"

Sure enough, somebody had, right in the doorway. Tutting with annoyance – she just *knew* this was going to happen – she went to the kitchen in search of a mop. Megan was already there, filling a bucket at the sink. She gave Kitty a rueful smile. "Here, let me help."

Good old Megan. You could always rely on her to lend a hand. Kitty thanked God, or at least the god of home floor coverings, that they had tiles in the hallway.

"It's OK, Meg. I can manage – you go and see if you can find Bruno," she said, pointedly. She wanted Megan to be motivated by the spirit of communal down-letting of hair and go and claim Bruno for a dance, to just – well, grab him. Go up to him and sparkle, be as uninhibited as Bella, so Bruno couldn't resist her. She was hardly going to be irresistible smelling of sick.

But Megan wasn't to be persuaded. "No, it's OK. I'll go and get the air freshener, shall I?" she said.

Puke-mopping duties over, they went back to join the action in the sitting room. Amazingly, everything had calmed down in there. There were considerably fewer bodies around – astonishing how a spot of vomiting clears the room, Kitty thought, drily – and someone had replaced Blondie with a slow smoochy number at a much lower volume. Megan followed behind Kitty, nattering in her ear about something: Kitty didn't really hear what she was saying because there – centre stage, as it were – in the middle of the room, swaying gently together to the soft rhythm of the music and so close you couldn't have slid a credit card between them, were Bella and Bruno.

I'm gonna getcha getcha getcha getcha. . .

Kitty stopped dead, then turned to look at

Megan who was standing as if petrified, an expression of such aghast horror on her face that Kitty thought she was going to fall down on the carpet in a faint, swooning like some Victorian literary heroine. But she didn't. She just uttered an inarticulate little cry and ran from the room with her hands pressed to her mouth, brushing past Rhys who was standing in the hallway chatting to some college mates.

"What's up with her?" he enquired, raising an eyebrow. "Is she about to have a conversation with God on the big white telephone, too?"

"What?" Kitty snapped, not having a clue what he was on about.

"You know – 'Oh God,'" he moaned, leaning forward as if retching into the loo.

"Worse than that. It's those two in there." Kitty indicated Bruno and Bella with her head, shortly. She could see them through the doorway, still clamped tightly together, apparently oblivious to anyone else in the room. "Oh, never mind. I'll tell you later. I'm just going to see if she's all right."

She found her in Owen's room, lying on the bed face down, wracked with sobs. Two Action Men sat incongruously on the pillow near her head, in full camo gear and with automatic weapons cocked and ready for action.

"Megan," Kitty said, sitting on the bed next to

her and placing a soothing hand on her friend's back. "Are you OK?"

For answer, Megan shook her head wildly from side to side. One of the Action Men toppled sideways, its arms and legs sticking out, and Kitty picked it up.

"Poor Megan," she said, in a deep, husky, soldier-type voice. "Bruno's a pig, isn't he?" She picked up the other, straightened its legs and walked it along the bed to face the one she held in her hand. "Yeah," she made it say, this time in a higher-pitched Cockney accent. She wiggled it from side to side. "'E's a bleedin' git, an' no mistake."

Megan sat up slowly. Her face red and swollen and blotched with tears, she looked at Kitty, and then at the two Action Men in her hands. Following her gaze, Kitty put them down on the bed sheepishly.

"Sorry," she apologized. "It used to work sometimes with Owen, when he was upset about something." She didn't tell her it was a trick she'd learnt, years ago, from Bella. Something told her Megan might just have full-on hysterics if she mentioned Bella's name.

"Well I'm not Owen." Megan's face crumpled. "Oh God, Kitty. I just love Bruno so much. What'm I going to *do*?" she wailed, and threw herself back down on the bed.

"I could slap him," Kitty said. "I told him. I did tell him."

Megan reared up in alarm. "What did you tell him? Not how I feel about him?"

"No, no. Don't panic – I didn't mention you at all. I just told him – well – not to bother with Bella because she's not interested."

"Oh right. Not interested. Course she's not." Megan's voice held a deeply gloomy blend of sarcasm and defeat. "She looked pretty interested to me." The last word ended on a sob, and she buried her face in the pillow again.

Kitty patted her shoulder, feeling inadequate. "I know. He's a bastard."

"It's not him. It's her."

"Well yeah, both of them," Kitty agreed.

"No, Kitty. It's not Bruno. It's her." Megan took a deep, shaky breath and sat up, drawing her knees up and encircling them with her arms. "She's man-mad. She can't leave anything in trousers alone. It's a fact."

Kitty said, doubtfully, "Well. . ."

"It's true. She arrives with Mel, the poor guy who's been panting after her since Day One at college, she tarts around all Rhys's and Bruno's mates the entire evening, and then she goes in for the kill with Bruno himself. *And* she was flirting with Rhys earlier," she added, as if to prove her point beyond question.

"No! Was she? When?" It didn't sound like Rhys.

"Earlier on. In the kitchen."

"Where was I, then?"

"Dunno. Not there, obviously."

"What was she saying?"

"It wasn't what she was saying. More what she was doing."

"OK, what was she doing, then?"

"Oh, you know. The usual. Giving him the old Princess Diana look – you know, simpering at him from under her eyelashes." Megan was on a roll now. "Touching him on the arm every five seconds when she was talking to him. Crossing her arms and sticking her boobs out at him. She could have any man she chose, but she has to hit on somebody else's. She's a total bloody *cow*." Her mouth folded in on itself again, and she laid her head on her knees, away from Kitty and towards the wall. Kitty felt acutely sorry for her. She knew exactly how it felt to be hopelessly in love with somebody who was oblivious to your existence. She'd had her fair share of desperate crushes – well, hadn't everybody? Everybody apart from Bella, that is, to whom the exact opposite appeared to apply. She probably left a trail of broken hearts behind her wherever she went. But on the other hand, Bella had her own problems to contend with.

"Don't be too hard on her," she said to Megan. "She hasn't had it easy."

Megan gave a giant snort down her nose. "Oh yeah," she said, with enormous scorn. "Well, who has, come to that?"

"No, I mean it. Take her mother, for example."

"What about her?"

"Well. . ." Kitty hesitated. To tell or not to tell, that was the question. She looked at Megan's swollen tear-stained face, her hair that she had French-braided so carefully and was now sticking out frizzily all over the place as if she had stuck her finger into an electric socket, her new silk kimono top in that particular shade of greeny-blue that suited her so well all crumpled and creased – and all for Bruno's benefit. Bruno, the dim, insensitive, hormone-led sod. She didn't want to gossip – it was Bella's life, Bella's past, and as such up to her to tell people about if she wanted to – but Kitty couldn't let her take all the blame for Bruno getting smoochy with her. "Bella's dad used to beat her up. She had to go to a women's refuge when she was pregnant, and when Bella was born she—"

"Oh please!" Megan almost yelped, interrupting. "Not that one again!"

Kitty was startled. "What, you knew?"

"She told me about it, yeah. Years ago. If that counts."

198

"What d'you mean, if that counts?"

"Well, you didn't believe her, did you?" Megan leant forward, still clasping her knees, and looked incredulously at Kitty.

"Well – yes. Why would she lie about something like that?"

"For the same reason she lies about anything else, I suppose. Attention-seeking. Or trying to get sympathy. Or maybe she doesn't know herself why she does it." Megan shrugged. "Beats me. I never could figure out her motivation."

"But –" Kitty scratched her head, nonplussed. "Do you mean you don't believe it about her mother, then?"

"Of course not. It's just one of Bella's little inventions."

Kitty couldn't understand why Bella should invent things of that nature. But Megan seemed so positive. "What little inventions? Are you saying she makes stuff up?"

"Are you kidding!" Megan gave another of her mighty snorts. "She lives in a total fantasy world. Or at least," she amended, "she used to. She lied all the time when she was living with us. I don't suppose she's changed that much. People like that don't," she added, darkly.

"So what sort of thing did she tell lies about?"

"God, Kitty, I don't know. I can't remember. It was bloody years ago. I just remember it caused endless aggro at home – 'Who crayoned on the wall, Bella?' – 'Not me!' – 'Who's eaten all the biscuits, Bella?' – 'It wasn't me!' Even when we caught her doing stuff, she still always denied it was her."

"But that's just kids' stuff. All kids tell fibs to get themselves out of trouble; I used to do it myself."

"Yeah, granted. But it wasn't just that kind of thing." Megan cast around for another example. "Sometimes at home she used to speak this gobbledegook that she told me was a foreign language."

"What foreign language?"

"Just a foreign language. It took me years to work out she was making it up. And before she came up with the women's refuge story she used to try and con me that her dad was a gypsy." Somewhere at the back of her memory Kitty could recall Bella telling her some such thing, years ago; how her parents had to meet out on the moors because her mother's family didn't approve of them being together. "Well, you know where she got that load of crap from, don't you?" Megan was saying. "*Wuthering Heights!* I recognized it straight away when we did it for GCSE."

"What? You mean she read *Wuthering Heights* when she was a kid?" Kitty laughed. "Come on!

We were all more into Enid Blyton than Emily Brontë when we were little!"

"Bella probably still is," Megan muttered, nastily. "Anyway, I'm not saying she read it. Maybe she saw it on TV or something. But what I do know is, the tales she used to spin me about her parents all came out of *Wuthering Heights*. Even her name comes from it, apparently."

"What, Bella?" Kitty frowned. She couldn't recall a character with that name.

"Isabella. She was thingy's sister – Edgar. You know, the one Cathy married."

"How did you know her real name?"

"She told me. Why – didn't you know?"

"Yeah, but not until recently. I always thought she was just Bella. She never told me anything about her background – her family." Kitty looked closely at Megan. If she was disturbed by her friend's assertions that Bella was a liar, she was even more disquieted by the knowledge that, after all these years, she still so badly wanted to know the ins and outs of Bella's past. "Didn't your mum ever tell you?"

"No. Mum's never told me anything about any of the foster kids. I don't think she's allowed to – you know, Social Services rules and regulations. They strike you off or defrock you or something, if you're a foster parent and spill the beans about the kids you look after. They always seem to have more dos and don'ts than you can shake a stick at."

"But you're her daughter!"

"It doesn't make any difference. It's just the way things are, Kitty – it's the way it's always been, all my life. Mum's never told me stuff, so I don't even bother asking." She got up from the bed suddenly, went over to the dressing-table and regarded her reflection in the mirror. "God, what a mess. No wonder Bruno can't stand the sight of me."

"You know that's not true. Anyway, you're upset – you looked fab earlier. Don't be so hard on yourself."

Their eyes met in the mirror, and Kitty could tell Megan wasn't convinced. "I'm not. Face it, I'm just not his type, am I? He's obviously more into the stick-insect, brainless bimbo type." It seemed a bit harsh, but Kitty didn't say anything. She had to make allowances; Megan had been distraught. It was unlike her to be so catty.

"You know, I don't really think Bella's his type either," she began, but the look on Megan's face stopped her.

"If she's what he wants, then good luck to him," she said, slowly. "But I tell you, Kitty; I don't give it five minutes. She's a compulsive liar, and if there's one thing Bruno can't stand it's dishonesty."

Kitty wondered, briefly, how Megan came to know so much about Bruno's moral standards. Then she realized that she was absolutely right. Whatever else her cousin might be, he was as straight as a die. Even as a kid he'd found it impossible to tell even the mildest fib as it always showed on his face as extreme discomfort. She and Bella used to tease him about it, calling it his constipated expression. Even so, interpreting Bella's childhood embroidering as evidence of being a compulsive liar was surely going it a bit.

"Maybe she just had an over-active imagination."

"That's one way of putting it, I guess." Megan turned from the mirror to face her. "Look, cool party and everything, but I think I'm going to nick off."

"What? But you can't go yet – it's not even midnight! Don't. Please stay." Kitty touched her friend's arm in dismay. Perhaps if she went downstairs and forcibly removed Bella and Bruno from each other, persuaded Bruno to have a dance with Megan – bribed him, even, if that's what it took – perhaps she could make everything OK again. Megan couldn't leave like this. Kitty had organized this do at least partly to clear the air between everyone, for Bruno to realize he had another admirer and leave off Bella, for Megan and Bella to resolve their differences. . .

But Megan was shaking her head. She smoothed her top down over her hips. "I feel like cack. I just want to go home. Sorry, Kitty."

There was nothing Kitty could say to make her change her mind. They went back downstairs together, and Megan gave her a brief hug and slipped quietly out of the door.

Kitty went back into the sitting room to survey the scene. Slightly to her surprise, Bella was standing with her back to the door, holding a glass of what looked like Coke and innocuously chatting to Mel. Bruno was nowhere to be seen. *I wonder if he knows how Megan's feeling*, she thought, murderously. She didn't really know what she had been expecting to see. He and Bella would hardly have been locked together in a passionate embrace on the sofa, after all. Not in front of everybody.

"*There* you are," said a voice in her ear. She turned. It was Rhys.

"Oh, Rhys," she murmured, slipping an arm through his. What she suddenly needed, more than anything, was a hug.

But to her surprise and consternation he withdrew his arm roughly, an unreadable expression on his face. "Am I with you, or what?"

"Sorry?" She couldn't think what he meant.

"It's nearly. . ." He tilted his arm to look at his

watch, the gesture making him lurch against the door jamb in a way that made Kitty realize he'd had too much to drink. "Nearly midnight, and I've sheen nothing of you. Seen," he corrected himself, carefully.

"I'm sorry." She took his arm again, carefully, wondering if she should steer him into the kitchen and make him a coffee. "Bit of a crisis." She smiled at him, willing him to understand.

"What crisis?" he slurred.

"Megan. You know when she went charging upstairs. . ." she began to explain, but he was in no mood to listen. He shook her off again.

"Oh, Megan, is it. Not Bella thish time. Makesh a change, that."

"Rhys." She put a careful hand on his arm. She didn't need this, not now, not after all the stuff with Bruno and Bella and Megan. "Come in the kitchen. I'll make you some coffee."

"I don't want coffee." He looked at her, his face full of admonishment. "I just want my girlfriend."

"But you've got me!" She laughed, in an attempt to lighten the tone. Bad move.

"No I haven't. Bella's got you. Megan's got you. Even bloody Bruno's got you. Not me, though. There'sh nothing left over for me."

Kitty, who was feeling emotionally frayed after the scene with Megan, could only stare at him, dismayed.

"Go on then!" he challenged, truculently, as if he'd lured her into a trap. "Deny it! Ha – you can't, can you! I sometimesh wonder jusht who you're going out with."

All of a sudden, Kitty had had enough. She couldn't deny she hadn't seen much of him that evening, but it wasn't like she'd deliberately been avoiding him – she was the host, so that brought its own responsibilities (such as the mopping-up duties), and then her friend had needed her. Just like she needed Rhys now – to understand, to support, not get all pity-me about feeling neglected.

"I'm going out with you," she said, tiredly. "You know I am. Now come and have a coffee – you're pissed."

"I'm pissed off," he said. *Pished off*, it came out as. "Pissed off at being taken for a ride." And with that he fumbled drunkenly with the door latch, flung it open with an air of triumph, and disappeared into the dark drizzle, leaving the door open.

"Lover-boy had a skinful?" It was Bruno, coming downstairs, zipping up his trousers and with an amused grin on his face.

"Where on earth have you been?" she demanded. Could the evening possibly get any worse?

Bruno started in surprise. "In the bog. If that's OK with you."

"Well, since you ask –" She took him by the arm, steered him through the loud thump of music that filled the house, out through the back door and into the garden and relative peace and quiet. "What the hell were you doing with Bella?" she hissed at him.

"Sorry?"

"Bella. Shall I spell it out? B – E – double L – A."

"Kitty." He removed his arm from her grasp, pointedly. "I haven't a clue what you're on about."

"OK, I'll enlighten you, shall I? In there. Earlier on. Stuck to each other like – like Mr and Mrs Evostick."

"You what?" In the light spilling from the back door she could see him frown with incomprehension.

"You were dancing with her," she declared accusingly.

"*Ooh*." Bruno sucked on his teeth and took a step back, lifting his arms as if fending her off and feigning hurt and shock. "That's a terrible thing to say. I mean, dancing – on New Year's Eve. With a girl. Whatever is the world coming to."

"Don't be so bloody smart," she snapped.

"Well, Jesus." He sounded annoyed now. Most unlike him – he was normally so laid-back about everything. It was why Kitty bossed him around: because he let her. "What's my crime, exactly?

Dancing with a girl I've known since we were kids? OK, so hang me."

"You weren't just dancing. Dancing would've been fine. You were – you were *snogging* her!"

"I was not!"

"You promised." All of a sudden, Kitty felt exhausted. Dealing with all Megan's outpourings and revelations about Bella, and then to top it all that stupid unnecessary scene with Rhys, had taken it out of her. She felt close to tears herself. "You promised you weren't going to come on to her."

"I wasn't coming on to her."

"That's not how it looked to me."

"Well, I can't help that."

"But poor Megan –" She stopped. *Shit!* There went the cat, right out of the bag.

"What about her?" Bruno looked baffled, and then the penny dropped with a loud resounding clang. "Ah! So she's my mystery fan, is she?" He smiled, a smug self-satisfied smirk that made Kitty want to smack him one.

"You really think you're something special, don't you?" she spluttered, furiously.

There was a silence. Then: "No I don't," Bruno said, slowly. "I don't think I'm anything, particularly. Apart from hassled half to bloody death by you, for fancying one girl, for not fancying another. Any bloke with blood in his veins would fancy Bella, Kitty. She's fanciable – can't you understand that? I can't help being attracted to her. I don't have any say over who I fancy and who I don't. It's a – a chemical thing. It doesn't mean I'm going to *come on* to her, as you keep putting it. And if you ask me, you want to stop interfering in everybody else's lives, and stop going on about who fancies who and who's allowed to be friends with who. Just stop all the control freakery, and start concentrating on your own relationships. For a change."

"Were you eavesdropping on me and Rhys?" Kitty demanded, but it was too late. He marched off into the kitchen, leaving her standing by herself on the damp patio flagstones.

chapter eleven

"Good party, was it?" Kitty opened her eyes. Her father was placing a mug of tea on her bedside table, level with her head.

Kitty groaned, and looked at her alarm clock. It was nearly midday. *God.* She groaned again. Well, that's what came of not getting to bed until gone two a.m. "What time did you and Mum get in, then?"

"Oh, about ten."

"Sorry?" Kitty blinked, bleary eyed, her brain still fuzzy with sleep. "Ten o'clock?"

"Ten this morning. We stayed over – we decided it was safer not to drive back, what with all the champagne and everything. We knew you'd call us if you were worried. We did try ringing to tell you, but there was no answer."

That'd be because some joker unplugged the phone. She'd discovered it in the course of her post-party house-cleaning activities, at Christknows what time.

"You dirty stop-outs." She yawned widely, and sat up. "S'pose I'd better get up."

"No hurry. Drink your tea first." He patted her

knee through the duvet, fondly. "So, was it a good do, then? Happy new year, by the way."

Oh yeah. It was fantastic. What with mopping up sick, and all Megan's traumas, and Rhys taking the huff and pushing off early, and then majorly falling out with Bruno. Not to mention having to shoo away a whole houseful of uninvited guests, and then carefully obliterate all traces of their presence when all I wanted to do was go to bed. It was just groovy.

"Thanks. Same to you. It was OK." Oh well, look on the bright side. At least after a start to the year like that, the only way was up. She would ring Rhys as soon as Dad had gone, to try and make it up with him. With any luck he wouldn't remember much of the exchange between them. And at least Bruno had helped with the cleaning-up operations, not to mention the eviction process; one of the advantages of having a cousin two years your senior who is six-foot plus, and built like a brick outhouse to boot. Nobody argued with him; they just went. He clearly had a glittering career awaiting him as a nightclub bouncer, if the law thing didn't work out. *And* she hadn't had to ask him to help with the clearing up, either; he'd just got on with it. *And* he wielded a mean vacuum cleaner, too. Not that he'd said a word to her all the while. He was clearly still pissed off with her. She'd have to ring him later, too – do a bit of grovelling, apologize for beating him round the head about him and Bella. She hadn't meant to come on quite so strong about it, it was just having Megan so distraught, and then falling out with Rhys had really upset her. It seemed so unfair for him to accuse her of – whatever it was he was accusing her of, when all her crime amounted to was caring about her friends. Which reminded her. . .

"Dad? You know Bella and me, when we were little?"

He scratched his head. "I think I can just about remember you, yes. What about it?"

"What did you make of Bella?"

"When you were small? Well now. " He pursed his lips, trying to recollect. "She was a grand little girl. Wanted to please. Very polite; always said please and thank you. No trouble to have around the place at all. Which was just as well, given that she virtually lived here." He smiled; he'd been very taken with Bella as a child. Just looking at her had always seemed to put a smile on his face.

"She was round here a lot, wasn't she?"

"She certainly was. I know your mother got quite concerned about it at one point. She always seemed to be here at mealtimes, and Mum didn't want Enid Roberts thinking she was treading on her toes by constantly feeding the child."

Kitty hadn't known that. With typical childish

lack of awareness of the complexity of adult politics, she had just enjoyed having her friend around so much.

"Did Bella tell lies?" she asked her father suddenly.

He blinked, taken aback. "Lies? What about?"

"About anything. Just – lies."

"I don't recall any. Not what I'd call lies, as such. Although she had a vivid imagination, that's for sure." He chuckled at the memory of it. "And whimsy. Ah, I loved her sense of whimsy. She'd talk to Heinz as if he was a person, do you remember that? She'd credit him with all kinds of opinions and ideas that no dog ever had, to my certain knowledge. And she said she saw a fairy, once, in our garden – up in the tree house, or so she claimed."

"Did she?" Kitty couldn't recall that one.

"She did. And knowing Bella, I wouldn't be surprised if she really had. Perhaps she had the gift of seeing the little people – I always thought there was some Irish in her, with that colouring. County Kerry, I thought, the first time I set eyes on her."

"Are you sure it wasn't a leprechaun she saw?" Kitty teased him. He was always claiming Irishness in all kinds of unlikely people, as if he considered it a huge compliment.

"Ah, mock if you will," he said, with studied

dignity. "It was such a shame, what happened with her and the Robertses."

"What d'you mean?" Kitty leant forward a little, sensing new confidences, but Dad just shrugged.

"Well, she left them. Moved away. As you know."

"I never knew where she went, though." Kitty leant back again, against the pillows, and picked up her mug of tea. "I mean, she'd been living with them all that time, and then she suddenly left and nobody seemed to know anything about what happened to her. Where she went, what she did, or anything."

"Could you not just ask her?"

"I kind of have, but she doesn't seem to want to talk about it. And I don't want to press her; it doesn't seem that – that *relevant* any more." As soon as she said the word she knew she was wrong. It *was* relevant, and becoming ever more so. It was relevant not just to understanding the simple, on-the-surface reality of what had happened to Bella in the years since she left, but to a whole load of other things as well; the intricately woven fabric of their friendship, the part Megan had to play in it, both then and now, and why Kitty was beginning to feel differently about Bella. Or maybe it wasn't a case of feeling differently, more an understanding that despite the length of time Bella had been in her life, she didn't really know much about her at all. She personally didn't think that wanting to know about your friend's past and what happened when she moved away five years ago was being nosy; just caring and interested. OK, she acknowledged, maybe nosy as well. Just a tiny bit. But if it had all happened to her, the whole fostering/moving thing, and one of her close friends had asked her about it, she felt pretty sure she would have told them. Isn't that what friends do – share things with each other? But Bella quite clearly didn't want to share this aspect of herself, and her dissembling on the occasions Kitty asked her, her fobbing-off, was beginning to make Kitty wonder just how much of a friend Bella considered her.

"She doesn't want to talk about it," Kitty told Dad. "It's like her whole life is some big mystery."

"Ah, I don't suppose there's much of a mystery about it. My guess is she just wants to forget about that whole time. I expect she's embarrassed to recall how she behaved and the fact that her bad behaviour got her sent away. She's probably ashamed that she became too much of a handful for Megan's mother – but then, Enid Roberts was more used to the little ones, wasn't she? And of course her own daughter was quite the opposite. A good girl, Megan was; just like yourself, in fact.

But Bella was into the lads at a pretty young age, wasn't she? I daresay her going off the rails a bit was all tied up with that."

Into the lads. . . . A memory came back to Kitty, as sharp and clear as if it had happened yesterday.

They are sitting at the kitchen table at Kitty's house. She has been feeling guilty at not seeing much of Bella for some time now, and has invited her round for what Mum calls "a working tea", which means tea and homework, and strictly no TV until the homework is done. Bella has been fine with the tea bit, but doesn't seem too keen on the homework aspect. She has got as far as taking out her English book, the front of which is covered with multicoloured doodles and scrawls as well as a fair number of inkblots. Adorning its centre is a huge heart, pierced by an arrow, surrounded by curlicues and containing the legend *CG 4 BJ* in characters five centimetres high. Kitty looks at Bella's handiwork in some astonishment.

"Doesn't your teacher mind you drawing that stuff on your book?"

"Old Smellypants? Are you joking? He couldn't care less what we do, long as we don't get up from our desks and start fighting."

Bella's English teacher, the unfortunately named Mr Oliphant, is known around school variously as Elephant and Smelliphant as well as Bella's even less respectful variation. Kitty knows for a fact that some of the cheekier members of Bella's English set even call him these things to his face. She doesn't even dare wonder what her own English teacher, Miss Sterndale, would do if anyone in Kitty's class were to call her names. Kill them, probably, and hide their bodies in the staffroom. She is fine when everybody is behaving, but as soon as there is the slightest hint of any mucking around she gets this seriously fierce expression, which quells the troublemakers in an instant. Megan calls it her death stare.

"Do you ever get the feeling that some of the teachers in our school are a bit – you know?" she asks Bella.

"Bollocks?" Bella grins.

"Sshh!" Kitty pulls a warning face at her. Owen is playing on the floor, seemingly engrossed in his favourite wooden train set, but you never know with him. He has got Kitty into trouble before, repeating things he has heard her say that Mum and Dad don't like ("you're a bloody little pest" springs to mind), but if he repeats what Bella has just said they will really go mental. She changes the subject hastily. "Who's CG?" She nods towards Bella's book.

Bella glances at it. "Craig Griffiths."

"Craig Griffiths? I thought you hated him."

217

"He was my serious crush last term, but I'm like so over him now. I like Brad Flower now. You know, Ben's brother? He's a stud – majorly cool."

Kitty stares at Bella with some consternation. It is as if she is speaking a foreign language. Kitty has the uneasy feeling that she is out of her depth, and all she can think of to say is, "But he's in Year Nine!"

"So?" Bella shrugs. "Sadie says I should go for him anyway. She's seeing Ollie Millington now, and he's in Year Ten."

Kitty can't imagine going out with any boy at all, let alone one three years above her. Boys in her own year are deeply childish and rush around the playground at break times with their shirts hanging out and probably only wash when their mums stand over them and threaten, but many of the boys in Year Ten don't look like boys at all, they look like men. Young men who swear and shave, some of them, and possibly even have *sex*. . . With Sadie Williams, maybe. She has the worst reputation of any girl in Year Seven, quite possibly in the whole school. Even Bruno says she is a slapper, and he generally doesn't say that kind of thing about girls. Kitty can't imagine what Bella wants to be friendly with *her* for.

"Oh," she says, rather lamely.

"I'm going to cover my book," Bella goes on, with determination, "and put BF on the front instead. Just as long as Ben doesn't think I mean him – God, how pants would that be, if *he* thought I fancied him!"

"Doesn't BF mean Bloody Fool?" Kitty asks carelessly, suddenly feeling really daring and brazen. "It's what my dad says about his partner at work – he's such a BF at times."

Bella laughs. "Does he?" She repeats the phrase in Daddy's soft Irish voice, and Owen looks up from his train on the floor and says, "Bloody fool! Bloody fool!" and the three of them fall around laughing although Kitty knows for a fact that Owen doesn't understand what they are laughing at.

"It was being in different sets at Brynglas," Kitty said, sipping her tea. "That's what started it." It was obvious, now she came to think of it.

"Started what?" Dad wasn't with her. "Made Bella's hormones kick in early? Surely not!"

"I didn't mean that." Although come to think of it, it was probably Bella's hormones that made them get put in different sets in the first place. Bella's interest in boys had begun well before they'd started at Brynglas, where at the age of eleven Kitty, ever the good little girl, had been placed in the top set along with Megan, whereas Bella, with her more esoteric interests of boys, make-up and pop music, had been somewhat lower down the academic pecking order and hence, in a school of getting on for fifteen hundred pupils, pretty much out of Kitty's line of vision.

"It pulled us apart." Even as she said the words they sounded overstated, melodramatic. She put her tea back down. "We were in different classes, we didn't see as much of each other as before. So we made different friends, and then we kind of drifted apart."

"Well, that's understandable. To be honest, your mother and I were quite relieved, in a way."

"That Bella and I drifted apart?" Another revelation. "Were you? I thought you liked her – you never said you were relieved when she went away."

"Well, no. We wouldn't, would we? But it was pretty obvious to us, as observers, that Bella started going down the wrong track at Brynglas. Getting in with the wrong crowd – that Sarah child, what was her name now?"

"Sadie. Sadie Williams."

"Ah yes. That's right. The tales that did the rounds about her! The concern to us as your parents was that you shouldn't do the same – following your great friend Bella into bad company. It was a bit of a relief to both of us when she moved away, if I'm to be honest. But look." He patted her knee again. "It's all worked out for the best, hasn't it? Look at Bella now – a fine young woman, and not a bad company to be seen!"

God, what a party! Bella yawned, and rolled over. She was aware of a banging sound coming from outside. No, not outside – on her door. She sat up. "Hello?"

"Isabella, my dear, it's the phone for you."

Who could possibly be ringing this early in the morning on New Year's Day? She glanced at her watch, still on her wrist. Ahem. This early in the *afternoon* on New Year's Day.

"All right, Auntie. I'm just coming."

She pushed the duvet back and sat on the edge of the bed for a moment, waiting for the room to stop its faint spinning. Surely she couldn't still be drunk, could she? She really must try to lay off the vodka a bit in future. Maybe it should be a new year's resolution.

She got off the bed and went downstairs, barefoot, to the middle landing where the telephone lived on a small mahogany console table. The phone sat on its side, off the cradle, the red In Use light winking brightly. Bella picked it up.

"Hello?"

"Bella, hi. Sorry – did I disturb you?"

"Oh hi, Bruno. Yeah, I was asleep."

"Lazy cow."

Bella made a little mooing noise, and she heard Bruno laugh softly at the other end. "So why are you ringing? I hope it's worth having my sleep disturbed for."

"What? Isn't talking to me always worthwhile?"

"What can I say?" She grinned to herself, and then yawned, loudly. "Oh, sorry. Look, d'you mind if we cut to the chase? Only I'm standing here in my pyjamas, and it's *freezing*." She gave a theatrical, noisy shiver, to prove her point.

"You weren't joking then? You really were still asleep?"

"Yeah." Bella mooed again, and they both laughed. "So what time did you get home?"

"Can't remember. It must have been gone two by the time we finished cleaning up."

There was a small, guilty pause. "Oh God. The cleaning up. Should I have stayed to help, d'you think?"

"No. Why should you? It wasn't your party."

"It wasn't yours either, but you helped."

"I'm Kitty's cousin."

"And I'm her –" She was going to say "best mate", but stopped. Was she still Kitty's best mate? She wasn't sure any more. When she had first come back, things between the two of them seemed to have reverted to the way they had been when they were kids. It was as if they were ten years old again, skipping across the playground with arms linked, heads inclined towards each other, giggling about something. Bella and Kitty against the world. *I belong to you and you belong to me.* The image was so clear, it was as if she had seen it in a film, or as an illustration in a book. It was amazing, really; once Kitty had got over her not having kept in touch, they had just picked up where they had left off. It was as if all the time in between had never happened.

But now; now she wasn't so sure. The vibe had changed, definitely.

"You're her what?" Bruno prompted, down the line.

"Her friend. I'm her friend." Bella fought down a childish urge to add *aren't I?*, to seek reassurance. She changed tack. "So. What are you up to today?"

"Not a lot. It's why I was ringing, actually. To see if you wanted to hook up later on."

"What?" Bella was startled. "Hey, Bruno! Are you asking me for a date?"

Bruno chortled merrily, as if this was the funniest thing he'd heard in a long time. "As if! No, I'm just at a bit of a loose end. I thought, if you were too. . ." He trailed off. "Course, if you're busy. Seeing wossisname; Mel. Or whatever."

"Mel? Why would I be seeing him?"

"I thought you and he were – you know – 'an item'." He put inverted commas around the phrase, ironically, and laughed again, as if to show that, really, it couldn't matter less to him whether they were an item or not.

"We're not an item," Bella said, firmly.

"No?"

"No. Where d'you get that idea?"

"Not sure." Bruno coughed, embarrassed. He was perfectly well aware of where he'd got the idea; Megan, that's where, chatting with her friend – that blonde girl, what'shername; Nicci – in the kitchen last night when he'd gone to get another beer. *Isn't it nice to see Bella's found herself a man*, Megan had said. *At last*, and then she had laughed in that catty, suggestive way some girls have when talking behind someone's back. To be honest, it was partly why he'd danced so enthusiastically with Bella – he didn't much like the implication that she found it hard to get a man. She was gorgeous; in his opinion, she could get any man she chose. Of course, when Kitty had let slip later on that Megan was his secret admirer, her comments, or rather the loudness and timing of her comments, began to make rather more sense to him. "That must be why Mel didn't mind us dancing last night," he remarked.

"I didn't see you dancing with him. I didn't realize he was your type."

"Ho ho. Funny lady."

"I'll tell you someone who did mind, though."

"Yeah, I know. Kitty."

"Kitty? No, I was going to say Megan. Why Kitty?"

"Why Megan?" he countered. He had the uncomfortable feeling that he was being led into dangerous waters and that, if he wasn't careful, he could be setting himself up for more stick with his cousin.

"Didn't you see her face? She looked as if she'd caught us at it, not just dancing. Then she went belting out of the room." She sighed. "It was only a dance. Just a bit of a laugh."

"Exactly."

"And we've known each other for years. It's not as if we're after each other, or anything like that."

"My point precisely." They were both carefully avoiding mentioning the slow dance that followed the bit of a laugh, he noticed. Interesting, that.

"So what was Kitty's problem, then?"

"I'm not really sure. Something to do with Megan liking me, I think." What a liar. He knew damn well what it was. It just seemed a bit big-headed to say, because Megan Roberts apparently fancies the pants off me and Kitty thinks I should respond just to be polite.

"Oh, right," Bella said, gloomily. "So Kitty

doesn't think we should have been dancing together either?"

"Who cares what Kitty thinks?"

"Me. I care. She's my friend – I don't want to upset her." There was a small silence, then; "Do you think she'd mind if I saw you later?"

"What's to mind? It would all be perfectly innocent, wouldn't it? Like you said, we've known each other for years."

"Yeah. But I don't want to cause any trouble."

"How would spending an hour or so with me, watching a DVD, cause trouble?" His voice rose slightly, and Bella could picture his expression. He was a good bloke, and there was a definite shortage of good blokes in this world, in her experience. Surely it wouldn't hurt anyone to go round and see him, just for a bit. He was a mate.

"Well, OK. If you're sure."

"Sure I'm sure. Look, Bella – I'll tell you what I told Kitty, last night." Or a revised and/or edited version, at any rate. "Just because someone fancies me, I can't help it if I don't fancy them back."

"Who are we talking about here?" She sounded faintly alarmed.

"Megan, of course."

"Oh, right. Yeah. Of course."

"Kitty needs to get her head round that, and get over it. I mean, I think she's great and all that, most of the time, but she does have this tendency to try and manipulate her friends' lives."

"It's only because she cares," Bella murmured.

"I know. But she tries to ambush people's emotions. She's got to learn that we can all choose our own mates. That we're allowed to spend time with whoever we want." He coughed, slightly embarrassed; this was all getting much heavier than he'd intended. "So anyway – are you up for coming over here later? Or shall I come over to you?"

"Oh God, no," she said, hastily. "There's nothing to do here. I'll come over to yours."

"Terrific. Say, about three? And Bella?"

"Hmm?"

"Don't worry about it. It's cool. Like you said, it's not as if we're after each other. We're just mates, hanging out together. OK?"

"OK."

She hung up, thinking *What harm can it do?* Neither Kitty nor Megan need ever know about it. They were probably tucked away with their respective families today: New Year's Day, along with Christmas, was supposed to be a time for families, wasn't it? Well, given that it wasn't possible for her to be with her real family on these occasions (apart from Aunt Susan, who didn't really count), spending them with people she'd known for so long they *were* practically family now seemed a reasonable alternative. And besides, this time of year held too many difficult memories for her, when the entire universe seemed to be OD-ing on festive jollity, and she was the odd one out.

She didn't want to spend the day alone. *Been there, done that.* Well, she didn't have to now, did she? She was going to see Bruno, and if anyone objected, well, it was just tough, frankly. So there.

Bella is hungry. Very hungry. She pads through into the kitchen and opens the door of the fridge. Not much in there – a bit of cling-wrapped cheese with fluffy green stuff growing on it, two squashed tomatoes in the bottom bit, a yoghurt with a picture of a strawberry on it. She takes the yoghurt out and opens the drawer for a spoon. No spoons. She puts the yoghurt down on the worktop next to the fridge, carefully, and goes out of the kitchen and into Sylvie's room.

It is very quiet in there. The curtains are closed, and on the bed she can just make out the hump that is Sylvie, lying almost completely covered by the duvet. There is a funny smell in the bedroom, an unpleasant sour kind of smell. Bella goes to the window and opens it, thinking perhaps a bit of fresh air might help. It is Sylvie's cure for almost everything. *Got a cold? Have a bit of fresh air. Headache? Bit of fresh air. Tired? Bit of fresh air.*

The noise of the squeaky catch on the window wakes Sylvie. She stirs and then turns over.

"Hello, funny bunny." In the gloom of the darkened room, Bella can see she has opened her eyes. "What are you doing?"

"Opening the window."

"I ought to get up." Sylvie gives a sigh, a huge sigh as if just thinking about getting up is the most exhausting thing in the world, ever.

"Are you all right?" Bella goes up to the bed and leans on it, peering into Sylvie's face.

"Yes. No." Sylvie closes her eyes again, and two tears escape from beneath her closed eyelids and track their way down the sides of her nose to the corners of her mouth, where they disappear. "I'm just a bit tired, that's all."

"It's a new year," Bella remarks. She finds this interesting. Where does the old year go? When does it change from being new to being old? And how do people decide that yesterday was still the old year, but today is a new one? How did they know in the olden days, before things like calendars were invented? She would like to discuss all this with Sylvie, but she knows this is going to be another of what Sylvie calls One of My Bad Days. It started the day before yesterday, which makes three Bad Days now, all in a row.

"Is it?" Sylvie opens her eyes again, and looks into her daughter's face as if searching for something. "Happy new year." She reaches out an arm and puts it around Bella's neck, drawing her towards her.

"I'm hungry." Bella squirms away, out of her grasp.

"Oh Bella." Sylvie sighs again. "Can you find something for yourself? Some Weetabix?"

"There's no milk."

"I'm sorry." More tears escape, and Bella wonders where they all come from. Sylvie was crying all day yesterday, for reasons that Bella couldn't understand. She can never understand what causes Sylvie's bad days. She is just surprised that there is so much water inside her: Bella herself can never cry for more than a few moments before the tears dry up, no matter how hard she tries to make them last. "I'll go shopping tomorrow, I promise. But can you just find something for now? Only I'm so tired. . ."

Bella loves Sylvie and is sorry that she is sad again, but at the moment her own hunger is all she can really think about. "There's a yoghurt."

"Oh good." There is a long pause, and then Sylvie says, in a tired quiet little voice, "I'm sorry, honey bunny."

Bella is about to tell her that there are no clean spoons, but Sylvie has fallen asleep again. So she wanders back into the kitchen and finds one underneath the mountain of dirty dishes piled in the sinkful of cold scummy water, rinses it off under the tap, and takes it and the yoghurt into the sitting room. She sits cross-legged on the floor in front of the television and eats her yoghurt and watches a programme with a whole load of people playing music in a great big glittering ballroom, lovely happy swirly music that makes her wish Sylvie was in there watching it with her because, you never know, the music might cheer her up.

Mum was in the conservatory, palely toying with a mug of coffee and what looked like a hangover. Surely not – Kitty didn't think mums were supposed to get hangovers. Especially not mums who are nurses and not only know all about alcohol-induced brain-cell death, cirrhosis of the liver, etc. etc., but lecture their teenage daughters about such things at every given opportunity.

"Hello, love. Have a good evening?" She took a glug of coffee and grimaced. Yup – definitely a hangover, then. "You've left everything nice and clean and tidy. I must admit I was rather dreading what we might find when we got back."

"Oh ye of little faith," Kitty said, breezily. Probably best not to mention the vomit, then. She was feeling much more cheerful after a long, initially apologetic and then decidedly saucy phone conversation with Rhys – who didn't appear to remember much, if anything, about the previous evening and hadn't referred to the way he'd left, so Kitty didn't feel inclined to remind him. She sat down on a wicker chair. "You had a nice time too, Dad tells me."

"A bit too good, to be honest." Mum stared into the bottom of the mug as if wondering how it had got into her hand. "I'm just feeling a bit – jaded."

"Oh, OK." Kitty nodded sagely. "Jaded."

Mum leant her head back and closed her eyes. "So. Who did you have round last night, then? Anything interesting happen?"

Er. . . "No, not really." She mentally crossed her fingers and hoped that none of the neighbours would comment later on how many guests the Doyles seemed to have had, and what a good time they all appeared to be having, judging by the loudness of the music. "It was just the usual crowd – you know, Rhys, Megan, Bruno, Bella."

I'm gonna getcha getcha getcha getcha. . . She could suddenly see them, entwined together with not a hair's breadth between them, moving sinuously in time to the music.

"Mum, would you say Bella's man-mad?"

She wasn't quite sure where the words came

from. She certainly hadn't intended asking Mum any such thing. But it was too late now – it was said. Mum's eyes snapped open.

"Why?" she asked, suspiciously. That was exactly why she shouldn't have asked Mum – the automatically suspicious response. *What's been going on in my house?* "What's been going on?"

"Oh, nothing," Kitty reassured her hastily. "It's just something somebody said."

"About Bella?"

Kitty nodded, and Mum raised her eyebrows and then pursed her lips and nodded back, slowly, in an evaluating no-surprises-there-then manner.

"What does –" Kitty copied Mum's facial expression and gesture – "mean?"

"Only that it's not totally unexpected."

"So you *do* think she's man-mad," Kitty declared, aware of her voice getting louder but not quite understanding why.

Mum winced, and put a hand up to her forehead. "Ouch. Don't shout, Kitty. You did ask."

"Yeah, OK," she conceded. "Sorry. So why do you think she's –" She waved her hands around, not wanting to use the phrase for a third time. "You know."

"Maybe man-mad's putting it a bit strongly. After all, I hardly know her these days, do I? Not like when you were both small. But I saw the way she was acting round Ged on Boxing Day. I don't know, maybe I'm turning into an old fogey, but it seemed a bit unnecessary to me. Even though he quite obviously thought it was great, the big daft lummox." She gave a small fond boys-will-be-boys smile at the memory of her nephew's enthusiastic response to Bella's come-hither manner. "She just seems to have this – I don't know – kind of *air* about her when she's around men."

"An aura," Kitty murmured.

"That's it, yes. An aura. She's what's used to be called a man's woman – it doesn't matter how old they are, if they're male she can't help herself responding to them. Flirting with them, you could say. I mean, look at how Owen goes all ga-ga whenever she's around."

"I know. What's that all about? He doesn't even *like* girls!"

"He can't help himself. It's the aura. I don't think she does it deliberately. It's just the way she is; she's probably always been like it. She was certainly interested in lads far earlier than you were."

"That's what Dad said."

"You've spoken to Dad about it?"

Kitty nodded.

"What did he say?"

234

"Not much. He really likes her."

"He's a man," Mum said, as if that proved her point. They looked at each other, and both said, "It's her aura," together, at exactly the same time, and then laughed, although Kitty felt a pang of guilt. Bella was her friend. Wasn't she supposed to confide in her friends about her mother, rather than the other way around? *Oh well – in for a penny. . .*

"When we were little, did Bella ever tell lies?"

Mum sat deep in thought for a moment, her face quite impassive. "Has something been going on with her?" she asked, eventually. "Something you want to tell me about?"

"No, no." Kitty flapped her hands around dismissively. Well, it was true. Nothing had been *going on*, not really. Just a few comments from Megan, and an incident or two that she could easily have misconstrued. Quite a few, come to think of it. Over the years. "I just wondered what you thought, that's all."

"It depends on your point of view, I suppose. You could say they weren't lies, exactly – more exaggerations. There again, if you wanted to be damning, you could interpret some of the things she came out with as a sign of a pathological liar."

"Is that the same as a compulsive liar?"

"More or less. Why?"

"It's what Megan called her." She was beginning to get an uncomfortable feeling about this. Was it only her who'd taken everything Bella had said as gospel, while everybody else had seen through it? "She said she used to lie about everything."

"Did she?" Mum raised her eyebrows again. "Well, I'm not saying that; it's just how some might interpret it. Anyway, I daresay Megan has her own agenda with Bella."

But on the other hand, wouldn't Megan know, with Bella having lived in her house for all that time?

"So what did she exaggerate about?"

"Oh, heavens." Mum gave a gusty sigh, as if Kitty were asking her something impossibly demanding. "I can't really remember. It was a long time ago." She gazed unseeingly through the conservatory windows to the garden, which dripped unbecomingly outside in the January gloom. "Oh yes. . . There was the time she said she'd once been to a party at Buckingham Palace."

"So how's that exaggerating?" Kitty pulled a face. "Sounds like a total lie to me."

"But we don't know that, do we? To be fair. She may well have visited the place at some point, in some capacity. We don't know what happened in her life before she came to Penllan, do we? Oh, and she used to say her father was a gypsy. Do you remember that? She said that for ages, then she suddenly stopped talking about him. When I asked her after a while if she'd seen him lately she just looked at me blankly and said she'd never met her dad. And you remember how much she used to love Heinz? She told me once that she used to have ten dogs just like him in her old house." She looked at Kitty. "Like I say, only fairly small things, but even so. . . Oh, and she told you she was being adopted. You got really upset about that, thinking she was going to be moving away from you."

"Bella says she's being adopted."

Kitty sees Mum and Dad looking at each other across the table.

"Is that right?" Dad says, and smiles at her kindly.

"What's dopted?" asks Owen.

Kitty ignores him, and leans forward to spear another potato. "She says she's going to live in England, in a big house in London near the sea, and have her own bedroom. It's got its own little bathroom and everything. And –" she cuts up the potato and pops a piece of it into her mouth – "she's going to have her own telly," she says, through the potato.

"I wouldn't believe everything Bella tells you," Mum says, crisply. "Don't talk with your mouth full, Kitty."

But Kitty does believe her. Bella knows every detail of the house she is moving to, and of the family – an older sister and a younger brother, two cats and a dog – even down to their names. Even the pets' names. She feels a little prickle of crossness towards her parents. What do they know? It's Bella's life – surely she knows what's happening in it. Then on top of the crossness comes a dawning realization. Her face crumples.

"She *is* being adopted, and I'm never going to see her again," she wails, and tears spring from her eyes, and bits of potato fall out of her mouth and on to her plate.

"I remember the adoption thing now." Kitty felt slightly stupid, as if everyone but her had known that Bella made things up. It added to her growing feeling that the Bella she thought she knew was gradually being revealed as having been someone else all along. "Why didn't I realize she wasn't telling the truth?"

"She was your friend – you believed what she said. You know, when you tell the truth yourself, you just assume everybody else does the same. You trust them. But I wouldn't worry too much about the past, love." Mum leant across and patted Kitty on the knee. "It's what's going on in the here-and-now that's important."

After everything else, it felt like a warning.

chapter twelve

Bella had seen plenty of Bruno when they were kids, but she'd rarely gone to his house. Twice, maybe – once for a birthday party and once for. . . She couldn't remember. Some family occasion she'd been invited to, along with Kitty, no doubt.

She looked up at the house now, appraisingly, as she walked up the drive. Nice. Four-square, cream-painted, with what looked like a new slate roof. Bella had become a bit of an expert on roofs, as when she'd first moved in with Aunt Susan the roof was in its final stages of being replaced, and she'd had to sleep in the guest room for the first week or so, with all her belongings piled around her in bags and boxes.

"Are the aliens landing?" Bruno was standing on the front step in his socks, his hand on the door latch.

"Sorry?"

Bruno grinned, and looked up to the sky. "What's so interesting? I can't see any UFOs."

"I was just looking at your roof."

"Oh, OK. Well, whatever floats your boat." He

grinned again, and the thought suddenly passed through Bella's mind: *You. You float my boat, big time.* Then she was immediately flooded with a hot tide of embarrassment mixed with annoyance. *For God's sake! What's the matter with me? I've known him for ever, I don't feel like that about him. Anyway, what's with the embarrassment? Like he can read my thoughts, all of a sudden?*

She shoved her hands deeper into the pockets of her charity shop fur coat. "So am I coming in, then, or what?"

"No, I thought we could put a couple of chairs in the porch and chat out here." He peered at her solemn face. "Joke."

"Sure. I knew that."

She seemed a bit on edge. Bruno guessed she was still concerned about what Kitty might think about the two of them hanging out together when he was supposed to be taking an interest in Megan because she fancied him. He thought that was how it went. Hard to tell with Kitty, sometimes. She was so intent on managing her friends' lives that her thought processes tended to get a bit complicated. Not to mention her sense of what was realistic, and what was wishful thinking.

"Don't worry," he said, gravely. "She won't find out."

Bella frowned. "Sorry? Who?"

"The Wicked Witch of the West." She still looked blank. "Kitty. Cousin Catrin."

"Won't find out what?"

"That I'm committing the ultimate sin of spending the afternoon with you, instead of trying to get it on with Megan, or whatever it is she wants me to do." He took her coat and hung it on the newel post at the bottom of the bannisters.

"Oh, that. I'm not worrying about that any more. I've made it a new year's resolution."

He turned round from the stairs. The top thing she was wearing was exactly the same shade of blue as her eyes. It was strange, but he'd never noticed before just how blue they were. Unless they'd got bluer since she was a kid. But surely people's eye colour didn't change as they got older? Plenty of other things did – in fact, just about everything else you could think of – but you were stuck with your eye colour for life.

Suddenly aware that he'd been staring like a loony into Bella's eyes for a good ten seconds, he blurted out awkwardly; "I never make resolutions. Unless it's not to make any resolutions this year. I only break them, and then I feel a failure the rest of the year."

"I don't usually, either. Only this year, I've decided I'm going to stop being bothered about what other people think, and just get on with it."

"Just get on with it?" He regarded her, amused. "That sounds like an advertising slogan."

"Nah, Nike have already nicked that one. Or nearly." Bella smiled, a sweet little smile that made her look, Bruno thought with a prickle of attraction, dead sexy.

"Not really," he protested. "They just did it. You're just getting on with it. It's not the same at all. I think it could have legs."

"Wow!" she exclaimed, teasing him gently. "Have you ever thought of a career in advertising?"

"Yeah, right." He looked down and shuffled his feet in a bashful aw-shucks kind of way. Weird. Nobody had ever made him feel like that before. Self-conscious, yes. Downright embarrassed, for sure. But bashful? No way. There must be something in the air, something that was making them both – Bella was currently scrutinizing the hall wallpaper as if it was the most fascinating thing she'd ever seen – act as if they were on a blind date, rather than mates from way-back-when, spending an afternoon together chilling because neither of them had anything better to do.

"Don't get me wrong," Bella said suddenly, looking away from the walls and directly at him (*Jeez, those eyes! How come he'd only just noticed them?*). "I don't want to upset Kitty. But I honestly can't see anything wrong in us hanging out together if we want to."

"Good. Me neither." He turned on his heel and began to lead the way along the passage.

"Even though we've never spent time alone together before. Do you realize that? In all the time we've known each other, there's always been other people around."

They reached the kitchen. Bruno strolled over to the kettle and began to fill it. "Cuppa?" he asked, brandishing it at her.

"Yeah. Lovely."

"Or coffee? Or –" He looked round the room, scratching his head. What did people offer each other to drink on these occasions besides tea or coffee? Apart from alcohol, of course, and given the previous night's excesses he didn't think that was necessarily a good idea. Besides, it was only three o'clock. "I think that's it. Tea or coffee," he said, apologetically.

"That's fine. I'll have whatever you're having."

"Tea, then." He plugged the kettle in, and took a deep breath. It was ridiculous; his heart was going as if he'd done half an hour's weights, not just walked up the hallway and lifted the kettle. What was the matter with him?

"So what are we going to do?" She plonked herself down on one of the stools beside the breakfast bar.

I know what I'd like to do. . . He banished the thought immediately. Somehow, he didn't think the kind of nudge-nudge wink-wink comments he was used to sharing with his mates were entirely appropriate here. Not only was Bella gorgeous, but he was quite surprised to be discovering that he really liked her as well. He didn't want to spoil it by treating her like some kind of sex object. "Well, I thought a cup of tea to start with. I don't know about you, but I woke up this morning with a mouth like an Aborigine's armpit."

"I didn't actually wake up until this afternoon, remember." She looked at him, an amused little half-smile hovering around her mouth. "What does an Aborigine's armpit taste like?"

"You don't want to know. Trust me."

The door opened and Bruno's mum came in. "Hello, Bella. Good to see you again. Happy new year."

"Thanks. Happy new year to you, too, er. . ." Bella didn't know what to call her. She tried to remember what she'd called her before, when she was younger. She didn't think she'd called her anything. She'd not really had cause to. She was always Auntie Carys to Kitty, but Bella could hardly call her that.

Bruno's mum (she couldn't really call her that, either) was taking some cake tins out of a cupboard. "Have you offered Bella a piece of Christmas cake to have with that tea, Bru? Or there's some of my biscuits here."

"Those ones with bits in?" He wrinkled his nose.

"*Bits?* In our language, we have a word for it. Walnuts. Wal-nuts," she repeated slowly, as if to a non-English speaker, and pulled a face at Bella behind his back, a kind of long-suffering, he's-a-guy-what-do-you-expect face. In that moment she looked just like Kitty. Bella felt a rush of warmth towards her. "Or would you prefer a mince pie?"

Bella had forgotten what a good cook she was. Round at the Peppermint House all those years ago, all the cakes and biscuits and jams – *bara brith*, scones, bramble jelly, marmalade – were inevitably provided by Kitty's Auntie Carys, who always seemed to make enough to feed an army.

Bella's stomach gurgled gently, and she remembered she had eaten neither breakfast nor lunch. "Would it be really greedy," she said, "if I had one of each?"

"That'll be cool," Bruno remarked airily. "Mum approves of people who like their grub, don't you, mother dear?"

"Just ignore him," she told Bella, cutting off a large wodge of Christmas cake. "I usually do.

And by the way." She looked up and smiled. "You must call me Carys, OK?"

"Bruno! Yay! Where've you been hiding?" Kitty had decided on the ultra-friendly, kissing-cousins approach. It tended to work better on these occasions than the bossy-little-sister one she usually adopted with him.

"Hiding? Nowhere."

Was it her, or did he sound guilty? "Oh, right. Only I rang a couple of days ago and your mum said you weren't around. And I left two voicemails on your mobile. Never mind," she went on, hastily, as Bossy Little Sister threatened to materialize after all, "you're here now. I just wanted to tell you something."

"OK."

Uncertainly, as if she was about to try and catch him out. Hmm. She'd have to be careful here, or they'd end up fighting again.

"I wanted to say thanks for helping with all the clearing up and everything the other night. I really appreciated it."

"No worries. It's what family's for, isn't it?" He put on an mock *EastEnders* accent – *famlee* – and she began to relax. She'd been wondering if he was avoiding her after their little run-in.

"Even so. It was dead kind of you, and I'm grateful." *Steady on. Don't want to overdo it.*

"You're welcome." A slight pause. "Was there something else?"

"Well, yeah," she confessed. "What did you mean when you said I should stop interfering in other people's lives and concentrate on my own relationships?"

"Did I say that?"

"Er – yeah."

"I was probably just pissed off at you for going on about me and Bella dancing."

"OK. Well, look, I'm sorry about that."

"It was all perfectly innocent, you know."

"Yeah. You said." *It just didn't look it, that's all*. . . Still, no point in going down that road again. "So what about the concentrating on my own relationships bit?"

"How d'you mean?"

"Well . . . what did *you* mean?"

Another pause. "I don't know. Nothing, probably."

"I just wondered if you'd overheard me and Rhys." He had never really got on with Rhys, had always referred to him in an irritatingly sing-song voice as Mr Shit-Hot Hot-Shot Lawyer until Kitty had lost it one day and told him to shut up.

"Did you?" Carefully. It told Kitty all she needed to know.

"So you *did* hear us," she declared.

"I couldn't miss it, could I? He wasn't exactly

keeping his voice down. If you want my opinion, though, you want to keep an eye on him – he was well sleazing it up at the party."

"He wasn't! He might have got a bit pissed, but after all it was New Year's Eve. And OK so we had a bit of a bust-up; but he wasn't being a sleaze."

"If you say so."

"So what did you see, exactly?" Kitty demanded, suddenly aware that she hadn't actually been around Rhys much that evening to notice what he'd been up to. Could Bruno possibly be right, rather than just biased?

"Nothing, probably. He had his arms round that mate of Megan's – Nicci – that's all. But like you say, it was New Year's Eve. Everyone was hugging everyone else."

"Exactly. He's not a sleaze. No way!" All that fuss just for a bit of hugging! Rhys could hug whoever he wanted – she wasn't going to get all possessive over just a hug.

"Whatever you say. He's your boyfriend." He sighed. "Look, you were cross with me for dancing with Bella rather than Megan, and I was pissed off with you for going on about it. That's what made me say what I did. Now can we please just get over it?"

"Only if you stop going on about Rhys."

"OK. I'll stop going on about him." He cast about for something uncontroversial to say. He didn't want her to start on about him and Bella again. "So. What're you up to?"

"Not much. I've got college work to finish before we go back next week, but I just can't be arsed at the moment. I hate January, don't you?"

Bruno had never thought about liking or disliking certain months. He was either enjoying life, or having a hard time – it had nothing to do with what month it was. "Er, yeah. Loathe it."

"I'm trying to focus on my eighteenth coming up, but I can't seem to raise much enthusiasm for that either. I don't know what to do for it."

"But you've got to do something! It's an important birthday – you've got to organize something or you'll just end up going down the pub. Tell you what – leave it with me. I'll sort it for you."

"Really?" She was overwhelmed.

"Really."

"Aw, bless. That's so kind of you." She was genuinely touched. "When are you back off to Manchester?"

"Monday." He suddenly had a brilliant idea. "Look, tell you what," he said, slowly. "Why don't we do something together on the weekend?"

"Like what?"

"I dunno. Go to a movie. Or, I know – bowling. We haven't been bowling for ages."

"What, just you and me? Bowling's no fun with two."

"Well, ask Mr Shit-Hot – I mean, Rhys. Ask him along too."

"It's not much better with three than two." She paused. Bruno held his breath, wondering if she would go for it. "Bru-no," she began, a wheedling tone in her voice. "How would you feel about Megan coming along too?"

"Whatever. I don't mind." He wouldn't normally have done it, he didn't want to encourage Megan, but under the circumstances. . .

"Really? Only I think she feels a bit stupid. You know – about what happened at the party. She rang me yesterday; she said she'd drunk too much, everything got out of hand, and she's afraid you're going to think she's lost it. I think she'd really appreciate the chance just to be friends with you again."

"I don't mind making up a foursome with her. I've never said I don't like her, remember. Just so long as she doesn't think it means we're now, you know, *Together*."

"Oh, she won't," Kitty assured him.

"Hey, I've just had a thought." *You liar, Bruno Lewis. No "just" about it.* "Why not see if Bella wants to come along as well?"

"What? Are you mad!"

"No. Along with Mel, I mean. Think about it.

If he and Bella are there, then there'll be those two, you and Rhys, and me and Megan. Six of us – so the vibe will be kind of diluted. Megan'll be able to see there's nothing going on between Bella and me, and the two of them might even start being civil to each other again. And you'll earn loads of Brownie points into the bargain for having organized it. Sorted." He didn't like being manipulative, it went against the grain, but it was worth it to get the chance of spending a couple of hours with Bella again. Just as mates, naturally.

"Well. . ." she said, doubtfully. "I don't know. We wouldn't want Megan throwing another hissy fit at the sight of Bella, would we?"

"At least suggest it to her, see what she says."

"What if she says she'll come, but she doesn't want Bella there?"

Hmm. Tricky one. "Then it'll just be the four of us," he conceded. Ah, what the heck? They would be in public, so Megan was hardly going to throw herself on him in a fit of unbridled lust. And if Bella wasn't going to be there he would just have to find another way of seeing her before he went back to Manchester.

Bella closed the front door behind herself, carefully.

"How was she?" Aunt Susan came along the

passageway from the kitchen, drying her hands on a tea towel.

"Oh, OK." Bella raked a hand through her hair, leaving it sticking up in spikes.

"You're wet, dear. Is it raining again?"

"Chucking it down. Are there any messages for me?"

"Two. I wrote them down." She rummaged in the pocket of her apron and withdrew a piece of paper. "Mel said could you call him back. And Bruno –"

"Bruno?!" Bella exclaimed.

"Bruno," Aunt Susan repeated firmly. "Bruno also said could you call him back." She looked at her great-niece over the top of her glasses. "Not very loquacious, these young men of yours, are they?"

"They're not my young men," said Bella, dismissively. "Did Bruno leave his number?"

"Yes. I've written that down, too. Here you are." She handed Bella the piece of paper. "Are you sure everything was all right? You look a little – unsettled."

"Everything was fine," Bella said shortly.

"She seemed a lot better the last time I went to visit. More positive. And it's good that Dorothy's money has meant she could go to that new place. It's much nicer."

"Yeah." Bella shrugged her coat off. "Is it OK

if I use the phone? I'll take it upstairs."

"Of course it is. Then why don't you come down and have a bite of supper with me? It's lasagne – I've made far too much, as usual."

Bella could smell it, the mixed aromas of tomato and herbs and garlic, wafting their seductive way from the kitchen. For a moment, she was tempted. She hesitated at the foot of the stairs, torn between a decent meal with some company for a change, and being alone with a packet of cigarettes and the remains of the vodka.

"Thanks," she said, with an apologetic smile, "but I've got something in the fridge I was planning to have."

"All right, dear. If you're sure."

She was sure. She needed to be by herself. These visits always shook her up. No matter how things were, it was always horribly, claustrophobically reminiscent of the first time.

"Come and say hello to Mummy, Isabella."

She doesn't want to. The auntie lady is holding her hand tightly, so tightly it hurts, and the other lady, sitting on the chair by the window, isn't even Sylvie. They can't fool her. She might be wearing Sylvie's lovely rainbow jacket, and even Sylvie's old scuffed red shoes, the ones she told Bella she bought in somewhere called Paris when she was a student, but it is definitely not Sylvie.

It is somebody who is about the same size and shape, dressed up in Sylvie's things, but it isn't her. This lady is sitting with her back to the room, rocking gently backwards and forwards, kind of plucking at her skirt, and – well, moaning. Not a person kind of noise at all, but more like the sound Mrs Briggs's dog makes in the flat downstairs when Mrs Briggs is out at work. Whining. As if she might start to bark at any moment. Sylvie would never make a noise like that. And she would never ignore Bella, either, when she walked into a room. Sylvie always knows where Bella is and what she is up to, every moment. If it was Sylvie she would turn round and say, "Hello honey bunny," and smile, and get up from the chair, and –

"Isabella." The auntie lady crouches down on the floor, still holding Bella's hand, so her face is level with Bella's. "Would you like to go and say hello to Mummy?"

Bella looks back at her. A funny feeling goes through her. What she really wants to do is reach forward and bite the auntie lady, right on the nose. But she doesn't, of course, and after a little while the feeling goes away. She doesn't say anything though, and after another moment or two the auntie lady says: "Don't be afraid. I'm sure your mummy will be ever so pleased to see you. And look, you've brought her book, haven't you? Why don't you go and give it to her?"

Bella looks down at the book she is holding. The wuthering book. When the auntie lady said she was taking her to visit Sylvie, and could she think of anything she might like brought to her, Bella thought of the wuthering book straight away. It is what she reads to Bella all the time, night after night. The auntie lady looked at her really strangely when she picked it up; wouldn't Mummy prefer some chocolates, she said, or some nice fruit. Some grapes. Or some peaches. But Bella knows it is Sylvie's most favourite book ever, so that is what she has brought.

She looks at the other lady now, the Sylvie imposter, sitting in her chair, rocking and whining and picking at her skirt, over and over. What would *she* want with the wuthering book? And then, just at that moment, something truly awful happens. The Sylvie imposter stops rocking and whining and turns her head, ever so slowly, and looks at Bella, straight at her, and Bella sees clear as clear that she isn't an imposter at all but Sylvie. Really Sylvie. Only not quite Sylvie, because there is something strange about her eyes. She is looking at Bella as if she has never seen her before and doesn't know who she is. Her eyes flicker past her and on to the auntie lady, and then she turns slowly back to the wall again.

Bella throws the book to the floor, wrenches her hand from the auntie lady's grasp and rushes from the room. The auntie lady follows her, and catches her just outside the door, and Bella can hear a lot of screaming that is drowning out Sylvie's moaning and then she realizes it is herself screaming. And then there is another lady, in a white coat thing, and both she and the auntie lady are patting her and talking to her, soothingly, saying things like: "It's all right, it will be all right." But Bella knows it is not all right, it is all wrong, and that nothing will make her go back in that room again. It was better when she thought it was a Sylvie imposter; much better.

"Perhaps I will have some of that lasagne with you." Bella gave Aunt Susan a tight little smile, hoping she would understand that her withdrawn mood was nothing personal. "I don't think I'll be much company, though."

"That's all right." The older woman turned, and made as if to go back to the kitchen. Then she changed her mind, and turned back. "I know it isn't easy for you. But your visits mean a lot to Sylvie. You are doing the right thing for her."

But who's doing the right thing for me? All of a sudden, Bella wanted to throw herself into the arms of her aunt – her formal, poker-straight, undemonstrative great-aunt who had never had anything to do with kids in her entire life – and ask her that question. *Who's doing that?* But she didn't. She just smiled again, reassuringly.

"I know."

chapter thirteen

"You mean, like a double date?" Kitty could hear the thrill in Megan's voice, mingled with a kind of stunned disbelief. "Wow!"

"Steady on. This is Bruno we're talking about, not David Beckham," Kitty joked.

Megan had a sense of humour bypass when it came to matters Bruno-esque. "You're so mean about him," she objected. "You can keep David Beckham – Bruno is far lusher than him. And smart, too."

Kitty was starting to hear alarm bells. Megan had promised her faithfully, had sworn on her cat's life after the party, that she was over Bruno now and wasn't going to be "like that" about him any more. I was getting too obsessed, she said. I was turning into a bunny-boiler. Getting in that kind of state over a guy was way embarrassing.

"OK," Megan said now, perkily. "What shall I wear?"

"Wear?"

"Yeah. Y'know, like, clothes? I thought perhaps my new denim hipster mini – what d'you reckon?"

Thinking she'd sound too much like her mother for comfort, Kitty bit back her instinctive response – *In January? To go bowling?* – and said instead: "Hmm. Trousers might be easier. You know – with bending over, and all that."

"I know." Megan gave a sex-kittenish little giggle that worried Kitty all the more.

"I thought you said you were over Bruno?" she said, with suspicion.

"I am."

"OK. So remind me, how does wearing your hipster mini to go bowling go with being over him?"

"Doesn't mean I can't *flirrrt* with him," she growled.

"He did say," Kitty started carefully, "when we were talking about this bowling thing, that he does like you but doesn't want you to think you two are an item. It's not, like, a proper date or anything."

"I *know*." Megan's voice changed instantly to wounded innocence.

"So flirting's kind of probably not a great idea?"

Megan sighed. "Give us a break, Kitty. I still like him. I always will."

"I know, hun. All I'm saying is –" *If you're going to be all over him in your denim mini, forget it. You won't see him for dust.* How could she say that? Answer: she couldn't. "All I'm saying is, if

260

you play it cool you might have more of a chance. Who knows? Hang out together just as mates a few times, and he might even get to realize what he's been missing." Genuine fondness for her friend, not wanting to hurt her feelings, made her expansive; even though a little voice at the back of her brain was telling her she shouldn't be saying such things, that it would give Megan false hope. "When we were discussing the bowling," she said, partly to try and introduce a bit of balance and partly because she wanted to get this bit over and done with, "we thought we might see if Bella and Mel want to come along too."

She braced herself for a typical Megan outburst, but slightly to her surprise none came. Instead, there was silence.

"Meg? You still there?"

"Yeah."

"Did you hear what I said?"

"I heard."

"So what d'you think?"

Kitty could hear Megan breathing steadily down the line. "Dunno," she said, at last.

"Well, initial reaction? Yes, no? Over my dead body?"

"I'm trying to work out whether I can put up with Bella being there for the sake of spending some time with Bruno."

"She doesn't *have* to be there. It was just, you know. A thought."

A bit more silence.

"I guess if Mel's there too. . ."

"Yeah."

"And I guess it'll reflect well on me?"

"You bet. You'll look dead mature."

"We-ell. OK then. But Kitty?"

"Mm-hm?"

"If she comes on to him again, I can't be held responsible for my actions. You've heard of 'Murder on the Dancefloor' – well, this'll be Murder in the Bowling Alley."

"Don't worry. It'll be just fine," Kitty assured her, pushing aside the slight feelings of misgiving that she'd had since Bruno first suggested the whole thing.

Bella hadn't seen Kitty since the party on New Year's Eve. She hadn't been avoiding her, exactly, but according to Bruno, Kitty had been annoyed about the two of them having that dance; and when you added Bella going round to Bruno's the next day into the equation, you were approaching some pretty major unpleasantness potential. She had no idea whether Kitty even knew she'd been to Bruno's, but she didn't want to take the risk just yet – her head was in a mess at the moment, and she just didn't need anything adding to the stress. She loved Kitty, but she did have this ability to go on about stuff and make you feel you should apologize for things you hadn't done, or that weren't your fault. She didn't want to be on the receiving end of Kitty's no doubt well-meaning rant about why Megan and Bruno were just perfect for each other, so therefore she, Bella Jones, shouldn't talk to him, touch him, acknowledge his presence in any way and probably even breathe the same air as him. . . All in all, it seemed much better just to keep out of Kitty's way for a while.

So she was rather surprised but very relieved when Kitty rang one evening, perfectly normal and chirpy and apparently utterly rant-free, to ask if she wanted to go out on Saturday night.

"Yeah, sure. Anywhere in particular?"

"We thought bowling."

Two things about that sentence – the we and the bowling.

"Who's we?" she asked, to give herself space to think about the bowling bit.

"Me and Bruno. He wanted to do something before going back to uni next week, so we thought bowling would be cool. You know – Bruno, me and Rhys, you and Mel. D'you reckon Mel'd be up for it?"

"I reckon. I'll ask him, shall I?" Bella had done the sums in her head. "That's five of us."

"Oh yeah, and, er – Megan," Kitty said, trying to be casual. Bella could practically see her on the other end of the phone, examining her fingernails in a studiedly nonchalant way.

"Megan," she repeated, gravely.

"Yeah. Problem?"

"No, no," Bella assured her, trying to suppress a smile. Kitty's matchmaking efforts were so transparent. It was sweet, really, even if it hadn't ever occurred to her that, if Megan and Bruno were destined to get it on together, they would surely have done so by now. If it was true that you can't hurry love, it was even more true that you can't compel it, either.

They agreed when and where to meet on Saturday, and after they had hung up Bella was genuinely pleased Kitty had rung, despite her thoughts being even more confused now than before. One fact, however, was beginning to detach itself from the rest of the murk in her brain – she really wanted to see Bruno again, even if Kitty had him lined up as Megan's date for the evening. She wasn't sure what it was she was feeling for him, or when whatever it was she used to feel for him changed to these new, strange and unaccountable emotions. She didn't know how she was going to play it, either – she certainly wasn't going to make any kind of move on him, she had no desire to upset either Megan or Kitty, and you could bet your life that one or both of them would throw a total mental if she so much as smiled at him too much. But for the moment, just having another opportunity to be in his company was enough.

The only slight snag was the bowling.

Sylvie had said it was going to be an adventure but Bella didn't know you had to change your shoes before having an adventure. She is standing in front of the desk in her socks while the man holds her trainers and looks at first them and then her, doubtfully.

"What size?" he asks Sylvie.

"I don't know. One, two?"

"How old is she?"

"Nearly seven."

"Shouldn't she be in bed?"

Now he is looking at Sylvie, a hard disapproving look that Bella is beginning to recognize. Sylvie just looks straight back at him, smiling her sweet unconcerned smile, and says nothing.

"It's gone half ten," the man persists. "Hasn't she got school in the morning?"

"This is educational," she says. She leans towards the man and her eyes begin to gleam. "I'm sure you mean well, but she's my daughter and I know what's best for her."

Please don't say anything back, Bella begs him, inside her head. She doesn't know what Sylvie might do if the man begins to argue. She might push her face right up to his and shout at him, like she did with the man who came to read the gas meter that time. Or she might do what she did to the man at the market who Sylvie said gave her the wrong change (and Bella thinks this would actually be worse) – she might pull an evil face, and lift up her T-shirt and show him what she is wearing underneath. Which is nothing.

But to Bella's relief the man just shrugs, and hands her a pair of funny-looking shoes that are half red and half blue, as if a red shoe and a blue shoe have been cut down the middle and stuck together. "As long as you're paying, I suppose," he mutters. "Lane three, then."

Even after that bad start, the bowling is fun to begin with. Sylvie shows Bella how to hold the ball, with her first two fingers and thumb in the holes (although Bella has to use her other hand underneath it as well because the ball is so heavy), and how to roll it carefully down the lane towards the skittles at the end. Bella is enjoying herself, and so absorbed in the game and waiting for her ball to come popping back up the little chute that at first she doesn't notice Sylvie's mood changing. Then she realizes that she is jumping around more and more after each go, punching the air with her fist and shouting "Yes!" and "Way to go!" People are starting to nudge each other, and stare at them.

"Sshh," Bella tells her.

"What? Why? I don't want to sshh," Sylvie replies, really loudly. "It's fun. Don't you think it's fun?" And she starts to sing, louder still, a song about coconuts and rolling balls, and loads of people have stopped playing and are staring at them now and Bella's face feels red and hot with shame. Still singing, Sylvie takes her ball from the chute and half runs, half stumbles to the end of the lane and lets the ball go. It thunders down the centre of the lane and then veers off suddenly to the right, knocking down just one of the white skittle things.

"Bugger!" Sylvie shouts. She whirls round to Bella, her face creased with temper. "Did you see that? It's a fix! It's a fucking fix!"

And before Bella can stop her she skids and slides her way down the lane. Just as she reaches the end where the skittles are being lifted up and set back down again she loses her footing and tumbles down to the floor; face first, and as her arms go out to save herself she manages to knock down another five or maybe six, Bella is not sure, because all of a sudden the whole place seems full of men shouting and rushing down the lane towards Sylvie.

"All right, missus!" It's the man from the desk, the shoe man. "Out! Come on, out! I knew you were trouble the moment I saw you!"

He and the other man (there are actually only two of them, it just seemed like more) take Sylvie under her arms and lift her up, roughly, and march her back to where Bella is standing. Nobody is playing any more, everyone is staring at Sylvie and some people are laughing. "Now get your stuff and go," the shoe man tells her. "This your mum?" he asks Bella. She nods, dumbly. "You poor little cow," he says, and this is the worst thing of all, not that Sylvie sang too loudly and shouted out bad words and fell over and showed her pants and made people stare and laugh, but that this man feels sorry for Bella for having Sylvie as her mum.

It had put her off bowling for life. Well, clearly not for life, because here she was now agreeing to going again. But it would be the first time she'd gone within a mile of a bowling alley since.

They automatically teamed up as Boys v Girls – Kitty, Megan and Bella against Bruno, Rhys and Mel. Nobody suggested they should play the game like that, but it just seemed the natural thing to do – the girls dashing over to enter their names first on the computerized score chart, and then cheering each other on wildly whilst rather unsportingly (Kitty acknowledged with total lack of shame) booing the lads' efforts and trying to put them off.

It was a real laugh. Kitty was pleased to see that Megan and Bella were being friendly towards each other. It was all pats on the back and obligingly handing each other the ball and high fives at any score more than an eight – such a contrast (especially on Megan's part) from the last time they had been together, when Megan had given the impression that she never wanted to set eyes on Bella again, far less spend any time in her company. Yet here she was now, making like Bella was her new best friend, and it all seemed – Kitty couldn't get over this – totally genuine and unforced. Amazing. She was even being sensible around Bruno, talking to him of course, and smiling and joking, but not being at all over the top. Kitty felt like hugging her. She appreciated how hard it was to behave in an apparently natural manner around someone you wanted to impress. And then there was Bruno – paying Megan exactly the right amount of attention, just being nice and, well, friendly.

Even Bruno and Bella were behaving impeccably towards each other, no sign of the oh-no-we're-just-mates palaver that had so agitated Megan before. In fact, come to think of it, they didn't seem to have much to say to each other. They were almost avoiding speaking to each other, which under the circumstances was probably best all round.

The only slight fly in the ointment was Rhys, who was all over her this evening like a rash, putting his arm around her at every opportunity and trying to plant kisses on her when it was her turn to bowl and she was trying to get to her ball before the people in the adjoining lane nicked it. He had these needy moments – something to do with his moon being in Pisces, according to Megan – but sometimes it was just plain irritating. Then she felt an immediate stab of guilt; she had so loved Rhys's keenness for public displays of affection at the beginning. When did she start thinking of it as neediness? Besides, she ought to just be glad that they'd made up after her party, and he'd apparently stopped kicking off about her spending time with other people.

The boys won by the narrowest of margins despite the girls' gamesmanship, and thanks mainly to a run of last minute strikes by Bruno, who looked more astonished than anyone else at his good fortune.

"Bloody hell," he said after the deciding third one, scratching his head in bewilderment.

Mel let out a whoop of triumph. "I thought you said you were crap at this, man!"

"I am. Well, I always have been before."

He and Bella exchanged glances and Kitty felt a twinge, sensed the tiniest bat's squeak of something, a mysterious significant undercurrent between them. *She's not going to throw her arms around him and congratulate him is she?* she thought, anxiously, remembering Megan's comment about murder in the bowling alley. But no. Bella just went over to where the computer was spewing out the score sheet, and started to talk to Mel. They all stood around looking at each other, slightly awkward now the reason for their having come together in the first place was over, the slightly artificial but nonetheless hearty game-generated camaraderie gone with the printing-off of the score sheet.

Megan broke the silence first. "What shall we do now?" she said, brightly.

"Another game?" Kitty suggested, but Mel shook his head.

"Can't. I'm cleaned out." He turned out his jeans' pockets and pulled a mournful face.

Megan shot Kitty an agonized glance, which Kitty instantly understood meant, *Think of something, quick! I don't want to go home yet!*

"A drink, then." She nodded towards the bar.

"Haven't got the dough for that, either." Mel's woebegone look deepened, and Bella put her hand on his arm.

"It's OK. I'll buy you a drink."

"Hey, babe, no," he began to protest, but Bella linked her arm through his and smiled at him.

"It's fine. Flippin' heck, it's only a drink – anyway, I owe you one."

"Why don't we have a kitty," Bruno suggested, calmly.

"Some of us have already had one." Rhys gave an amused snort, and Kitty felt a sudden surge of annoyance with him.

"Good idea," she declared, trying to glare at him without everyone else noticing. "We could all put a few quid in. Why don't you guys go and grab a table and organize the cash, and I'll go and get the drinks in."

"I'll give you a hand," Mel suggested.

The bar was packed with rowdy post-bowling groups, and troops of lads downing a few loin-girding pints before going into battle with each other, judging by how it sounded – they were all menacing each other with cheery threats of "I'm going to slaughter you" and "You don't stand a chance, mate". As Kitty stood at the bar with Mel, waiting their turn to be served, she turned to ask him why it was that guys always seemed to view competition – even competition as mild as a game of bowling – as a fight to the death. Then she realized she didn't know him well enough to ask him such a thing. In fact, she barely knew him at all. He might take instant and lasting offence on behalf of his sex. She had to say something, she had her mouth open and he was looking at her with polite expectation, waiting for whatever-it-was to issue forth from her lips. So instead she said: "Well then. How's it going with you and Bella?"

"Oh, groovy. She's one cool lady, but she's just, like, a mate."

"Just a mate?" Kitty smiled in a who're-you-trying-to-kid way. "Are you sure?"

"Unfortunately." He shrugged. "I mean, I'd like it to be more, obviously, but she's not up for anything heavy. She told me so right at the beginning, so hey, what could I do?"

"I thought you were spotted snogging at college?" She cocked her head to one side, giving him her best come-on-you-can-tell-me smile.

Mel looked alarmed, and spread his hands in denial. "Not me, babe. Not guilty. She'd knee me in the goolies if I tried that kind of game with her."

Kitty frowned. "But Rhys said —" She stopped. Perhaps he'd got his wires crossed. "Oh well, you never know. She might come round in time. Are you still going to the evening class together?"

Mel frowned. "Evening class?"

"Yeah. Martial arts or something, isn't it?"

Looking baffled, he frowned and shook his head. "Not my scene, man. I'm a pacifist."

"So what is it?"

"What's what?"

"The evening class you and Bella go to."

He was beginning to look at her as if she was delusional. "We don't go to any evening class."

"Haven't you given her a lift there? On a Friday evening?"

"No."

"That's funny. . ." She racked her brains, trying to remember exactly what Bella had said about the class, but Mel was continuing.

"We never went to any evening class. We just sat in the car."

"Sorry?"

"We just drove, and sat in the car."

"When?"

"When I gave her a lift." He enunciated the words carefully, as if explaining them to a dimwit.

"So you did give her a lift?"

"Yeah. I just said. Not to an evening class, though."

"Forget the evening class." Kitty shook her head, impatiently. "Was the lift on a Friday night?"

"Dunno. Can't remember. Some of them might have been."

"So there was more than one occasion?"

"Yeah." The word ended on a rising note, as if followed by an inaudible *So?* Kitty realized she was quizzing him rather forcibly. She smiled again, reassuringly.

"Sorry," she apologized. "There I go again, fuss fuss fuss. Don't mind me. It's just –" What? Just what? What could she say to cover the fact she was interrogating him in order to try and catch out Bella, whom he quite plainly liked a lot? "Er, just that she was asking if Rhys might be able to give her a lift on Friday," she improvised. "I thought it was to an evening class but, um, I might have got that bit wrong," she finished, lamely. Luckily Mel didn't seem to notice how feeble her explanation was. Too chilled, or something.

"Cool," he murmured, making it rhyme with jewel. *Kewl.*

"So, um – where did you go, exactly?"

"Just to this road."

"Which road? What was in it?"

"Nothing. Well, not exactly nothing, obviously. Just a whole bunch of houses."

"A residential street?" Her voice sounded pompous even to her own ears.

"That's the one, yeah. A residential street."

"And –?" she prompted him.

"And nothing. Like I said, we just sat in the car."

"And talked?"

"Some. But mainly she just sat and looked."

"What at?" This was deeply puzzling.

"One of the houses."

"And what could you see?"

"Dur, somebody's sitting room?" From the depths of his hip, laid-back soul, Mel summoned up a hint of sarcasm. "The people who lived there?"

"Didn't you think it was odd?"

"None of my business." He shrugged, then looked at her with some suspicion. "Why are you asking me all this? Why don't you just ask Bella?"

"Sorry," she said again, with another breezily apologetic smile. "Sorry sorry sorry. Just call me nosy. I'm always getting into trouble for it."

At that moment the barman turned to Kitty to take her order, which saved her having to give Mel any more explanation but left her totally nonplussed by what he had just told her.

"Bella!"

She turned round. Bruno was standing in the entrance with one hand on the open glass door and a guilty expression on his face. Grinning, she exhaled the smoke through her nostrils.

"God, what have you been up to? You look like you've been caught with your hand in the cookie jar."

He came towards her. "Can I bum a fag off you?"

"Sure." She dug around in her jeans pocket and held out a slightly battered pack of Marlboro Lights and a Bic lighter. "I didn't know you did."

"I don't, not usually. Just the odd, you know, social occasion." He shook a cigarette out of the pack and lit it, cupping his hands around the flame. "Can we hide round the side for a bit? I don't want any of the others coming out and spotting us."

"Are you afraid Megan will go off you if she discovers you're a closet smoker?" she teased him.

"No, I'm scared Kitty will go off on one if she sees me out here with you instead of in there with – you know."

"Miss Dream Date?" Bella lifted an eyebrow. "Bruno Lewis, you're not scared of your cousin, are you?"

"Terrified of her," he admitted, cheerfully. "Anyway, what d'you mean, lady – Miss Dream Date?"

"Well, this whole thing is about getting you and Megan hooked up, isn't it?" She took another drag on her cigarette, not looking at him.

Bruno groaned. "Don't say that. I feel like a spoilsport for not liking her back in the same way."

"So what's the problem? She's OK. And she's quite pretty too, in a Charlie Dimmock-y kind of way."

Bruno snorted. "Charlie Dimmock-y? Give us a break! What makes you think I'm into lady gardeners who don't wear a bra?"

"I thought you dug them," Bella said, solemnly, and then started to giggle. "Dug them – geddit?"

Bruno started to laugh too. "No, they're too *down to earth* for me," he said, with heavy emphasis.

Bella gave another snort. "Bet Kitty thinks you're a sod because you don't."

"Yeah, but don't grass me up, will you."

They snorted and spluttered for a few moments, lost in amusement at their own feeble wit, until Bruno choked on the cigarette smoke and Bella had to thump him on the back.

"Oh well," he said, when he had recovered. "Guess we'd better go back in, or they'll start to wonder where we've got to."

"Where did you say you were going?"

"The bog. How about you?"

"For a ciggie," she said, with a shrug, as if it was obvious. Bruno smiled. She was the only person he knew who would go outside for a cigarette when she had been sitting in a smoke-filled bar, and then speak as though it was perfectly normal. She looked up at him then. It was too dark to see her eyes properly, only pinpoints of light from inside the bowling alley reflected in them, but Bruno remembered when he'd first noticed their extraordinary colour and beauty on New Year's Day. A strange shiver passed through him.

"Oh, right," he said, inadequately.

"Actually," Bella said, hurling the cigarette butt to the ground and grinding it beneath her foot, "I just needed to be by myself for a bit."

"I know what you mean." Bruno smiled empathically. "It was getting a bit lairy in there."

"Yeah. And I've got a lot on my mind right now."

Their eyes met again. "Yeah?" Bruno said, softly. There was total silence. Silence, that is, apart from the racket issuing forth from the building. The air between them seemed to sing with some kind of charge, or promise. He was aware of standing utterly still, apart from his head, which appeared to be being pulled towards Bella's, slowly, slowly, as if by an invisible thread. For one mad moment he thought he was going to let his face be drawn right up to hers, nose to nose, until he was kissing her – he could taste that kiss, feel her soft lips beneath his, smell the faint tang of her scent. . .

"Yeah," she said. She turned, her eyes dipping away from his, and the moment was

279

broken. He felt a wash of emotion, disappointment and frustration, and anger at himself for bottling it.

"Bella?"

She turned back. Did she look eager? Probably not. It was just his wishful thinking. "Mmm?"

"Why don't you come and see me sometime?" *Shit! Where did* that *come from?*

"Sorry? Is this a 'come up and see my etchings' moment?" She grinned at him, and he grinned back, sheepishly.

"No, really. Come and visit, when I'm back at Manchester. If you fancy a bit of a break from round here." Well, why not. She could only say no, after all. Or no way. Or I'd rather boil my head in a bucket.

But to his immense surprise, she said none of these things. Her whole face lit up, as if someone had shone a torch on it. "Really? Do you mean it?"

"Sure. If you'd like to," he added, making certain she understood it was absolutely her decision and in no way influenced by anything he might say or do. Or want.

"Do you know," she said, with a little sigh, "I can't think of anything I'd like more at the moment than a bit of a break from round here."

"Cool! Let's do it! Bring it on! I'll give you a ring, yeah?" *You do realize you sound like a complete gibbering prat, don't you?* "Er, shall we go back in now?"

He even held the door open for her, like the total gent he suddenly, desperately wanted her to consider him to be.

chapter fourteen

The nugget of information that Mel had imparted to Kitty sat lodged in her consciousness like a piece of information. There was no evening class; there never had been. Which meant, quite simply, that Bella had deliberately lied to Kitty.

It seemed such a stupid thing to have lied about. Why hadn't she just told the truth about what she was doing that evening, when Kitty had called round unexpectedly? Instead of all that bollocks about self-defence classes, and fancying the instructor – and then afterwards, saying that Mel had given her a lift there. Which was another lie. Kitty remembered how suspicious and doubting she had felt at questioning Bella about it at the time, and how guilty when Bella had stuck to her original account without batting an eyelid. But now Kitty knew for a fact that she had been lying all along.

It was all she could think about for weeks; for if this was a lie she had inadvertently uncovered, what else had Bella lied to her about? She couldn't seem to stop her thoughts, which tumbled through her mind like a river over rocks.

And just as water, in time, wears away the hardest of stone, Kitty could feel her trust in Bella becoming slowly eroded by her thoughts. What kind of friend deliberately tells you lies? Kitty didn't know. It perplexed her. She found herself evading Bella, not returning her calls and ducking into classrooms if she spotted her in a corridor at college. She couldn't face even talking to her just now. And if she couldn't avoid speaking to her she used looming exams next term and the pressing need to revise as an excuse not to make a date to meet up.

She needed to talk to someone, though, pretty urgently. She needed a sounding-board, somebody to confide in and spill it all out to, someone who knew both her and Bella and the ins and outs of their relationship. And really, there was only one person who fitted the bill.

Sat in Megan's bedroom with a mug of coffee apiece and a plate of biscuits between them, Kitty was pierced with a splinter of recognition, a sharp sense of *déjà vu*. It reminded her of the first year at Brynglas, the second or third term, when Bella had been hanging out more and more with Sadie Williams and Megan had come to school each day with a scandalized air and fresh tales of the dramatic goings-on at home. The tantrums, the rows, the slamming of doors and the swearing. As Kitty and Bella had seen increasingly less of each other, so she and Megan became drawn to each other once more, going back to how they had been before Bella had come on the scene.

If Kitty had felt any guilt in those days at being closeted away with Megan, absorbing gossip about Bella if not actively contributing to it, then it was diminished by the knowledge that for weeks Bella had increasingly chosen to be with Sadie (mad, bad, dangerous to know) over Kitty. And that guilt was totally demolished when she was there to witness for herself the exact kind of scene that Megan had been so vividly describing for so many weeks. (The front door slamming, raised voices downstairs, then shouting, then positive yelling, then thumping elephant footsteps coming upstairs, the door to the bedroom – which Bella and Megan still shared – flung open. Bella standing there, uniform skirt hitched up to mid-thigh, school shirt knotted around waist, thick black tights ripped at both knees, hands covered in ink scrawls. Arms folded with boredom, a sneer spreading across her face – "Oh. *You're* in here, are you?" – then the whole thing in reverse, thudding on the stairs, yelling at Megan's mum, screaming, shouting. A final, shocking "Just *fuck off*!" as a farewell, the front door slamming with window-rattling force. Kitty and Megan looking at each other in wide-eyed thrilled horror at the drama of it. See what it's like round here these days. How *could* Bella behave like that? End.)

Now, though, Megan looked neither wide-eyed nor thrilled. Nor horrified, come to that. She passed Kitty the plate of biscuits, took one herself, bit into it, chewed it and swallowed before saying: "I see," in such calm tones that Kitty wondered whether she had actually heard what she'd said.

"Did you hear? I said, Mel told me there's no such class. At least, not one he goes to with her."

"Yeah. I heard. When did he tell you all this?"

"When we went bowling."

"That was weeks ago."

"I know. I've been trying to get my head round it – that's why I didn't tell you before."

"So what does Bella say about it?"

"Are you joking? What's the point of asking her about it? She'd only deny it."

Megan nodded, wisely. "More than likely. Probably no point, then. So why are you telling me now?"

"It's been doing my head in." Kitty ran her hands through her hair, as though to smooth down the thoughts which bubbled in a granular mass just under her scalp. "I needed to tell somebody that she's been lying to me. God,

Megan," she groaned suddenly, "I know what you're going to say."

"Do you?" Megan's carefully composed features shifted, ever so slightly. "What's that?"

"That you've never trusted Bella all along."

"I wouldn't say that, exactly," Megan protested. "She's just been majorly pissing me off with her antics with Bruno, when according to you she's like, *Oh, no, we're just good friends.* Hey, did you know he's been texting me from uni?"

"Who?"

"Bruno." Megan spoke his name with satisfied pride. "And –" She paused for a moment. "*And* he's said we could meet up in the Easter holidays."

"Wow." Kitty was momentarily speechless. Glad for Megan, naturally – but speechless. Bruno had been so dead set that he didn't fancy her back, that he was only agreeing to the double-date thing (or triple-date, as it turned out) to be friendly. And now here he was texting her and suggesting they meet up again, or so Megan said. This would explain why she was feeling more forgiving towards Bella.

"Cool, eh?" Megan beamed happily.

Somehow, the thought of it all turning out happily ever after with her and Bruno didn't quite ring true. Kitty smiled back at her friend slightly doubtfully. "Well, go, girlfriend! I hope it all works out – I've never seen you so upset as you were at my party. You were convinced Bella was after him; you said she was a compulsive liar, remember?"

"I know. I felt quite bad about that, afterwards. But you know, I'd, like, set my heart on snaring Bruno, and then along comes Bella and before you can say *Robert est votre oncle* she's wrapped round him like – like –"

"A big sheet of wrapping paper?" Kitty suggested.

Megan smiled. "Yeah. Like a big *extra-wrappy* sheet of wrapping paper. I could've poked her eyes out, if you want to know the truth. Easily. I hated her. I don't think I've ever hated anyone in my life that much before. Ever."

"I noticed."

"And I was like, how come it's all so easy for her? How come the rest of us struggle and have sleepless nights and can't eat and agonize over planning how we're going to get *him* to notice us, stop *him* thinking of us as his annoying little cousin's annoying little mate and start seeing us as potential girlfriend material, as a hot funky babe –"

"Which you are," Kitty put in.

"Which I am. Thank you. And then Bella comes along and just – just kind of *pole-vaults* over all the other poor suckers standing in line for all the cool guys, and gets to the front of the queue. How does she do that? That's what I want to know," she finished, slightly breathlessly.

"Me and mum reckon she's got an aura."

"Yeah? How does that work?"

"It's like, I dunno, a kind of force-field thing, that attracts guys."

"Really? Where d'you get one of those from, then – Auras R Us?" Megan sighed, gloomily. "You know, I wanted to kill her for copping off with my man. Tear her hair out, smother her in that stupid bloody look-at-me coat she wears. All of that. But I was wrong to say she's a compulsive liar."

"I thought you said she made things up all the time when she was a kid?"

"She did. She lived in a fantasy world. But that's not the same as being a compulsive liar – that's a serious mental thing, it's a psychological condition."

"And you don't think Bella's got it?"

They looked at each other gravely for a moment, both of them thinking about the evening-class-that-never-was.

"I don't know," Megan said, slowly. "Do you?"

As time went by, Kitty found herself wondering just where Mel had taken Bella – just an ordinary house in an ordinary street, according to him. They had sat in Mel's car, parked at the kerbside, and she had looked at – what? What was the attraction? Kitty considered how she could go about asking Mel just where this house was. Would he think there was something suss about Kitty questioning him again about it all, and blow the gaff to Bella? Probably not. He was such a space cadet, he'd probably forgotten he'd ever told Kitty about it. Maybe even forgotten he'd taken Bella there. Unless he was still taking her, of course.

Just what did she know about Bella, exactly? Not much, when all was said and done. She still knew nothing of her life before the age of seven, nothing of the years in between leaving Penllan and returning. With hindsight, theirs seemed always to have been a pretty one-sided relationship, or at least the exchange of information had been. Why hadn't she asked Bella more about herself when they were kids? Had she really been so accepting, or just incurious? Kitty had no answers, just an increasing number of questions that wouldn't go away and leave her in peace.

"Did you never wonder about Bella? When she was living with you?"

"Nope."

"So you never found out anything about her background, or why she was being fostered?"

Megan sighed, patiently. "I've already told you. No."

"And you never bothered asking your mum because you knew she'd never tell you anything."

"Correct. Kitty, why are we still talking about this?"

"I'm just beginning to realize," said Kitty, slowly, "that I don't know anything about Bella either."

"Or only what she's chosen to tell you. You know that much."

That, plus what Megan had told her back in Year Seven, about the stuff Bella was getting involved in with Sadie Williams.

"You'll never guess what!" Megan's eyes are big round Os.

"What?"

"Bella was caught smoking at break yesterday."

"*Bella*? But she hates smoking!" It was only the other week that she and Kitty were standing outside the newsagent's in the village, pretending to be doing a survey for school and asking people what they were intending to buy, and if they said cigarettes pulling revolted faces and going, "Eurgh!" and, "What a dirty disgusting habit!" Or rather, Bella had. It was her idea, of course.

She said it would be doing the National Health Service a big favour because of the amount of money it has to spend on smoking-related illnesses. Something like that, anyway. She hadn't even been put off when Mr Evans from down the road told Kitty off and said he'd tell her mum she'd been hanging about on street corners, haranguing folk. That's what he'd said – haranguing. Come to think of it, perhaps it was the other month, rather than the other week.

"Not any more she doesn't." There is something triumphant in Megan's voice. "She's been nicking off behind the sports hall for a cigarette with Sadie Williams and her gang. They were all caught."

"How?" Kitty wants proof, rather than just gossip.

"Mr Stanley was on duty." Mr Stanley is the deputy head, and the scariest teacher at Brynglas. He prowls the corridors looking for troublemakers, and invariably finds some. "Mum had a letter from school this morning, he wants her to go in for a chat."

"Blimey." Mr Stanley's chats are legendary. "What did Bella say?"

"I can't tell you what Bella said. I don't use language like that." Megan manages to sound both prim and gloating at once.

*

"Bella didn't come home from school until half-past nine last night."

"Why? Where was she?"

"She wouldn't say. Mum rang the police, and everything. She was dead worried."

"But was Bella all right?"

"Of course she was." Megan sounds scornful. "She was with Sadie."

"I thought you said she wouldn't say where she was?"

"She wouldn't. But Nicci saw her. You know her cousin Rich? Well, he lives in the same street as Sadie. Nicci was round there with her mum and she saw a whole bunch of people going into Sadie's house, and Bella was one of them."

"What do you think about Bella hanging round with Sadie?" Kitty asks Megan.

Megan makes a snorty noise down her nose. "What do you think I think! Of all the people to choose as a friend. . . Mum says she's a terrible influence on Bella, but I think she's wrong."

"What, don't you think she's as bad as people say?"

"No, I think they're both as bad as each other. If you ask me, they make a great team."

"But Sadie's much worse than Bella. Isn't she?"

"Is she?" Megan shrugs, not interested in comparing their badness. "You don't see Bella much any more, do you?"

Kitty tries to think back to when she and Bella last spent any time together, and realizes with a little lurch that she can't actually remember when that was. She does recall having Bella round for tea sometime before Christmas, but surely that can't have been the last time? That was nearly four months ago!

"Not much," she confesses.

"Well, I think you should be glad she doesn't want to be friends with you any more," says Megan. Kitty is about to say she's not sure that Bella doesn't want to be friends as such, more that they just don't really bump into each other these days, but Megan is carrying on. "She's always stropping around at home – that's when she's there. And she's in trouble at school the whole time. And you should hear what Nicci's cousin Rich has to say about that Sadie Williams! He says one of her brothers is in prison for drug dealing, and the other one goes off stealing cars the whole time."

"It doesn't mean Sadie's the same," Kitty puts in, for the sake of fairness. She doesn't quite understand why she feels she has to be fair – she doesn't even know Sadie, only what she has heard about her from other people.

"Of course she is," Megan declares, with a toss of her head. "My mum says Bella's going right off the rails. She says we can't be expected to cope with her any more. She's going to ask for her to be moved away. Just think; if you were still friends with her you could be getting into all this trouble, too. I think you've had a lucky escape."

Kitty privately thinks that Megan can't know her very well if she thinks *she* would ever have anything to do with someone like Sadie Williams, but she doesn't bother saying so because she knows it can't be very nice for Megan to live with all the trouble that Bella is bringing home. Just about every week at school she seems to have something newly sensational to report, some fresh bit of scandal that Bella has caused or become involved with.

And then, all of a sudden (or so it seems) comes the news that Bella is moving away. It is dinner time at school and Megan is telling Kitty all about the latest goings-on at home, her face alight with the drama of it, and Kitty doesn't see Bella until she is there, right in front of them, almost colliding with them.

"Oh," Kitty says, a little embarrassed and hoping she didn't overhear what Megan was saying about her. Not that it matters, especially – Bella is most probably well aware of what Megan thinks about her by now. "Hello."

Bella looks at her, thrusting her chin forward in the slightly belligerent fashion she has adopted since taking up with Sadie (who does exactly the same thing whenever anyone outside her little gang speaks to her, including teachers. Especially teachers). Her eyes narrow and she looks as if she is about to say something rude and four-lettered, but instead she looks down at the floor.

"Hi," she mutters.

By now Kitty is certain Bella did overhear them talking about her. She casts around for something inoffensive to say. All she can think of is the looming end of term. "Nearly the holidays. I can't wait, can you?"

Bella's expression clears slightly. "No. Especially as I'm not coming back here afterwards."

"What?" Despite everything Megan had told her about how bad things had got at home with Bella, Kitty hadn't been expecting this.

"I told you," Megan is whispering, nudging her. "See? I *told* you!"

"So where are you going, then?"

"Dunno. Just away. To another foster family." Bella shrugs, offhand. She doesn't seem to care one way or another. Kitty feels a pang, for how things used to be when they were blood sisters. It was only a few months ago but it feels like years.

"Really?"

Megan is nudging her again. "*Told* you!"

Bella's face is filled with hate, a despising scorching hate that seems to encompass both

Kitty and Megan and makes Kitty wonder when their closeness, their blood-sisterhood, turned into this. Then the hate is gone, wiped out. Bella's mouth turns up at the corners in a sketchy smile that doesn't reach her eyes.

"Yeah," she says. "It's cool. Won't have to come to this dump any more, anyway. See ya around, then. Maybe."

Kitty watches Bella go, stalking disdainfully across the playground in her clumpy black shoes with her school uniform skirt hitched up round her waist as high as she dares wear it, and she suddenly feels a huge ache inside her for their lost closeness. Tears make her nose prickle and she has to bite on her lower lip to make them go away.

"How slaggy does she look? Talk about a Sadie Williams clone," Megan is saying, scornfully. "I'll be glad to be shot of her, at least there'll be peace and quiet at home again."

"Yeah," Kitty says, with a sigh. Megan is probably right. Bella isn't the same person since she got in with Sadie, and her moving away from school and from the area is probably the best thing all round.

And anyway, why should Kitty care, when Bella so obviously doesn't?

"Why do you think Bella moved away?"

Megan answered without hesitating. "Because

she went off the rails and became uncontrollable. Mum and Dad had had enough, so they asked Social Services to place her with another family."

"Did they tell you that?"

"They didn't have to. I worked it out all by myself." She looks closely at Kitty. "Didn't you realize that at the time? I thought I'd told you about all the stuff that was going on."

"Yeah, you did. I just wondered if there might have been another reason as well. I mean, it just seems a bit harsh – she'd been living with all of you for years, then she hits adolescence and BOOM! – she's suddenly out on her ear."

"Boom?" Megan curled her top lip in disdain. "There was no boom about it. It had been coming on for months. She was a little cow, Kitty. You've got no idea what total bloody hell she made our lives."

"I think I do. You told me, remember."

"Yeah, well, being told's not the same as having to live with it. Just imagine Owen in the worst strop he's ever had, then multiply it by about five thousand. That's what it was like, every day for – oh, I don't know. Months and bloody months. There's doors in our house that still have dents in them where she kicked them. And there's still an orange patch on the kitchen wall from where she threw her supper at Mum. Plate and all. Spaghetti bolognaise, it was. Mum scrubbed at it with bleach and everything, but it's never come out properly. And you talk about boom!"

"OK, OK. Calm down, already! I'm not saying it wasn't that bad."

"Well good, because it was that bad. She only just missed Mum when she threw that plate. She was aiming right at her, too. She could have killed her."

"All I'm saying is, maybe there was something else. Not instead of – as well as."

"Like what?"

"I don't know. That's what I'm trying to work out."

One Friday evening a week or so later Kitty was in her room, headphones clamped to her ears and urgent overdue English assignment spread out all over the bed, when she became aware that she wasn't alone. There, framed by the doorway, stood Megan. Her face was ashen, her cinnamon freckles standing out in relief against its waxen pallor, and her eyes red-rimmed and rabbity-looking from weeping.

Startled, Kitty tore the headphones from her ears and stood up. "What on earth's the matter? What's happened?"

Megan immediately began to apologize. "Sorry, Kitty. Your mum said to come on up; I didn't mean to scare you."

"It's OK." Kitty cleared all the papers off the bed by the simple expedient of sweeping them all to the floor. "Come on, look. Sit down. Tell me what's wrong."

Megan sat, and took a deep breath that juddered at the end, like a gate catching on its hinges. "It's Bruno."

"What? What's happened to him?" She only realized later that, had anything serious happened to her cousin, Megan would hardly have been the first to hear. At the time, though, she could only think that some major catastrophe must have befallen him up in Manchester for Megan to be in such a state. "Tell me, Megan!"

Megan sat and stared tragically at the carpet for a few moments, as if debating whether she should. Then she said, "Bella's gone up to stay with him."

"What? When? Why?" She only needed where and how for the full set. Realizing Megan could only answer one question at a time, she repeated, "When?"

"This afternoon, apparently. She's gone for the weekend."

"But I thought he's been texting you and – and suggesting you meet up and stuff? So how come he's suddenly entertaining Bella for the weekend?"

Megan gave a doleful shrug. "Dunno." She looked up at Kitty. "She's won, hasn't she?"

"The Battle for Bruno?"

"Don't take the piss!" Megan's face crumpled, and Kitty put a hasty arm around her friend's shoulder.

"I'm sorry, hun. I didn't mean to. But look –" She cast around wildly for something positive to say, some crumb of hope to offer Megan, which given the evidence was pretty hard. "How did you find out?"

"From Nicci, this afternoon. Bella told her."

"Well, she might have got it wrong."

"Oh sure. Bella might have said, Well I'm off home to wash my hair now, and Nicci mistook it for, Well I'm off to Manchester to see Bruno for the weekend. Thanks for trying Kitty, but I don't think so."

"She definitely said Bella was going to Manchester to see Bruno?"

"Yes! Bloody yes! I've just said so, haven't I! Don't keep repeating it – it just makes me feel –" She didn't finish the sentence. She didn't need to. Kitty could see perfectly well how it was making her feel.

"I can't believe it. They both swore blind they were only friends. Bruno I can just about get my head round – don't look at me like that, Meg, he's a guy, it's brains-in-trousers territory – but Bella. . . If she told me there was nothing in it once, she told me a hundred times." Something else occurred to her. "I've just thought of something. I was feeling a bit bad about hardly having seen her this term, so I asked her on Monday if she wanted to go and see that new Ben Affleck movie tomorrow night. And do you know what she said?" Megan shook her head, dumbly. "She said she was snowed under with revision for her modules, but next weekend would be better!"

"You don't expect her to have told you what she was really up to, do you?"

"Well she wasn't exactly keeping it to herself, was she? She told Nicci – she must have known it was going to get back to you."

"No, she told Nic not to breathe a word, apparently. Nicci only told me because she said she thought I ought to know. She knows how I feel about Bruno." She sighed, a huge exhalation that seemed to contain all the fed-upness in the entire world. "D'you know, she seems to have this knack of taking over the people I care about. You – Bruno – Nicci. But do you want to know what the real belter is?"

"You mean there's more?"

"Oh, there's more." Megan's lips twisted together, grimly. "Nicci also said Bella told her weeks ago that she was after Bruno. She said – and I'm quoting here – 'He might think I'm thick but I could get him just like *that*'." She snapped her fingers on the last word. "Nic's only just told me. She said she didn't want to tell me before because she didn't want me to think she was stirring, but given the circumstances. . . So." She looked bleakly at Kitty. "It looks as if Bella's had us all fooled over this one, doesn't it?"

chapter *fifteen*

Bella worried all the way up to Manchester. What was Bruno's motivation for having asked her to go and stay? Come to think of it, what was her motivation for having said yes? Was he expecting to sleep with her? Did he think she was expecting to sleep with him? Where exactly was she going to sleep, anyway? If he made a move on her and she knocked him back (which she would, of course she would, she totally didn't think of him in that way), would that be the end of their friendship?

By the time the train arrived she was thoroughly confused, not to mention exhausted. She'd been intending to have a snooze during the journey, but all her thoughts had been jostling for position while not providing any answers, only other, even more baffling and unsettling thoughts, and she had been unable to banish them for long enough to drop off, even for a few moments.

He was waiting on the platform. She didn't see him at once, battling as she was with her bag which had decided to get wedged behind somebody else's suitcase. Then, as she stepped off the train and down on to the platform there he was, standing a few metres away, scanning the length of the platform in his battered leather jacket with a long knitted stripy Dr Who-style scarf wrapped around his neck and his hands shoved into his jeans pockets. He saw her at that exact moment, and as their eyes met Bella's stomach gave an odd lurch, the sort of flip you get on a fairground ride, or when you get an unexpected piece of good news. He smiled at her, his eyes twinkling, and hurried towards her.

"Hi!" he greeted her. "Good journey?"

"Yeah, it was OK."

He put his hands on her shoulders and surveyed her for a second, at arm's length, and then enfolded her in an enormous hug. As she hugged him back her body relaxed into his, and she thought how right it felt. How absolutely perfectly appropriate. There was nothing remotely sexual in that hug; it was the hug of two friends who were genuinely pleased to see each other. It felt, to Bella, like coming home.

Bruno shared a house with four other students and a ginger cat called Mike.

"Why Mike?" Bella enquired as they climbed

the stairs to the top of the house, cradling the cat to her as he purred ecstatically.

"The other three lads are all called Mike, so it seemed the obvious name. Saves us having to remember a different one." Bruno grinned, and threw open a door. "This is you, Madam. No luxury spared."

To Bella's relief the room contained a single bed, covered with a purple and gold Indian throw. Church candles of every size from tiny to enormous crowded the wide window sill, which had a piece of filmy gauze pinned to the sash for privacy and looked out on to a square of scrubby grass and a leafless sycamore where two fat pigeons sat cooing at each other. The room smelled faintly of incense and its owner was clearly female.

"The last housemate, I presume," said Bella, putting the cat down on the bed. "What's her name – Michaela?"

"Close. No, Mia. How did you know she was a girl?" Bruno put Bella's bag on the scuffed wicker ottoman under the window.

"Oh, I'm psychic. That, plus the red satin kimono." She indicated it with her head; it was hanging on the back of the door, its back adorned with a ferocious-looking tiger-cum-dragon embroidered in black and gold.

Bruno pouted camply. "That's my favouwite fwock."

"It's not a frock, stupid. It's a robe."

"Favouwite wobe, then."

"It's not your colour, sweetie. Now, pink. . ."

He aimed a playful blow at her. "Watch it, smarty-pants, or you're not getting any supper."

"Aw, Bruno – are you cooking for me? Sweet!"

"Nah." He wrinkled his nose. "I thought we'd go out. I would cook, only two of the Mikes are in tonight, and I thought – you know. Ve vant to be alone."

Bella wasn't sure she liked the sound of that. (In which case, why had her stomach done another one of those flips?) "Do ve?"

"Ve absolutely do. You don't know the Mikes – trust me on this one." He turned as if to go. "You OK, then? Anything you need?"

"An en-suite shower would be good."

Bruno turned back, looking slightly anxious. "Oh, sorry. I never thought. The bathroom's down on the next landing, but I could always ask Mike if he'd do a swap – he's got a washbasin in his room. What?"

She was smiling. "It was a joke," she explained. "I'm sure I can manage to haul myself down to the next landing – I can always borrow the wobe to preserve my modesty."

"Oh, OK. If you're sure."

"Sure I'm sure. So where's Mia, then?"

"Gone to Norwich for the weekend. Home," he

explained. "So she said you could have her room."

Bella bent over her bag and began to take out her things. "She your girlfriend?"

"Er, no. I'm not her type."

"No?"

"No. She's got a girlfriend of her own."

"Oh. I see. So what does she do? Not with her girlfriend, I don't mean," she said hastily, feeling slightly flustered. She stood up. Bruno was grinning at her. "I mean, at uni."

"I know what you mean. She's a post-grad metallurgist."

"What's one of them?"

"Christ knows. She did try explaining it to me once, but gave up when she saw my eyes beginning to glaze over."

"I'm glad I'm not the only one who's dim."

"You're not dim. Don't say that." There was a slight edge to Bruno's voice that hadn't been there before. They stood regarding each other for a second or two, and Bella felt herself tensing to accommodate his change of mood. Then he smiled again. "You probably want to freshen up after being on the train. I'll be down in the midden, when you're ready."

"The midden?"

"Yeah. Otherwise known as the kitchen. I'll stick the kettle on."

*

307

They went to a tapas bar for supper, a noisy studenty dive down a warren of back alleys with cheap food and a smoky comfortable atmosphere. Bella was hugely relieved; she'd had a picture in her mind of being taken to a more select establishment, all white linen tablecloths and discreet subservient waiters, surrounded by fearsomely bright students with sports jackets and centre partings, all earnestly discussing Proust. Or something. God knows why – the tapas bar was much more Bruno's style, not to mention budget.

"This is my treat," Bruno said, as they sat at a table with their drinks and were handed laminated menus the size of broadsheet newspapers.

"Get off." Bella turned her menu the right way up and smiled kindly at the waitress, who looked about fourteen. "You're a student. You can't afford to treat people."

"You're a student too. And you've had to pay for your train fare. Anyway –" he took his wallet from the inside pocket of his jacket with an Ebenezer Scrooge-like leer – "I bin savin' up."

"Bless. But you really don't have to."

"But I really want to. Really really."

"Bruno." She was about to lay her hand on top of his, on the table, but changed her mind, thinking it might seem condescending or, worse, flirty. "I've got plenty of money. Seriously."

"Yeah? Why didn't you say so before?" He put his wallet back in his pocket and leant across the table towards her, taking her hands in his. "Will you marry me?"

She laughed, tilting her head back. Her hands slid from his grasp. "It would shake you if I said yes, wouldn't it?"

"No it wouldn't. I'd just leg it and leave you with the bill." He looked at his menu. "The roasted pimentos are supposed to be good."

"Stuff the roasted pimentos."

"I think they already have been."

She ignored him. "Don't you want to know about the money?"

"What, you mean you were serious? I thought you were messing around."

"I never mess around when it comes to money. My grandmother left me a whole pile when she died."

Bruno looked at her over the top of the menu. "Define whole pile. Are we talking major wonga here?"

"Major-ish."

"Hundreds, thousands?" His eyes gleamed. "Millions?"

"Thousands." She nudged him gently under the table with the toe of her boot. "You can close your mouth now. You old gold-digger, you."

"Sorry. I just –" He gave a theatrical fake gulp. "I didn't know you were an heiress, or I'd have been serious when I asked you to marry me."

"And there was me thinking you were." She smiled. "Don't look so gobsmacked – it's not that much. Just enough for me to live off while I 'finish my education'." She put ironic inverted commas around the phrase, and pulled a wry face. "Such as it is. I don't think Grandmother was thinking of a Leisure and Tourism Diploma at the local tech, somehow. I think she was more intending somewhere like this."

"Don't knock it. You could still come somewhere like this."

"Oh, sure. With my super-brain, I'd be a shoo-in. I don't think so. It'd be more like, Bella Jones – you are the weakest link, goodbye."

Bruno opened his mouth to say something, but was interrupted by his mobile bleeping at him from the table top.

"Hold on. Got a text." He picked it up and pressed a button. "Fuck. Fucketty fuck."

Bella was mildly taken aback. He hardly ever swore. "What's wrong? Bad news?"

"You could say that. It's from Megan." He put on an I-am-reading-this voice. "Bruno, hope you are enjoying your weekend with Bella, love Megan. Kiss kiss kiss."

"Ah. So she knows I'm here, then."

"Seems like it. Bugger. I'm sorry – I don't know how she found out. I didn't tell her."

"I think it might be my fault. I told Nicci I was coming up to see you; I knew as soon as I'd told her that I shouldn't have, that she'd most likely go straight back to Megan. Anyway, does it matter?"

"Yeah. It matters because I don't want Megan and Kitty giving you a hard time."

"I can handle Megan and Kitty." She took his mobile from his hand and looked at the message. "What's with all the kisses?"

"She's been sending me these weird texts ever since we went bowling that time. She kind of tricked my mobile number out of me." He looked sheepish. "She said something like, We ought to do this again sometime, and I said, Sure why not, and then she went, Maybe in the Easter holidays, and I went, Maybe, and now she keeps texting me saying how much she's looking forward to seeing me again. And stuff like that."

"Did you text her back?"

"Once or twice, at the beginning. Just to be polite. But not for a while now; she's obviously read more into it than there is, and I don't want to encourage her. I didn't mind going bowling, but. . . To be honest, she's got really scary. She's so – avid."

"Then you've got to tell her you're not interested."

"I already have. Well, kind of. I've told Kitty."

"It's no good telling Kitty. That's the easy way out. You've got to tell Megan to back off."

"Seems a bit harsh."

"Maybe." Bella shrugged. "But it's way harsher to carry on letting her think she's going to have a date with you in the holidays, and texting you kisses. Obviously, you don't have to say it in those words. Just that you're not interested in her in that way. It's the only fair thing to do, trust me."

"You think so?"

"I know so. I had the same kind of thing with Mel when I started college – he wouldn't leave me alone. He was being a total pain in the bum. But I put him straight, and now we're just mates. It's cool."

"And you don't mind being mates with him?"

"Course not. He's a sweetie. I just don't want him as a boyfriend. I don't want anyone as a boyfriend right now, come to that."

"Because. . .?"

"Because I don't do relationships. Too much hurt involved."

"So young, and yet so cynical." Bruno spoke casually, trying to ignore the disappointment that was curling round his soul like a smothering hand. This was clearly a barely camouflaged personal message for him.

"Not cynical. Realistic."

"And are you speaking from experience here?"

Bella shot him an I-don't-want-to-talk-about-it glance, and busied herself with lighting a cigarette. Bruno felt a sudden, irrational desire to kill whoever it was, whichever lad, who had hurt Bella in the past. "Well, I'm not sure I want Megan as any kind of friend any more." He took a slug of his beer. "Like I say, she's scary."

"So tell her the score." Bella exhaled a cloud of smoke and crinkled her eyes at him, sympathetically. "You know it makes sense."

A tide of music as Bruno opened the front door indicated that at least one of the Mikes was in, but there was no visible sign of anyone. Bruno made coffee for both of them, and removed a pile of magazines, two empty Coke cans, a pair of trainers, a birthday card and a paper folder of photographs from the kitchen table to make space for them to drink it.

"Here you go. Take a seat." He pulled two stools out from under the table. "Sorry about the mess."

"Don't worry. It's fine." Most guys probably wouldn't even have noticed there was a mess, she reflected.

There was a small silence. Bruno cast around for something to say to fill it. "So. I never even asked you how college was going for you."

She curled her lip. "Don't bother."

"Not good?"

"No. I don't think I'm cut out for studying. It's just such a *boring* course."

"Maybe it's not the right subject for you."

"No, I think I'm just stupid," she said, in a Noo York accent. *Stoopid.*

"Don't keep doing that."

"Doing what?"

"Calling yourself stupid. Selling yourself short. You're probably the least stupid person I know."

Bella allowed herself a tiny little preen. But only a tiny one. "You don't have to be kind," she told him.

"When was I ever kind? You're not stupid."

"Compared with you I am."

"You're *not!*" He smacked the table with his hand for emphasis. "You just haven't had my – I don't know. Opportunities. Family support. Nice middle-class mum and dad, chivvying me along to do my homework and paying for extra Maths tuition in the holidays. Stuff like that."

"I never knew you had extra Maths tuition in the holidays."

"I'd never have passed the GCSE otherwise. I was crap."

"I got a B for Maths. I thought it was quite easy."

"Well, there you go then. You're not stupid, are

you? I only managed a C." He looked closely at her. "I thought you said you screwed your GCSEs up?"

"I did. I only got five."

"That's not what I call screwing up."

"I was entered for ten. Everyone else passed them all – one girl got all A stars. The school I went to after Brynglas, my efforts were considered screwing up, big style."

"Even so. Five GCSEs – you could do A-levels with those. Or NVQs, or some other qualification. Whatever you fancy. You could go on to university, if that's what you want to do. You can do whatever you want – the trick is identifying what you're good at, and what you enjoy, and doing that. Just don't keep putting yourself down all the time, OK?"

"OK, OK! I give in!" She laughed. "It's funny you should be saying all this. I've been seriously thinking about jacking my course in, but I didn't have a clue what to do instead. I think you're making up my mind for me." She glanced at him, her eyes sliding sideways. "So go on then."

"Go on what?"

"Tell me I'm crazy."

"Why should I say that? It's your life – it's up to you what you do with it."

"God." Bella took a careful sip of her coffee. "I think you're the first person who's ever said that to me. Everybody else seems to want to run my life for me."

"Well that's pretty normal, isn't it? For someone your age."

She laughed. "Someone my age? I'm only two years younger than you!"

"Oops." He made a noise like a siren. "Patronization alert. Sorry, I mean for someone *our* age. My parents are always telling me what I should be doing. Or what they *think* I should be doing. I sometimes think my dad'll be telling me how I should be spending my money and my mum tutting over my choice of girlfriends when I'm forty."

"I wouldn't know," Bella said, darkly. "Parenthood is a bit of closed book to me."

"Parents, foster-parents." He shrugged. "It's all the same principle, isn't it?"

"Is it?" She looked at him, her forget-me-not blue eyes shadowed by some unreadable emotion, a tiny crease between her brows, and Bruno felt a small wave of trepidation lap at the edges of his consciousness. *Careful. Do I want to go there? Does she?* It was uncharted territory, potentially shark-infested waters – in all the years they had known each other she had never revealed the slightest detail about her life before and beyond the here-and-now reality of Penllan, living with the Robertses and her close connection with Kitty and her family. To be honest, Bruno had never thought to question it; Bella was fostered, end of. The whys and wherefores were none of his business. But something about the way she was looking now – dammit, the way she was looking at *him* now, with those huge blue eyes of hers – made his heart quiver in his chest.

He took a breath, and dived in amongst the sharks.

"I don't know," he said, softly. "Wanna tell me?"

Bella's eyes never wavered from his for twelve seconds. He knew it was twelve seconds because he counted them, along with the battered alarm clock on the window sill that Mia claimed was an essential cooking aid. Then Bella lowered her gaze, carefully pushed her empty coffee mug into the exact middle of the table, and stood up.

"Nothing to tell. I'm off to bed now – thanks for a fab evening. Night."

"Hello, Isabella. I'm Auntie Enid." She is smiling expectantly.

Bella scowls up at her, her bottom lip jutting out crossly. "I'm not Isabella, I'm Bella. And I don't want another auntie," she says to the social worker at her side. "I want Sylvie."

She sees the two women look at each other across the top of her head.

"Poor lamb." The new auntie puts a kindly hand on Bella's shoulder. Bella wants to throw it off, to run out of this clean neat tidy living room that is so unlike home and run and run until there is no run left in her. Trouble is, there is nowhere to run to.

"Bella." The social worker crouches in front of her. "We've already explained. Your mum is poorly again. Auntie Enid is going to look after you until she's better. But I promise you, you'll be able to go and visit her often. All right?"

Bella thinks, *no*. It's all wrong. *I don't want to go and visit her, not in that horrible place where they do things to her, where they keep her face but change inside her head. I want Sylvie back, I want her to come and get me and take me home.* She opens her mouth to say all this but what comes out is, "All right."

The door to the clean neat tidy living room opens and a head pops round, a head with a freckled face and ginger hair like a cat's fur.

"Ah," says Auntie Enid. "Here's Megan. Come in, *cariad*, and say hello to Bella. You're almost exactly the same age, isn't that nice? I just know you're going to be the best of friends."

"Where have you *been*?" Megan's sulky voice is raised, annoyed.

"Sshh. To see Kitty."

"She's my friend, not yours. Besides, you're not supposed to. You're not allowed to go down the lane by yourself. I'm going to tell my mum of you."

But somehow she never does. Bella likes to think it is because she is too scared of what Bella might do to her, but she knows it is more likely that Megan likes the thought of getting her into trouble more than the reality. The Roberts family doesn't like Trouble. They have never said this, it is just something that Bella is coming to understand. It is the social worker, a lady called Gail who is actually quite nice really, who always goes with Bella to visit Sylvie, rather than Auntie Enid or Uncle Phil. Not because they don't want to, or can't be bothered, Bella is sure of that, but because it is Trouble. It is like a sum at school – Sylvie plus Bella equals Trouble. Bella is slowly coming to see this, as well.

Bella and Kitty are sitting in the back of the car with Owen strapped in his seat between them. They have been singing to him for miles and miles ("the wheels on the bus go round and round, all day long") and now he is asleep, his plump legs inside their red shorts dangling down and jumping slightly as the car goes round bends and over bumps in the road. His bare feet still have sand from the beach in between the toes. His face is flushed and rosy from the day in the sun, with a fuzzy bloom upon his cheeks that looks exactly like one of the peaches in the fruit bowl Kitty's mum keeps on the table in the dining room. Bella can smell the wet fur of Heinz who is lying fast asleep on his side in the back of the car, legs stuck straight out like a dead dog's and dreaming no doubt of finally catching one of the waves he has been chasing all day.

Bella's eyes meet Kitty's across Owen's slumped sleeping body and they smile at each other, a smile that is about everything and nothing at all, and Bella is suddenly filled with an enormous rush of feeling that seems so huge her body doesn't seem big enough to contain it. She doesn't know the name of the feeling, only that it is a good one and that she has never felt it before. She settles her head back against the headrest and closes her eyes.

After a bit – it could be seconds, it could be minutes or even longer, Bella is not sure – she is aware that the air inside the car has somehow changed. She opens her eyes, just a crack, and through her eyelashes she can see that Kitty's mum has twisted round in her seat and is looking at the back of the car, smiling.

"They're all asleep," she says to Uncle Mike, who is driving. He replies something Bella can't hear over the sound of the engine. Then Kitty's mum says, "Well, it's not as if she's any trouble, is it? She's virtually our second daughter," and turns back to face the right way.

Bella squeezes her eyes shut again, tight. She knows that they were talking about her. Quietly, so nobody will hear, she draws in her breath and holds it, as if she is about to blow out all the candles on a birthday cake. This thought leads to another, and she thinks she will make a wish. She knows exactly what to wish for. *Please let me come and live with them. I want to be their second daughter. Please please please.* Wishing with all her might, she suddenly understands what she was feeling just now, the feeling that was too big for her body. It was happiness.

"Bella! Gail's here."

Aunt Enid comes into the bedroom where Bella is sitting on the bed. "Come on, love. I thought you were ready. Get dressed now."

"I'm not going."

"What? Don't you feel well?" She puts a hand on Bella's forehead, but Bella shakes it off.

"I'm fine. I just don't want to go."

Aunt Enid stares at her, dismayed. "But she'll be looking forward to seeing you, *cariad*."

"No she won't. She doesn't even know who I am half the time. She's out of her tree."

"Bella!" She is shocked now. "Don't say that. They're changing her medication, that's all. Just a few weeks, and she'll be as right as rain."

What a stupid expression. What is right about rain? Bella scowls. "No she won't. They're always saying that. I'm not going. You can't make me."

Aunt Enid sits down on the bed beside her. "What's brought all this on?"

"Nothing." She doesn't tell her about the thing she read in one of Aunt Enid's magazines that said relatives of people like Sylvie are themselves more likely to get what she has got. It made her go all cold inside – she still feels cold now, as if she has swallowed a whole ice-lolly by mistake which is now stuck in a big lump just above her stomach. But she knows she will get into trouble if she confesses to having read the magazine. Aunt Enid doesn't let either her or Megan read them, she hides them away in her bedroom because she says they are Not Suitable for Children. So that's two things Bella would be in trouble for, reading the magazine and snooping around in Aunt Enid and Uncle Phil's bedroom.

"It must be something."

Bella jumps to her feet. "I just don't want to go, OK? Just leave me alone! Just – just butt out!" She feels a stab of shame at shouting at Aunt Enid, who looks really upset, but the shame is a

322

hot feeling and helps to melt the lump of ice-lolly so it's all right really.

Bella has discovered a new game at school. It is called Wind Up The Student Teacher, and the expert player is Sadie Williams. Sadie Williams is the coolest girl in the class because a) she wears make-up even though she is not allowed (thick black eyeliner and matching black lipstick that makes her look, or so Craig Griffiths reckons, like someone has just dug her up); b) she chews gum the whole time even though eating in class is supposed to be forbidden; c) she never hands her homework in on time, she just pins this bored look on her face and the teacher backs off instantly (most of them, anyway – Bella has noticed she picks which teachers she does this to); and d) she doesn't care what other people think of her. In Bella's eyes this is the coolest thing of all because she can tell that Sadie really, truly doesn't care rather than, say, Megan, who says it a lot but then goes off and boos in corners if anybody says anything even slightly harsh to her.

The student teacher in question is Mr Rankin, who has ears that stick out and thick sandy hair that springs back from his brow, and has come to teach them music. Bella knew from the moment he walked in the door that there would be trouble, as music is one of those subjects that everybody uses as an excuse for dossing around and nobody concentrates in (except bozos like Tim Mayhew, who plays the violin and wears a blazer, a proper one with the Ysgol Brynglas crest and everything, even though the uniform list says you can wear sweatshirts instead which is what everybody else wears).

Mr Rankin has written his name on the board in thick black letters with the marker pen. Now he is handing out singing books.

"What's this?" Ben Flower looks at the book in amazement.

"We're going to do some singing," the teacher says, hopefully.

Sadie's hand shoots up in the air. "Please, Sir, I can't sing."

"It doesn't matter." Mr Rankin smiles at her kindly. "Just do your best."

"No, Sir. You don't understand. I don't mean I can't *sing*. I mean I *can't* sing. I'm not allowed to. I've got this, er, medical condition."

The teacher makes his fatal mistake. "What medical condition?"

"I don't know what it's called, Sir." She looks at him, innocently.

"I've never heard of any medical condition that prevents singing. Is it laryngitis? You don't sound as if you've got that."

"No, Sir. It's not that." One or two of the lads are beginning to titter, and he starts to realize he is being blagged. He turns and walks to the piano.

"Just do your best," he repeats. "Now, I want you all to turn to page ten, please." He sits down on the piano stool, and shoots his arms out from his slightly frayed cuffs. This is his second mistake. At least four people copy him, and Sadie's hand goes up in the air again. He ignores her and plays some chords. Sadie jumps up and down in her seat and waves her hand around as if she has just seen her best mate across the playground.

"Please, Sir! Mr Wanking, Sir!"

Tim Mayhew tuts and goes red, but everybody else laughs. The teacher jumps up from the piano stool as if someone has burst a balloon behind him.

"Rankin! My name is Rankin!"

"Oh, sorry, Sir."

"So what's the matter?"

"I need to go to the toilet, Sir."

"Can't you wait? The lesson's only just begun."

"No, Sir. It's –" she lowers her voice to a stage whisper – "it's the *time of the month*, Sir. I need to go and – you know."

The deepening blush on Mr Rankin's face shows that he does indeed know.

"No she doesn't, Sir," Craig Griffiths yells out from behind her. "She's not on the blob yet. Don't take any notice."

Sadie turns and begins to hit him. Mr Rankin looks at them both for a moment or two, helplessly, and then goes back to the piano. Two other people have joined in the fight. Three more are playing Snake on their mobiles. Mr Rankin starts playing "*Ar Hyd y Nos*", and Tim Mayhew obediently starts singing along. "*Holl amrantau'r sêr ddywedant. . .*" Bella joins in, but instead of singing the proper words just sings Wanking, over and over, shouting lustily. Five others join in with her and Sadie, sitting next to her, breaks off from duffing up Craig Griffiths, shoots her an approving look and does the same while Mr Rankin tinkles gamely on.

Then the classroom door bursts open and there, on the threshold with an expression like Robocop, is Mr Stanley. Mr Rankin's piano playing tails off like a battery running out of juice.

"What in God's name is going on in here?" Mr Stanley thunders. He looks round the classroom and sees Bella and Sadie with their mouths still open from singing. He points an imperious finger at them – "You two girls. In my office. Now!" – and sweeps majestically from the room.

"Shall we try that again, class?" Mr Rankin suggests, timidly, as Bella and Sadie push back their chairs, noisily and in unison, and stalk haughtily from the room.

"So what's yer name again?" Sadie nonchalantly transfers the plug of gum to her other cheek, and examines her fingernails. The one on the little finger of each hand is painted black.

"Bella Jones."

"Yeah?"

"Yeah."

"Wanna know why I'm so *baaad*, Bella Jones?"

Bella shrugs, equally nonchalantly. "If you like."

"My mother doesn't love me."

Bella is silent for a moment. Then, "You wanna know something back?"

"Go on then."

"My mother doesn't love me, either. In fact, she hates me. She never wanted me in the first place, so she made me go and live somewhere else."

"Yeah?"

"Yeah."

Sadie considers her, recognizing she has met her match. "Cool," she says. "You wanna be in my gang, Bella Jones?"

*

Bella slams the front door behind her, as loudly as she can. Sure enough, out from the kitchen comes the Moaning Old Bag, wiping her hands on a tea towel and with a face on her like a smacked bum (a Sadie-ism that Bella especially likes).

"Where on earth have you been?"

Bella shrugs. "Out." She doesn't feel like telling her she had been hanging around the bus station with Sadie and Sadie's youngest brother and all his scally mates. She would find out soon enough; old Mr Doo-Dah from next door saw her when he got off the bus from Bangor, and gave her one of his looks. She is surprised he hasn't been round with the good news already. Anything to shit-stir.

"You should have been home hours ago!"

"Why, what happened?"

"Don't you be insolent with me, young lady!" She sniffs the air around Bella suspiciously, like a dog greeting another. "Have you been smoking again?"

"No." Bella raises her eyes heavenwards. "Just get off my case, will you?" She stomps upstairs and into the bedroom where she throws herself down on the bed. Good Little Megan is sitting at her desk in the corner, doing her homework. As per. She looks up.

"In trouble again?" she enquires, sweetly.

"Fuck off," Bella mutters, and pulls the pillow over her head.

"I didn't know where to put myself." *I can think of somewhere*, Bella thinks. *Like off the edge of the Great Orme.* "What were you thinking of, Bella? A packet of wine gums and a china mug. A mug! What did you want a mug for?"

"School project," Bella lies, and then wishes she hadn't. Silence is much better.

"It's not even as if you needed a mug," the Moaning Old Bag goes on, as if she hasn't heard her speak. "And wine gums! We give you pocket money, don't we? Don't we?"

"Yes." Sulkily.

"So why did you have to steal wine gums? You're lucky the manager didn't call the police. I'm telling you, child, if you don't pull your socks up and buck your ideas up, you're going to come to a sticky end."

And so on. On and on and on. *Oh shut up. I won the bet, didn't I?*

Slam. Out comes Moaning Old Bag. Wipe, wipe. Smacked-bum face.

"You've done it this time, my girl."

Tut. Look up to ceiling with long-suffering expression. "What?"

"Have you been out in cars with Gareth Williams?"

"No."

"Well, that's not what Mr Hughes-next-door thinks."

"Whatever." *Shrug. What's the point of carrying on denying it? She's made her mind up. Try to push past her and go upstairs but she blocks the way.*

"He said he saw you last night. With Gareth Williams and some other lad. In a red Fiat Panda." *He noticed the make? What kind of pillock is he, anyway?* "He's fifteen, Bella. Fifteen."

"Looks nearer fifty to me." *Stupid attempt at being funny. Bad move. Moaning Old Bag moves in for the kill.*

"How can you joke about it? Don't you know a lad got a girl killed on that estate the other week, a lass only a bit older than you? Crashed the car, he did, and nearly bashed his own brains out into the bargain."

Shock. She hadn't known. Mustn't show it though. Uncool. "So?"

"*So?*" Aunt Enid's shriek nearly blasts the front door off its hinges. "*So?* You're twelve years old, you're spotted joyriding on that God-awful estate with two fifteen-year-old lads, and all you can say is *so*?" Uncle Phil comes scurrying out from the living room, still holding the newspaper. "Well, that's it. I've had enough. No, don't say anything." She holds up a hand to quell Uncle Phil, who doesn't look as if he was about to say anything.

"I've made up my mind. Why should our family – our decent, law-abiding family – be tainted with all this –" she casts around for the right word – "this *behaviour*? Why? Well, I'll answer. Oh yes. I'll answer. We shouldn't. And we're not going to. Not any more." Bella is aware that Megan has appeared and is sitting on the top stair, silently, like a ghost. A ghost with an open mouth. "We've done our best for you – God knows, we've always done that. And I didn't expect thanks for it. Just a bit of common courtesy and consideration. But it seems that's too much to ask for. Well, I've had enough of it, Bella. You're out of control. More than that – in my opinion, you're going the same way as your mother."

Bella flinches, and Uncle Phil puts a restraining hand on her arm. "Now, Enid," he says. "That's enough. You don't mean that. You're upset."

Aunt Enid flushes an angry red, but she doesn't take back what she said. "Upset? No I'm not. I'm determined. That's what I am. First thing Monday morning, I'm ringing Social Services to tell them to get you out of my house."

She marches down the passage to the kitchen. Uncle Phil shoots Bella a nervous look and then scurries after his wife, and Bella is aware of a dull noise. She looks up; Megan, still sitting on the top stair, is slowly clapping her hands together.

"Not that anyone else is going to want you,"

she says, smugly. "You're damaged goods, you are."

It takes all the self-control Bella has to stop herself from hurtling up those stairs and pulling Megan down them, head over heels together, and never mind how much it would hurt when they landed at the bottom.

She can't sleep that night. There is only one thought in her mind, going round and round: *I'll never see the Doyles again.*

All she can think about that weekend is how much she wants to tell Kitty, but she hasn't been round to the Peppermint House for so long now that she would feel awkward and stupid if she were to just turn up out of the blue. And she isn't allowed to use the phone – at least, she assumes she isn't; in all the time she has been at the Robertses' she has never had cause or reason to make a phone call, and besides, she doesn't even know Kitty's number – so all she can do is wait on tenterhooks until Monday morning and school. On tenterhooks is an Aunt Enid expression. Bella has never really understood before what it means but it feels exactly right now, as if she is suspended on some kind of huge uncomfortable hook, dangling unpleasantly and not knowing what the future is going to bring. Any of it. But somehow it is enormously important to tell Kitty that she is going away, that she isn't going to be

able to see her any more, and most importantly –
so important that it feels to Bella like the most
urgent thing she has ever had to tell anybody in
her whole life – how much she is going to miss
her.

She has to wait until break on Monday
morning before she sees Kitty at last, coming out
of New Block with Megan and walking across the
playground, deep in conversation so that she
doesn't see Bella until she is almost upon her.

"Oh," Kitty says, looking at her, startled.
"Hello."

Bella looks back at her, her brain thronging
with all the things she wants to say that she has
been practising in her head all weekend. She
looks at Kitty, and then she looks at Megan, and
suddenly she cannot think of a single one of
those things.

"Hi," she says instead. She looks down at her
shoes, wishing Megan would go away, just piss off
and leave them alone for a few moments. Then
she looks up again. Megan is still there, not
showing any signs of going anywhere.

"Nearly the holidays." Kitty is talking brightly,
as if trying to find something to say. "I can't wait,
can you?"

"No," Bella agrees. "Especially as I'm not
coming back here afterwards."

"What?" For a moment, Kitty looks confused.

Then Megan digs her in the ribs with an elbow.

"I told you," she hisses. "See? I *told* you!"

"So where are you going, then?"

Bella shrugs. "Dunno. Just away. To another foster family."

"Really?"

"*Told* you!" Megan hisses again, and all of a sudden Bella wants to launch herself on her, slap her silly smug freckled face, grab handfuls of her stupid frizzy ginger hair and kick her in the shins and knock her to the ground, and batter her and shout and yell at her for stealing away the best friend she ever had. But all the time, a hard little voice at the back of her mind is telling her that it's her own fault, for hanging round with Sadie Williams. And Kitty and Megan were friends first, so in a way, Megan has only reclaimed what was hers in the first place. That's probably how she would see it, at any rate.

So with a great effort of will Bella stops herself from battering Megan, and smiles at both of them instead. It feels like a pretty wonky smile, but it is a smile nevertheless.

"Yeah," she says. "It's cool. Won't have to come to this dump any more, anyway. See ya around, then. Maybe."

And she turns and stomps off, back across the playground. She is blinking so hard she can barely see where she is going, the tarmac blurry through the stupid babyish tears she can feel gathering on her lower eyelids. She manages to get back inside without a single tear spilling over, but when she opens the door there is a smear of blood on her hands, and she realizes she has been clenching her fists so tightly that her fingernails have broken the skin on her palms.

It was early. So early, it was still dark. But it was definitely morning, because there were birds singing in the square outside. So much birdsong, it seemed to Bella that all the birds in Manchester – in Britain, in the world – had congregated outside the window and were joyously singing their feathered little heads off.

She lay in Mia's narrow bed for a few moments, listening, and inhaling the mingled scents of cigarette smoke and patchouli oil and incense that were so familiar despite her having never met their originator. Then she pushed back the covers, pulled the dragon-adorned kimono on over her nightshirt and padded down the first flight of stairs to Bruno's room.

He was asleep, huddled under the duvet and illuminated faintly by the orange sodium glow of the street light outside.

"Bruno. Wake up."

She put a hand on his shoulder, and he stirred.

"What? Wotisit?"

"It's me. Bella."

He sat up in bed, bolt upright. "What's wrong? You OK?"

"Yes. Well, no. Can we talk? There's things I want to tell you."

chapter sixteen

They talked all that day, and into the night. Various Mikes came and went, including the feline one who sat periodically on Bella's lap and purred comfortably. Bella twined her hands in his fur and ploughed on, on and on, all the shameful secrets and half-forgotten memories about her mother and her childhood that had lain buried in her subconscious for what felt like her entire life tumbling out in a jumbled unstoppable cathartic flood.

She did the lion's share of the talking. Bruno mostly sat and listened, fetching sandwiches and hot coffee and cold beer at intervals, and reassuring her that, no, she wasn't boring him and yes, it was perfectly fine for her to be telling him all this, and that the various tourist delights of Manchester and environs could wait for another time, another visit.

"You mean you actually want me to come again?" Bella took a bite of sandwich and laughed shakily. "God. I'd have thought you'd be barricading the doors. Or moving house and not leaving a forwarding address."

"Now why would I do that?" He looked genuinely puzzled.

"Well, you know. Using you as a free counselling service. Ruining your weekend with all this crying on your shoulder."

He ached to take her hands in his and tell her that his idea of paradise was just this, Bella in his house, trusting him enough to offload on to him, that he felt honoured and privileged and that as far as he was concerned she could make both his shoulders soggy as hell. He couldn't tell her that, though. She'd run a mile – either that or vomit from the cheesiness of it. So instead he just laughed back and said, "Don't worry. I'll just add it to your bill."

Bella woke on Sunday morning feeling spent; purged clean. She also felt faintly anxious, embarrassed at just how much she had divulged to Bruno. Being driven to the station by him, later, she said awkwardly; "Don't say anything to anyone, will you."

"What about?" Then he smiled. "Course not. What am I, a blabbermouth or something?"

They pulled in to the entrance to the station. "Just drop me here," Bella told him. "Don't come on to the platform with me."

"What? Don't be daft. I want to make sure you—"

She put a hand on his knee. "Please. I hate goodbyes."

"OK. If that's what you want." He manoeuvred the car into a parking slot, pulled on the handbrake and switched off the ignition. He was disturbed by the fact she considered this a goodbye. It seemed very final. Maybe now she'd told him everything about herself she was intending to do another runner, and he was never going to see her again. . . He looked at her, anxiously. Her face was turned towards him; she seemed oddly reluctant to get out of the car.

"I'll be home for Easter in a couple of weeks. I'll see you then, yeah? At Kitty's eighteenth?" He went to kiss her, then changed his mind and put out his right hand, cupping her cheekbone. She rested her face against it, briefly, and closed her eyes.

"I can't have a relationship with you, Bruno," she murmured. *Who's going to want you? You're damaged goods, you are.* Then she opened her eyes. He was smiling at her fondly.

"Soft girl. You've already got a relationship with me; don't you realize?" Something flared behind her eyes. She didn't contradict him. Encouraged, he went on: "I'm not asking you for anything, Bella. Just think about what I said the other night, OK? About identifying what you want, and going for it?" He brushed his thumb against her lower lip, gently.

Flustered, she pulled away, rummaged around in the footwell for her bag, then opened the door and half-stepped, half-fell out. "I've got to go. My train'll be here in a moment."

"Ring me when you're home, yeah? Let me know you got back OK."

"Sure." She bent towards the open passenger door and smiled. It transformed her entire demeanour, not just her face. "Thanks, Bruno. For – you know. Everything."

Then she slammed the door and was gone, walking briskly towards the station entrance, the fingers of her right hand wiggling above her shoulder in farewell, and as Bruno drove out of the station he suddenly felt as if he had been given something supremely precious. It was all he could do to stop himself punching the air and yelling aloud with joy.

Bella could feel the memory of Bruno's hand against her cheek the entire journey, the soft imprint of his thumb on her mouth. She had to lower her face into a magazine to prevent the rest of the carriage seeing her grinning like an idiot at the prolonged delicious memory of it.

She was still smiling when she reached home. Getting off the train and walking along the platform, she felt lighter in spirits than she could remember being for years, and wondered whether to be really indulgent and splash out on a cab the rest of the way home.

"Hello, Bella."

Lost in her thoughts, not expecting to see anyone she knew, she spun round. Kitty was standing at the bottom of the stairs, her hands in her pockets and an unfathomable expression on her face.

"Kitty! Hi! Flippin' heck, you made me jump! Where are you off to?"

"Nowhere. I've been waiting for you."

"What?" She frowned, not understanding. "How did you know where I was?"

"I rang Bruno. He told me what train you were on. So I came to meet you."

A small stab of alarm. "Did he tell you anything else?"

"Like what?" Kitty frowned.

Bella made a small helpless gesture. What could she say? Like the fact we were up talking from half-past five yesterday morning? Like he now knows stuff I haven't told another living soul?

Kitty was looking at her with suspicion. "What's going on between you two?"

"Nothing." Bella spread her hands. Bruno wouldn't have revealed anything she had told him – of course he wouldn't. He'd promised not to, and she trusted him. "He invited me up to see him ages ago, and I just felt like a break. We're just mates – honestly."

"That's one of your favourite words. *Honestly*. But it doesn't actually mean anything, does it?" Kitty's voice was full of bitterness.

"What do you mean?" Bella looked at her friend, closely. "Kitty, what's wrong?"

"That's what I've been asking myself, ever since you came back."

"You're talking in riddles." Bella laughed, but she knew Kitty considered it no laughing matter. She had never seen her look so serious. Her face was clouded and troubled, with the expression of someone who had been profoundly hurt or deeply wronged. Bella tried to take her arm. "We can't talk here; c'mon, Kitten, let's—"

"No." Firmly, Kitty shook her arm free. "I don't want to go anywhere."

"What then? Why are you here?"

Kitty regarded her for a long moment before she replied. "I'm not really sure. I had it all worked out in my mind, while I was waiting for you. All the questions I wanted answers for. But now you're here, I'm not sure there's any point. You'll only tell me more lies."

"What?" Bella was aghast. "I don't tell you lies!"

"Don't you? How about –" Kitty cast about and could only come up with something trivial. "How about that hat you were supposed to have bought me for Christmas?"

"What do you mean, supposed? I did buy it for you!"

"You bought it with your '*allowance*', I suppose." Kitty put inverted commas around the word, ironically.

"That's right. I did. You were with me when I bought it, in actual fact – or almost. Remember when we went shopping in Chester? We went off and did our own thing for the first hour, didn't we – that's when I bought it. OK, so then I kind of tricked you into trying it on – but I knew it was you. I knew you'd like it." She frowned. "Why are you looking at me like that? Don't you believe me? We're friends – friends don't lie to each other!"

"Friends? Are you sure? I always thought friendship was a two-way thing. All about sharing. But you don't want to share anything."

"How do you mean?"

"I know nothing about you. I never have. Nothing important, I mean. Your background, or what happened to you when you left Penllan. Your past, I suppose you could say. All those little things friends know about each other. And since you've been back, you've just used me to fill the gaps in your social life."

Bella's hand flew to her mouth. "That's not true."

"It feels like it from where I'm standing."

"Kitty." Bella appealed to her. "Don't be like this. I know we haven't seen much of each other this term, but we've both been busy. We've got exams after Easter, and then you've had to fit in seeing Rhys, and Megan –"

"And you've had to fit in seeing Mel, and Bruno," Kitty added, meaningfully. "But oh no, I forgot – you're 'just good friends', aren't you? With both of them."

"Yes. I am. I don't know what you're getting at." Bella touched her arm, urgently. "What *are* you getting at?"

Kitty looked at her incredulously. "Oh, come on. You're not telling me you don't know."

"I don't! Tell me."

"OK then," Kitty said grimly. "How about going up to see Bruno this weekend, but telling me you were too busy with college work to go to see a movie with me?"

"I was, when you asked me. But I managed to get through a whole load, and then Bruno rang later in the week, and I was feeling totally brain dead from all the revision, so—"

"And telling Nicci that you were intending to get Bruno," Kitty cut across her.

"Did I? When?" She looked nonplussed.

"You told her he might think you were thick, but you could get him just like that." She snapped her fingers, as Megan had done when relating the conversation to her.

"Ah yes." She flushed slightly. "I remember that. We were talking about, you know, brainy lads at college, and how they look down on girls like us who aren't doing A-levels. And then she mentioned Bruno, and then – well. I admit it. I was just showing off, I guess. I said I could get him, easy-peasy. I didn't say I was intending to, though," she added.

Kitty wondered what the difference was, but didn't have either the will or the energy to pursue it. "OK then. What about the self-defence class you told me you and Mel went to; the one he supposedly gave you lifts to. Tell me about that. There's no such class, is there!" she declared, triumphantly.

To her surprise, Bella didn't try to deny it. She stood motionless for a moment, then said, "No. You're quite right – I did lie about that. I'm sorry."

"So where were you going?" she demanded. "Where exactly was Mel taking you?"

"I can't tell you here."

"Of course you can," Kitty scoffed. "What's the problem? There's nobody around to overhear your deep dark secret." She indicated the Sunday evening near-deserted station with her head.

"It's not that." Keeping things secret from her

past had become a habit from Bella's early childhood. It had been a way of shielding herself from things, of cutting herself off emotionally to avoid getting hurt; but she now realized with a flash of insight that it hadn't solved anything. On the contrary, it was clear from what Kitty was saying that her refusal to trust anybody with information about herself had simply resulted in others mistrusting her. Misjudging her, even – viewing her with suspicion. She had been ashamed of her past, but she had nothing to be ashamed of – none of it had been her fault. She could see that now, as plainly as seeing her life held up before her. The time had clearly come to start putting the record straight. Confiding in Bruno had started the process, loosed the flow; it hadn't been easy, but afterwards she had felt more relief than she could have ever imagined. She knew now that she had to tell Kitty as well. She had kept things from her for too long, and as one of Bella's oldest friends she deserved to know the same as Bruno. She just hoped it wasn't too late.

"There's loads of stuff I should have told you. I want to tell you now, but it may take a while." She linked her arm with Kitty's, determinedly, and this time Kitty allowed herself to be led away. "Come on – we'll go to my place."

*

When Bella had finished talking, she lit a cigarette and sat in silence for a moment. Then she looked at Kitty.

"Is there anything else you want to know? Just ask me."

Kitty didn't quite know what to say. All the years of being fobbed off by Bella, of having the subject changed whenever it got too close to home, and now this sudden rush of all kinds of unexpected information. It almost felt like too much. She wondered what had prompted it. She was glad Bella had told her, nonetheless. She felt she ought to say something.

"So it was the joyriding that got you sent away."

"Yeah. I'd been a bad girl generally, but that was the — what's the word? The catalyst. Although I was never actually in that car. That was Sadie. I was just standing watching."

"Why did you ever get involved with Sadie in the first place? Didn't you realize she was trouble?" Kitty had never been able to understand it.

"Sure I did." Bella shrugged. "That was the appeal, I guess. She attracted attention, and I wanted some of it. And at that age, any attention is better than none – I was crap at school, you were palled up with Megan again, so—"

"We were in different classes," Kitty pointed

out, quickly. "We hardly saw each other. I didn't mean to abandon you."

"I know. I wasn't accusing you – just saying how it was. What happened to Sadie, do you know?"

"She was excluded in Year Ten – the word was she got involved in some drugs thing." Kitty sniffed with distaste. "You said you were fostered because your mother was ill – what was wrong with her?" Part of her didn't like asking, but on the other hand Bella had invited Kitty to ask questions.

Bella hesitated a moment. "She's got bi-polar disorder. Manic depression," she explained, seeing Kitty's blank look.

"Is that where you're up one minute and down the next?"

"That's one way of putting it. But it's more like weeks or months than minutes, and saying you go up and down is like saying Jesus Christ is good and the devil is naughty. It's much, much more extreme than that." Bella chewed on her bottom lip. Talking about it was clearly difficult for her. "Basically, there's periods of deep depression alternating with mania – mad activity, psychotic behaviour."

"Psychotic?"

"Delusions, hallucinations. Not pleasant. The problem is, it's very hard to treat – the medication for the mania can make the depression worse, and vice versa. Plus it can take years for the correct diagnosis. My mother was treated for major depression for nearly ten years, which just made the mania worse. Then there's what they call 'the tendency to self-harm' – I think the figures say something like twenty per cent top themselves, but up to fifty per cent attempt to. That's a hell of a high figure."

"Did your mother?"

"What, try or succeed?" Bella gave a bitter laugh. "You know, when I was about eleven I used to wish she'd just get on with it and stop faffing around with cutting herself up. Nice daughterly thing to think, isn't it?"

Kitty was shocked. She struggled to hide it, to find something helpful and supportive to say. "Understandable, I should think. It sounds like hell to live with."

"Well that's just it, isn't it? I didn't have to live with it. I was fostered."

"Before you were fostered, then."

"Before I was fostered I never knew how she was going to be from one day's end to the next. That's pretty scary for a little kid."

"I can imagine."

"No, Kitty." Bella looked down at her hands. "You can't. You can't begin to imagine. And do you know what the worst thing was?"

"No." It was all so painfully intense. Kitty wasn't sure how much good it was doing Bella, all this deep introspection, but she could hardly tell her to stop now. "What?"

"It started after I was born. Post-natal depression can kick the whole thing off, apparently. So you could say her illness was all my fault."

"You don't really think that, do you?" What a dreadful thing to have to carry around all your life.

Bella shrugged. "I used to. I don't know any more. Now, I kind of feel she's got it, and that's that. For years I used to worry that I was going to get it too, and I hated her for it. Then I decided I'd have to cross that bridge when I came to it. *If* I came to it," she amended.

"Do you still see her?"

"I do now. I wouldn't visit her for years, but then quite recently I realized the situation wasn't going to go away just because I was refusing to accept it. She's still my mother, when all's said and done. She wants to see me. Cutting her out of my life just seemed unnecessarily cruel."

"So how is she now?"

"OK." She shrugged again. "She's been back in hospital for the last six months, but she's on different medication now and it seems to be working. I don't see her that often. It's still difficult. Not just because of the illness. When I was small I had to cope with things that would have been difficult for a grown woman, and now I'm older my mother still seems to view me as a little girl. It's as if she's caught in a time-warp. It's not easy. But it's a start."

"Is that where Mel was taking you? To see her?"

"Something like that." Bella's eyes slid away from Kitty's. "I never kept things from you to shut you out, you know. It was because I was too embarrassed to tell anyone. That way, I almost managed to convince myself that it wasn't happening, that my life was normal like everybody else's. You know what you said about me telling lies? Well, I developed a very vivid imagination when I was a kid. I was probably trying to make my life seem better than it was. Do you understand?"

Kitty nodded. "I think so." It did make some kind of sense.

"It was a way of shielding myself from the truth, I guess. Having a mad mother wasn't exactly a bundle of laughs. But do you know what kept me going? You and your family. Having been fostered on and off since I was, I don't know, three or four, it felt like having a proper family of my own."

"But didn't you feel that with Megan's family?"

"No. Don't ask me why, I don't know – I just never truly felt part of their family the way I felt part of yours."

"What about your dad?"

"My dad was a bastard. He put my mum in hospital when she was pregnant with me, and then he pissed off. I've never met him." So that was true after all, then – not the gypsy story. Bella leant forwards and caught Kitty's hands in her own. "You'll never know how much your friendship meant to me. Still does. I'd never do anything to put that in danger. You do believe me, don't you?"

She looked at Kitty with a fierce intensity, her blue eyes bright with fervour. Bella's vehemence always faintly embarrassed Kitty, but how could she rebuff her after what she had just revealed about herself? It couldn't have been easy for her, either to live with or to talk about. She gave Bella's hands a sympathetic squeeze.

"Of course I do," she said. "We're soul sisters, remember?"

But even after all Bella's revelations, Kitty found herself continuing to go over things in her mind. If was as if the seed of doubt had been planted too deeply to be uprooted; she had been questioning Bella's truthfulness for so long that she couldn't stop. She felt sorry for her, there was no doubt about that – all that stuff about her mother was horrendous – but the unpleasant fact was, she didn't feel the same way about her as before, and she doubted that feeling would ever come back. It was something to do with not quite trusting her any more. Bella had shown herself to have the capacity for telling lies without batting an eyelid; and then there was the matter of her behaviour with Bruno conflicting with her continued insistence that they were "just mates". Not that Kitty herself had any particular axe to grind on that score – it was poor Megan who was affected there. Even though Kitty couldn't quite get a handle on her friend's passion for Bruno she did understand how unrequited love felt, especially if the object of your desire encouraged you, as Bruno appeared to have done with his texts and his suggestions of meeting up in the holidays, and then dropped you in favour of somebody else. She realized that she had actually wanted Megan and Bruno to get together, partly (it sounded awful to admit it, but it was true) as one in the eye for Bella, who seemed to be able to ensnare any man she wanted, but partly as a kind of compensation to Megan for having dismissed her misgivings about Bella for all that time.

The misgivings that Kitty herself was now having, big style. There was still something about all of this that didn't add up. Kitty mulled and deliberated over what it could be for some time, and when it finally hit her it was so obvious it was like being struck by a bolt of lightning.

She went round to Bruno's as soon as he was home for the Easter holidays. "I've got to talk to you about Bella," she said, when he opened the front door. "I've worked out what's been going on."

Something in Bruno's face closed up immediately, like curtains being drawn. "Have you."

"I think so, yes."

"And has it occurred to you that it might not be any of your business?"

"Of course it's my business – I'm supposed to be her friend, aren't I?"

"So you still consider yourself her friend, then?"

"Of course I do. Why wouldn't I?" She regarded him quizzically. "Look, can I come in? I really don't want to have this conversation on the doorstep."

He held the door open, reluctantly. "Come on, then. Only I don't want you slagging her off with all this bollocks about what a liar she is." He led the way into the kitchen. "D'you want a cuppa?"

"Not for me. I've just had one." Kitty sat down on a stool. "She does tell lies. She admitted it herself."

Bruno shook his head. "You're way off the mark, Kitty. She's the most honest person I know. She's told me stuff that she didn't need to tell me – personal stuff that would make your hair curl."

"Oh, I already know about all that," Kitty said dismissively.

"You do?" He looked surprised. "When did she tell you?"

"When she came back from visiting you. Which is when she told you, presumably."

"Well, yeah." He passed a hand across his jaw. "I just got the feeling it was the first time she'd ever told anybody. I'm amazed she then came straight back and told you."

"Cheers, Bruno. Just who's her mate here?"

"Only you haven't been that much of a mate to her lately, have you?"

"What d'you mean?" She was indignant. "I was her mate long before you were."

"This isn't a competition, you know. There's not going to be any prize awarded for being the world's best pal."

"I know that."

"It's a shame nobody told Megan. I put much of this down to her."

"Megan?" She stared at him. "What's this got to do with her?"

"Loads. She's got a lot to answer for, in my view. First she's jealous of Bella usurping her as your best friend, then she resents her having anything to do with me. That girl is so jealous, if you cut her in half she'd have a green streak a mile wide going right through her."

"She can't help how she feels."

"Granted. But she can help what she does about it. And what has she done? Turned you against Bella, and started behaving like some kind of stalker with me. I've got to tell you, Kitty – there's no chance of her getting it on with me. She's just got to get over it."

"She hasn't turned me against Bella," Kitty objected. "Anyway, I thought you suggested meeting up with her in the holidays?"

"Er, hello? *I* suggested it?"

"That's what she told me."

"I rest my case." He spread his hands. "The girl's away with the fairies. She's obsessed. *She* was the one who suggested it – I was just too soft to say no outright."

"Then perhaps you should have."

"Perhaps I should. It doesn't alter the fact that she's apparently making out we've got a relationship when we actually haven't."

"Well, OK. Whatever." They were getting off the point – Kitty hadn't gone round to Bruno's to talk about him and Megan. "So anyway, about Bella. . ."

He sighed, impatiently. "Must we? I really

don't think we should be discussing what she said. I don't know about you, but she told me in confidence."

"But if she told us both the same thing, it doesn't really matter, does it!"

"It's the principle, Kitty. Surely you can see that?"

"Well, yes, but –" She shrugged. "Look, there's something I need to tell you. Something important. What did she tell you about the reason she moved away from Penllan?"

"What she said to me was confidential. I told you."

"Oh come on, Bruno," she pleaded. "This is important. I'm not here to tittle-tattle, I promise. It's just. . . Just give me the general impression."

He said, calmly, "I'm not telling you anything. You'll only go running off to Megan with it, and then the two of you will use it to beat Bella round the head."

"We won't!" She stared at him, dismayed. "Is that what you think of us?"

"It's what I think of Megan. I'm not sure about you; you say you're Bella's friend, and then you—"

"OK, OK," she said hastily. "Just tell me this. Did she say it was because of getting in with the wrong crowd – Sadie Williams and co? And that the last straw for Megan's mum was being told she'd been spotted joyriding with Sadie's brother?"

"That kind of thing." He frowned. "If you already know all this, why are you asking me?"

Kitty persisted. "She definitely said it was the joyriding? Or was there something else?"

"No. She said it was the joyriding. Look, Kitty, what's all this about?"

"You know," Kitty said, slowly, "Megan used to come to school with horror stories about the trouble Bella got into when she started hanging out with Sadie."

"Now there's a surprise," Bruno muttered, darkly.

Kitty ignored that. "And I've always thought it a bit odd."

"Odd? Why odd?"

"Because it just didn't seem – I don't know – *serious* enough for Megan's family to want shot of Bella. Oh, I know it couldn't have been easy for them – some of the things Megan used to say went on were pretty bad. But I also know Megan's mum, and I know what she's like. She's kind, and patient, and – well, she's been fostering for years. You'd have thought she'd seen it all before; not that she'd have been fazed by a bit of teenage rebellion."

"Maybe it was more than just a bit of teenage rebellion."

"That's what I mean."

Bruno scratched his head. "Sorry, you've lost me."

"I've been thinking for a while now that something didn't add up about why Bella went away. That, OK, the Sadie connection was undesirable, and the joyriding thing was a worry, blah blah blah. But, like I said, it didn't quite seem enough. For the reasons I said. And then Bella told me about her mother." She looked at Bruno. "You know about her mother too, I presume? About her illness?"

"She told me, yes," he said, shortly.

"Well, after she told me that, I realized she'd been lying again." Bruno started to protest, but Kitty held up a hand. "Let me finish. Just hear me out, and then see what you think. Bella told me that she'd refused to see her mother for years, but she'd recently had a change of heart and Mel had taken her to visit her. She'd originally told me they were going to an evening class together, and I assumed she'd come up with that as an excuse because she hadn't wanted to spill the beans about her mother's illness. *But*." She took a deep breath. "Then I remembered what Mel had told me."

"Which was?"

"That they'd driven to a road and parked the car and just sat outside a house. Not gone visiting anybody – just sat. Watching."

"So? Maybe she felt awkward at first, as she hadn't seen her mother for a while. Maybe she went back later by herself, and went in."

"That's what I thought. To begin with. Then I remembered that Mel had said they'd gone there several times and always done the same thing – just sat outside in the car. And *then* I remembered that Bella had told me her mother had been back in hospital for the past six months. Not living by herself in a house – in hospital."

Bruno was looking at her with faint distaste. "So what conclusions did you jump to then, Inspector Morse?"

"I didn't have to jump to any conclusions. I discovered she wasn't going to see her mother at all, because I went there myself."

"What? How? You didn't ask Mel to take you, surely?"

"Of course not. He'd have smelled a rat, wouldn't he?" She hadn't wanted Bella thinking she was spying on her. Even though, in actual fact, that was exactly what she was doing. But there was no malicious intent, no plan of catching Bella out in yet another lie and confronting her with it. She just wanted to know the truth. After all these years, all the lies (even if some of them had been understandable and excusable), she thought she was entitled to know the truth. "I made up some excuse to get Mel to tell me where it was, and then I asked Rhys to take me there."

Rhys moaned like hell to begin with, about giving up his Sunday morning to drive to God-only-knows-where, but Kitty nagged and pleaded, and then bribed him with promises of how she'd make it worth his while, which put a smile on his face, albeit a small one.

"So where is it we're going?"

Kitty, knowing she had to give Rhys some explanation, had already worked out a detailed if slightly implausible excuse about delivering something to a work colleague of Mum's. She even had it with her as a prop – a couple of books wrapped in a Marks & Sparks carrier bag.

"Why can't your mum do it herself?"

"She's at work. And her mate's at home, on study leave. Ah, go on, Rhys – I said I'd do it. She does loads for me."

"And is your mum going to pay for the petrol?"

"Don't be tight. It's not that far. We can go and have lunch afterwards – on me."

So there they were, sitting in Rhys's dad's car in what Mel had correctly described as a residential street. He hadn't been able to recall the number of the house, but he'd said it had a red front door, a child's plastic slide in the front garden and a bus stop right outside, all of which

Kitty could see perfectly plainly. They weren't parked directly in front of the house but opposite it, on the other side of the road.

"What are we doing now, then?" Rhys asked brightly, when Kitty made no move to get out of the car. "Playing I-Spy?"

Kitty looked at her watch. "We're early. She's – er – still at church. We'll have to just sit here for a bit."

"Define a bit."

"An hour, maybe?"

"An *hour*? Bloody hell, Kitty! Why did you get me to pick you up so sodding early?"

Kitty wished she could tell him why they were really there. "I'm sorry. I didn't realize we'd get here so quickly. Please, Rhys. I'll buy you a lovely lunch as a reward."

So he turned the radio on, and read the computer magazine he'd brought with him, and grumbled a bit more, and eventually moved the driver's seat back and leant his head against the headrest and folded his arms and closed his eyes, and Kitty was grateful for the peace and quiet, even though they had been sitting there for almost an hour and she was beginning to wonder why they had come.

Then the red front door opened and into the garden spilt three noisy dark-haired children, a toddler of about two, a little girl of four or five and a boy of around Owen's age carrying a football, and as they played noisily together in their garden in the unseasonably mild March morning Kitty could not take her eyes off the little girl, and understood exactly why she came, and why Bella came too.

"It's no good." Bruno shook his head. "I'm rubbish at puzzles. You'll have to enlighten me."

"Come on! Isn't it obvious?" She was clearly going to have to spell it out for him. "The little girl – she was exactly the right age. I knew as soon as I set eyes on her. She's Bella's child."

chapter seventeen

Bruno felt as if he had been punched in the guts. Suddenly all kinds of things made sense: Bella saying she didn't do relationships, that she had been too hurt in the past. Bella saying that parenthood was a closed book to her – he'd assumed she meant her own parents, but she must have been referring to herself. Bella, abruptly removed from Penllan after five years of living with the same foster family. Bella, not wanting to divulge anything about what had happened when she'd gone. She'd got pregnant, and had gone away to have the child, and it had been taken away from her. Little wonder she'd screwed up her GCSEs later on. It all made sense now.

But he hated Kitty for having dug it all up. He hated how uncovering all this about Bella was making him feel, how it had suddenly and irrevocably altered his perception of her. How, despite having told him so much of her past, she clearly hadn't trusted him enough to tell him this. Even though part of him could understand why she hadn't. Pregnant at twelve. Man. That was heavy stuff.

"Are you OK?" Kitty was looking at him anxiously. "You look dead weird."

"I feel dead weird." He raised his gaze slowly, as if coming round from a coma. "Did you enjoy finding all that out? Did telling me give you a kick?"

Kitty's eyes filled with tears of injustice. "That's way harsh. Why would I enjoy it? I just wanted to know the truth, that's all."

"Well, I hope you and the truth will be very happy together. Because I'm sure as hell not."

Kitty's discoveries about Bella produced a new, tender and genuine pity for her – what an appalling thing to have gone through at such a young age – but most of all, she felt relieved at having got to the bottom of all the mystery and intrigue that had been going on for so long. There was no need for Bella even to know that Kitty had found out, not really. She was reasonably certain Bruno wouldn't say anything; he'd looked totally shell-shocked, it *was* a shock to learn that the girl you'd known since she was seven had been a teenage mum. Kitty herself had been shocked, shocked to her core. She'd had to come up with some story about feeling suddenly faint, and Rhys had had to drive them to a pub and buy her a brandy. But Bruno would get over the shock, just as Kitty had. And it wasn't as if he and Bella were a couple or anything like that. That *would* have been tough, to find out that kind of thing about your girlfriend. To find out she'd been keeping such an enormous secret from you.

And as far as Mel was concerned, Kitty had told him that she needed the directions to the house because Bella had asked Rhys to give her a lift there. She'd thought it a bit tenuous but he didn't seem to think it especially odd, or point out that Bella could just tell Rhys the way herself. But then, he was so spacey he probably wouldn't think it odd if Kitty had told him Bella was intending to hitch a lift there on a passing ice-cream van.

Kitty could just put it all behind her now; concentrate on her looming exams, and seeing more of Rhys (even though, since New Year's Eve, he seemed to have stopped being so jealous of the time she spent with others), and trying to help Megan through the inevitably painful realization that she and Bruno just weren't going to happen. And seeing Bella too, of course. Forging a new, more grown-up friendship, based on knowing at last exactly who Bella was and accepting that knowledge, rather than trying to recreate their childhood closeness. Living in the past just didn't work; she could see that now.

Oh yes. It was all going to be fine, mature and civilized and enlightened. She had it all figured out.

And then it was her eighteenth birthday, and all her carefully pre-calculated responses, her confident preconceptions as to how she was going to behave and act and feel, were smashed to smithereens.

Bruno had, as promised, organized what he described as "a small do" for Kitty. "You'll have to come round, though," he said.

"Round where?"

"To the pub," he said airily. "I'll meet you there, yeah?"

Kitty agreed, rather reluctantly – from that description, it didn't sound like it was going to be the greatest night out of all time – and when she duly arrived at the prescribed time she was even less impressed to be greeted by just one person. Bruno.

"Where is everybody?" she looked round. "Rhys said he was going to be here – what's keeping him?"

"Don't worry. I'm sure they'll be here soon."

"Who's they? Just who are you expecting?"

"Well, Rhys. Obviously. And Megan said she might show her face. And Bella said she's not sure but thinks she's OK for an hour or so."

He bought her a glass of wine which she drank with increasingly lowering spirits, and when he offered to get another she said, "Actually, if you don't mind, I think I'll just go home. Nobody else is coming, are they?" Just wait until she got home – she'd be on her mobile to her so-called boyfriend like a shot. It was her eighteenth, for Christ's sake – her eighteenth!

Bruno took one look at her face and burst out laughing.

"What? What's so funny?"

"You are, you plank." He put out a hand and ruffled her hair, affectionately. "You didn't really think we'd let you celebrate like this, did you? All by yourself?"

And he steered her out of the pub and along the half-mile of street to his house, where everybody – both sets of parents, Rhys, Bella and Mel, Megan, Nicci, Cousin Ged, even Owen – were hiding in the semi-dark, all leaping out when the front door was opened, shouting, "Surprise!" and blasting on those tooty things that unroll when you blow down them, and Kitty stood there in the hallway in stunned delight and accepted kisses and cards and presents from all of them. She should have known them better. They wouldn't have let her down, not on her eighteenth.

There was a proper sit-down meal laid out in the dining room on Aunt Carys's best damask tablecloth, with a fistful of cutlery apiece and more crystal glasses than you could shake a stick at.

"Wow," Kitty said. She turned to her aunt. "When did you do all this?"

"Oh, we just conjured it up from nowhere, me and your mum." She twinkled at her niece, and planted a kiss on her cheek. "You're worth it. Happy birthday, *cariad*."

"God, Carys, it all looks amazing." Bella was at her side. Kitty felt a prickle of something odd. Since when had Bella been on first-name terms with her aunt?

She had wondered how the seating was going to work out, half-envisaging a full-on cat-fight between Bella and Megan for the privilege of sitting next to Bruno, but even that was all right because he was sat between Kitty and her mother, with Bella and Megan miles away from both him and each other on the opposite side of the huge extended table. It gave Bruno the opportunity to play the gent, helping the birthday girl and his aunt to vegetables and gravy, and pouring wine with panache. Rhys was heavily on the wine, Kitty noticed – perhaps he was finding the family gathering hard work.

It was a fantastic meal, with plenty of chat followed by the obligatory champagne toast. Afterwards Rhys said in Kitty's ear, slurring his words slightly, "What now, then? Shall we go to the pub?"

Kitty's father overheard. "Good idea, Rhys. You

369

young 'uns go off and enjoy yourselves, and we'll stay behind and do the clearing up. Give us a good chance to talk about you all behind your backs!"

Ged declined, and it was Owen's bedtime, but the others all agreed it would be a good way to round off the evening.

"I'll just go and get my jacket," Kitty said to Bruno. She looked round. "Where's everybody gone?"

"The bathroom, I think. The girls, at any rate – major tarting-up operations."

Taking her champagne for company, Kitty used the en-suite bathroom off her aunt and uncle's bedroom to apply more lipgloss and fluff up her hair. She smiled at herself in the mirror. What a fab evening. She gave a small chuckle. And there was Bruno, playing along, pretending nobody could be bothered to come along – you had to hand it to him. He'd really had her fooled.

"C'mon, Kitbag!" His voice floated up the stairs. "What's keeping you? And round the others up, will you? It would be good to get there before it closes!"

"Nag, nag, nag," Kitty muttered fondly, under her breath. Now, where had her uncle put her jacket? Ah yes – in the guest bedroom, along with all the others. Still holding her champagne glass, she turned the doorknob with her other hand and went in.

The room was in darkness, and it took a few moments for Kitty's eyes to become accustomed to the lack of light. Fumbling for the light switch, firstly (inevitably) on the wrong side of the door jamb, she became aware that she wasn't alone in the room. There was a kind of scurrying sound, a rustling and an intake of breath, and as she located the switch on the correct side of the door and the room was abruptly flooded with the harsh overhead light she was able to see the source of the noise. For there, in the far corner of the room and wedged against the pine double wardrobes were Rhys and Bella, locked in a tight embrace. His back was to the room, his body bent hungrily over her slight form, his shirt untucked, her hands resting on his shoulders. Rhys turned to look at Kitty as the light went on, frowning and blinking at the sudden glare, and Bella's face, a pale oval with enormous startled eyes, peered at Kitty over the bulk of his shoulder.

"Sorry," Kitty said, and switched the light off again. Afterwards, she couldn't believe she had actually apologized. Shock, obviously. She set the champagne glass down on the nearest bedside table, carefully, so as not to spill any on Aunt Carys's lovingly starched and ironed antique linen cloth. Then she turned and went out of the room, closing the door quietly behind her.

"There you are!" Bruno was standing at the top

of the stairs. "You haven't got your jacket now – what are you like." Then he caught sight of her face. "What's up? You look as if you've seen a ghost."

Kitty couldn't answer. She literally couldn't speak. Even if she had managed to find the words to describe the scene she had just disturbed she couldn't have brought herself to utter them, couldn't have borne the humiliation, couldn't have coped with Bruno's response. Instead she walked past him, slowly, with dignity, and as she went down the stairs she heard the bedroom door open behind her and a voice – Bella's frantic voice – calling: "Kitty! Come back!"

She was moving in slow motion, as if underwater. As she descended the stairs a sea of faces looked up at her, at Bella who was stumbling down the stairs behind her, still calling her name. Various anxious hands clutched at her as she stepped, unseeing, off the final stair – her parents', Megan's, Ged's.

"Catrin! What's the matter?"

"Do you feel ill, *cariad*? Here, sit down."

A chair was fetched from the dining room, a glass of water from the kitchen. She brushed both aside. "I want to go home." She was amazed at how calm her voice sounded. She turned to Dad. "Please. Please take me home."

Megan was in front of her, taking her hands in

her own. "What is it, Kitty? What's happened? You can tell us – we're your friends."

Then Bella was there too, bobbing behind Megan, her eyes full of concern. "Kitty," she beseeched. "Please listen to me. You've got to listen to me."

Everyone was clamouring around her. *What's the matter – what's happened – are you all right – yes of course I'll take you home Catrin love – where's Rhys, someone ask him if he knows what's been going on – please Kitty, listen to me, LISTEN!*

It was too much. Kitty looked around at all of them, her friends and family gathered there to celebrate her eighteenth birthday, her coming-of-age. Ged was still holding his glass of champagne; she took it from him, stepped on to the last-but-one stair and raised it as if she were about to propose a toast.

"I'm absolutely fine. But I want to make an announcement," she declared. There was an immediate hush; they all looked up at her expectantly, obediently. "I want us all to drink to Bella."

"Please don't do this," Bella whispered. "I can explain. Let me explain."

"To drink to Bella," Kitty went on, firmly, "because – because. . . Well, simply because she's Bella." She felt dizzy, light-headed; drunk, only she'd barely had anything to drink. She could hear her own voice, as if from a long way away; it sounded disembodied, the words spoken by somebody else. "Bella – my best friend. My soul sister. Because as we all know she hasn't had an easy life, but in her own Bella-like way, she's managed to put it all behind her and grab herself a better one. Isn't she clever?"

"Please," whispered Bella, again.

"She's such a good friend. Such a good friend that she steals my boyfriend and lies to me for years. She's managed to forget about her loony-tune mother, and guess what – she's even rediscovered the secret kid she had when she was thirteen. Isn't that amazing?" She raised her glass, a fake smile stretching her lips across her teeth, rictus-like. "So. Here's to Bella."

Nobody repeated the toast. In the stunned silence that followed her eyes locked on to Bella's, the huge agonized pools kingfisher-blue in a face totally blanched of colour. They shimmered and shone, and tears seemed to gather along the lower eyelids. That couldn't be right, though. Bella never cried. Never.

Then Bella turned on her heel, pushing through Kitty's party guests, and was gone.

chapter eighteen

"You complete cow. You absolute total bloody bitch. Why did you say that? Why?"

"It wasn't my fault. I was provoked – I caught her with Rhys."

"That's no excuse and you know it. She told you all that stuff about her mother in confidence. She trusted you with it."

"I know she did. I'm sorry."

"You think sorry's good enough? It doesn't even come close."

"But seeing her with Rhys was such a shock."

"Oh, poor little you. How do you think she felt, having her most shameful secrets blabbed like that to a roomful of people? Whatever she's done to you, she didn't deserve that. You've betrayed her. And you call yourself a friend. You don't know the meaning of the word."

"I said I'm sorry. I feel dreadful."

"*You* feel dreadful? What about her? And what about that so-called boyfriend of yours? What's his part in all this? You didn't even give her a chance to explain, did you? Oh no. You just wanted revenge, didn't you? You spiteful, vindictive cow."

On it went, on and on, the voice inside her head. There was no respite from it, not even if she put her hands over her ears, or played music through headphones at top volume. Kitty wondered if her conscience was going to give her stick until the day she died. Probably. She deserved it, after all. After what she had done to Bella.

Megan came to see her, creeping into her room with a solicitous expression on her face as if Kitty were an invalid. She was even carrying the requisite box of chocolates.

"Are you OK?" she enquired.

Kitty wondered, not for the first time, why that was the first thing people always asked. Even when it was perfectly bloody obvious that you weren't OK, you had no reason or right to be OK, and would probably never be OK again. Like now, in fact.

She sighed. "I guess."

"Well. You certainly know how to make a party go with a swing." Megan tried a smile, to see if Kitty would respond. She didn't.

"That's one way of putting it."

"I've brought you these." Megan proffered the chocolates, timidly. "They're Belgian. Really yummy."

"Megan." Kitty lifted her eyes to her friend,

wearily. "Why are you being so nice to me?"

"What were you expecting me to do? Stand you in the naughty corner and give you lines – I must not be a bitch to my friends at my birthday party?"

"See. Even you think I was a bitch." She sighed, momentously, and slumped down on to the bed.

"Yeah, you were. Unanimous verdict, I think we can say. You're still my mate, though." She sat on the bed next to Kitty. "Is it true what you said about Bella – the mad mother, and the baby?"

Kitty nodded, wordlessly.

"That's really strange." Megan looked thoughtful. Not gloating, or triumphant, or any of the other things Kitty had come to associate with her expression when sharing a juicy scandalous titbit about Bella. Just thoughtful. "I never knew. I kind of picked stuff up about her mother – I knew she was ill, she used to go off to visit her in hospital – but I never even guessed Bella might have been pregnant when she left."

Kitty shrugged. "Like you always said, your mum was discreet." *Not like you. You wouldn't know discretion if it came up and bit you on the nose. . . Oh, shut UP!*

"It's all my fault, isn't it?" Megan said, suddenly.

"What? What are you on about? How can Bella getting pregnant be your fault?"

"I don't mean that. I mean this – this mess. You dissing Bella in public. All that."

"How do you work that one out?"

"I've done nothing but slag her off since she came back. Since *before* she came back." *Megan's got a lot to answer for, in my view.* The voice inside Kitty's head turned into Bruno's. "I was so jealous of her, Kitty. Firstly with you, when we were kids – then finally she went away, and I could have you all to myself again. Then, bugger me, back she strolls. Large as life and twice as gorgeous. And not only does she tempt you back again, but she has Bruno eating out of her hand too."

All Kitty could think of to say was, "It must have been hard for you."

"It was. Only I should have learned to live with it, shouldn't I? I should have grown up a bit, and realized that it's perfectly possible to be friends with more than one person. I should have learnt to share. And I should have understood that you can't stop someone fancying another person, and force them to fancy you instead. I know Bruno's never going to feel about me the way I feel about him – it was just good manners, him answering my texts and stuff. I shouldn't have tried to kid myself it was anything else." She looked at Kitty. "But instead of all that, I just dripped poison in your ear about Bella. It was me who wrecked your friendship with her, Kitty – not you."

She looked close to tears. Kitty put an arm around her shoulders. "Don't blame yourself. You had your reasons. I didn't have to listen, did I?"

"Maybe not." Megan sniffed. "But there's something else."

"Go on then," Kitty said, gloomily. "Hit me with it." She was getting used to all this sackcloth-and-ashes stuff. She'd been doing enough of it herself.

"It's about Rhys."

She sat up straight. "What about him?"

"You know you caught him and Bella together, at your party?"

"Yeah. What about it?"

"What did you actually see?"

"I went to get my jacket from the bedroom, and there they were. At it. Glued together at the lips. Sucking face," she expounded, just in case Megan didn't get the full picture. She contorted her own face in a googly-eyed attempt at comedy, to pretend that she didn't care really. It failed. The impact of it struck her all over again. Of all the people for Bella to hit on, she'd never have expected Rhys to succumb. She'd thought he didn't like her – he'd had such a problem with Kitty spending time with her. He'd even said that she wasn't his type, long ago, when they'd first met.

"It'll have been Rhys, not Bella. Jumping her.

He tried it on with Nicci, too," Megan said, baldly. "And me."

Kitty goggled at her, aware of her jaw hanging down somewhere near her knees. "What? Are you telling me my boyfriend came on to all the females under forty at my birthday dinner?" she wailed.

"Not then," Megan said. "This was other times. With Nic, it was at your New Year's party – apparently he nobbled her when you were upstairs with me, mopping me up. Remember?"

Kitty did remember. She also remembered how Bruno had told her she should keep an eye on Rhys, that he was sleazing it up at the party, and she had dismissed his comments out of hand, made excuses for him. "Why the hell didn't Nicci say anything? Why didn't *you* say anything, come to that?"

"Nic's only just told me. She thought it might have been her fault, before – that she was giving out the wrong signals, or something. She felt really guilty. But after you caught him with Bella the other night –" She shrugged, meaningfully. "And he grabbed me coming out of the loo that time at the bowling alley, but I smacked him one and he was all apologetic. Said he thought I was you. So I thought I must have just been mistaken. It's not something you want to believe about your mate's boyfriend, Kitty – you must see that."

"Well, yes, but. . . Why did you and Nic carry on being nice to him? Bloody hell, why did you even carry on *speaking* to him? Why –" She ran out of whys, subsided weakly on to the pillows. "Shit. You mean he's been hitting on other people, all this time, and I never knew? What a sleazebag. What a – a *fuckwit*."

"It was only when he was drunk."

"He's still a fuckwit. And he wasn't drunk at the bowling alley, was he? *Shit*." She sat up again, turned to Megan. "Have I been a stupid, blind fool, or what?"

"No you haven't. You trusted him."

"Yeah," Kitty said, grimly, "and we all know what a mistake trusting people is, don't we?"

Bruno, when he came round, had no revelations to offer her. Kitty made them both coffee, and her cousin stood in the kitchen doorway with his arms folded and his ankles crossed, regarding her coolly with the kind of expression he might have when watching a small, grubby and not very attractive animal at the zoo. She could feel his gaze boring into the back of her neck. She poured boiling water on to the cafetière containing Mum's best after-dinner blend of coffee, and took the cellophane off a new box of chocolate biscuits. Foil-wrapped and chunky, each one looked a meal in itself.

"Blimey," Bruno remarked, sitting down. "We are getting the VIP treatment."

"I know you like them." She pushed the box towards him and lowered her eyes, penitentially. "Don't say anything, Bruno. Please."

"Righto. We'll just sit here in total silence and drink our coffee, shall we, and then I'll piss off back home?" He leant towards her, across the breakfast bar. "I'm not going to tell you off, Kitty, if that's what you're worried about. That's not my role in your life. I'm not your dad."

"Why – do you think he should be telling me off?"

"I think you should be telling yourself off." He picked a biscuit out of the box and began to peel the foil off it.

"Do you think I haven't been?" she burst out. "All the time. Over and over again. I can't bloody stop."

"Good. You deserve it."

"I know. I know I do." She sighed. "You can't say anything that I haven't said to myself already. You can't make me feel worse than I already do."

"No?" He didn't look at her, just at the biscuit. He took a bite out of it. "I bet I could. I bet I could think of loads of things to say that would make you feel like a totally worthless piece of shite. Make you feel you want to hide away for ever, and never come out and see anybody ever again. Make you feel, in fact, like Bella's feeling right now." He swallowed. "But I won't."

"Have you seen her?"

"No. I told you, she doesn't want to see anybody. Have you seen Rhys?"

Kitty gave a mirthless laugh, down her nose. "No. I'm not intending to, either."

"Because. . .?"

"Because it turns out it was him coming on to Bella, not the other way round." She frowned. "But you knew that, didn't you?"

He lifted a shoulder. "Let's just say I've had my doubts about him for some time. I did try to warn you, but you were having none of it. According to you, you're the expert on relationships."

"OK. Fair point." She sighed again. There was a whole world of woe in that sigh. "What'm I going to do, Bruno?"

"About Rhys?"

"No, not about Rhys. I know what I'm going to do about him. About Bella."

"Depends what you want the outcome to be." He took a slurp of his coffee. "You don't have to do anything. You could just leave well alone. Now that would be a first."

She knew she couldn't do that. Somehow, she had to try and make amends. Trouble was, she didn't have the first clue how to go about it.

She picked up a spoon and stirred her coffee,

purposelessly. "I didn't mean to say all that stuff about her, you know. I didn't plan to. In fact, I've been wishing ever since that I hadn't known it – any of it. Then I couldn't have blabbed it all."

"That's the problem with finding out secrets, isn't it? They have a habit of escaping at inconvenient moments."

"I only wanted to know the truth." She looked down into her mug. She couldn't meet his eyes.

"Ah. The Truth. No such thing – don't you know that yet?"

"What do you mean? Of course there is!"

"I mean everybody has their own version of what's true and what's not."

"But what about – what about history? History with a capital H, I mean. William the Conqueror, and the Tudors and Stuarts, and all that. That's all true, isn't it? I mean, people accept that it all happened."

"History?" Bruno shook his head. "Bad example. History is always written from the victor's perspective. There are no losers' history books. Did you know that, until quite recently, kids weren't taught about the Holocaust in German schools? They'd just erased it from history – wiped it out. That was their version of the truth."

Kitty blinked. How come they'd suddenly got on to the Holocaust? "I've got to do something," she declared. "About Bella, I mean; I can't just do nothing."

"Up to you." Bruno finished his coffee and stood up, pushing his specs up on his nose. "Just don't be surprised if it all takes longer than you imagine. Some things take more than just an apology and a girly hug to fix them."

She fully intended going round to see Bella. Throwing herself on her mercy, apologizing profusely; telling her how wrong she had been, and how terribly, terribly sorry. But somehow, she couldn't face her yet. Couldn't pluck up the courage necessary to just go and do it. And the longer she waited, the more difficult it was to do.

A week after her birthday, Kitty looked out of the window of her room and saw Cushion padding up the garden with a bird in his mouth. She shot down the stairs and outside.

"Cushion! Bad cat! Drop it!" she yelled, windmilling her arms in distress.

Startled, the cat did just that, then retreated to a metre away, tail flashing sulkily, as Kitty advanced on his lovely present and crouched over it protectively. It was a female blackbird, still warm, its claws drawn up underneath its body and its half-closed eyes milky with death. There was not a mark on it – it must have died from shock.

"Poor little thing." Kitty put out a finger and stroked the silky feathers on its breast. It probably had babies somewhere, waiting to be fed. At this thought, two tears spilled over and tracked their way down the sides of her nose. She looked at Cushion, who was clearly waiting for his chance to pounce on the bird anew, snatch it up and leg it. "Don't you dare, you horrible creature!" He gave up and stalked off with dignity, tail swishing.

"Don't be so hard on him. He was only being a cat."

She spun round. Bella was standing at the garden gate, watching her. Kitty stood up, hastily wiping the tears from her face. "Do birds have babies this time of year?"

"No idea." Bella shrugged. "Natural history isn't really my thing."

They looked at each other, guardedly, not sure what to say next, what the other was going to say. Then they both began to speak at the same time.

"Do you want to come –" said Kitty.

"I was just coming to –" Bella said. She gave a small, rueful grimace. Not a smile, though. Nowhere near a smile. "You first."

"I was going to ask if you wanted to come in."

"No thanks. I was just calling to say goodbye."

"Goodbye?" Kitty was transported back to that day in the playground, all those years ago. Megan by her side, whispering in her ear, and Bella standing before her, tough uncaring Bella (*pregnant Bella. . .*), saying she was going to another foster family. "Where are you going?"

"Away for a bit. It seems the best thing to do." She didn't say why. She didn't have to. *Small place like Penllan. All the gossip. . .*

"You're moving away again?" Kitty whispered. *You did this. You've driven her away.*

Bella nodded. "Yup. It's no biggie."

But it is! Kitty took a step towards her, her eyes welling up with tears again. "Bella. I've been meaning to come round to see you."

"So what kept you." It was a statement, not a question. Kitty looked at her, expecting to see hatred stamped across her face, but her eyes were filled not with loathing but uncertainty and wariness.

"I don't know. I'm a coward. I'm sorry. I'm so, *so* sorry."

Another long moment of silence. Then Bella sighed. "Yeah well. I'm sorry too."

"Sorry you ever met me?" Kitty's lips twisted. "I wouldn't blame you for feeling that."

"Don't be stupid. I don't feel that. I did, a week ago. But I don't now." More silence. "What I'm sorry about is keeping things to myself for all those years. That I wasn't more honest from the start. Then people wouldn't have had to fill in the blanks for themselves."

"Bruno says you're the most honest person he knows," Kitty offered.

"Yeah?" The shadow of a smile flitted across Bella's face, then was gone.

"Do you think –" She didn't know how to put it, what to say that wouldn't sound stupid or gushy or self-pitying. But she had to say it, nonetheless. "Will you ever be able to forgive me?"

Bella looked straight at her. "I don't know. That's the honest answer." She picked at a bit of the laurel hedge that framed the gate. "How many years have we known each other?"

"Ten, eleven?" Kitty hoped she was going to go on and say, after all that time I have to forgive you. Something like that. But she didn't.

She said instead, "Most of our lives, right? But I realized that night I don't really know you at all. Maybe we never really know anybody else. Not truly, deep down. But I'd never have guessed you could have done something like that. You can cry over a dead bird, but still go and –" With an effort Bella stopped herself, took a deep breath. "Anyway. You want to know what the worst thing was?"

No. "Go on." She steeled herself, telling herself she deserved it, whatever it was.

"That you could think I'd go off with your boyfriend under your nose." She paused. "He just grabbed me when I came upstairs, and bundled me into that room. I was trying to get him off me when you came in, not – not *encouraging* him. You do know he's pretty much tried it on with all your mates, don't you?"

"I do now."

"And?"

"And I've blown him out." No need to go into detail, about how much it had hurt, about the excuses and near-to-tears apologies from Rhys she'd had to turn a deaf ear to. Bella didn't want to hear about that. "And I never knew. And yes, you're absolutely right, I should have given you chance to explain." She made a contrite sincere face. "And sorry again."

"Actually," Bella said, briskly, "I didn't just come to say goodbye. There's something else you were wrong about that you need putting straight on. I never had a kid."

"Sorry?" For a moment, Kitty didn't understand.

"The child you saw. The one you told Bruno about? She's not mine."

So Bella knew she'd been spying on her, too. Her face flamed. "I'm sorry, it wasn't – I didn't mean to – I just assumed—"

"Damn right you assumed. You put two and two together, and came up with thirty-five."

Or perhaps she just saw what she wanted to see. Something to prove her nasty sordid little theories about the girl she used to call her best friend. "So –?"

"So who was it? What was I doing, sitting outside a house in Mel's car and watching some kids playing?"

"You don't have to tell me." Kitty's embarrassment deepened.

"I know. But I'm going to tell you anyway." She took a deep breath. "It was my brother. Not the little girl, obviously – she's no relation. The older boy. That's who I was watching."

"Your *brother*?" Bella had a brother? She'd never mentioned him to Kitty, not once.

"My half-brother. You know I told you how my mother's illness started after I was born? Well, when she got pregnant with him, she got really ill. That's when I went to live with Megan's family. He's been in care all his life, poor little sod. I'd never even seen him before. Though at least the family he's living with now are more long-term – they've just adopted him." She put a hand on the gate and examined her fingernails. "I only found out recently where he's living and everything. I just – really wanted to see him. To make sure he seemed OK, and looked after, and stuff."

"But why did you have to sit outside his house? Couldn't you go and visit him properly?"

Bella shrugged. "I don't think he even knows about me. He's been fostered his whole life – I wouldn't want to disrupt him now. That's why I didn't tell anybody about him."

"But wouldn't he want to know about having a sister?"

"He's got a sister," Bella said, roughly. "You saw her, remember." The little girl. Kitty had been so convinced she was Bella's. How could she have jumped to that conclusion, with so little real evidence? "I'd always wanted a little brother, too. Remember how I loved Owen so much?"

"I remember. You don't fancy taking him off my hands now, do you?"

Bella didn't smile back. "You know something? You need to stop making assumptions, and start appreciating your family more. Family is everything. I mean it. *Everything.*"

"I know," Kitty said, humbly. "I do know. So where are you going?"

"To stay with some friends of Aunt Susan's for a bit. In Scotland. Then in September –" Another deep breath. "In September I'm going to Manchester, moving in to the student house where Bruno lives. One of the post-grads is leaving in the summer, so I can have her room. I'm going to do some A-levels at college, and then I want to study Psychology. My other course wasn't working out and it's something I've been interested in for a long time. Bruno persuaded me I should give it a go."

"Does this mean you and Bruno are a couple?" Kitty felt no surprise; their joint protestations of being just mates had never rung true.

"No. Oh, I don't know. Maybe in time. I know he cares about me, and I care more about him than I realized. More than I thought I could care about anyone. So who knows?" She shrugged, and Kitty was flooded by a wave of emotion – of abiding fondness for her, of compassion, and regret, guilt and shame. Most of all shame. She put out a timid hand and touched Bella's, still resting on the top of the gate.

"And what about us? Will I see you again?"

"I expect so. You're his cousin, aren't you? You'll see both of us." They looked at each other, a long, long look that seemed to stretch on for ever, back in time as well as forward. "I still think of you as my friend," Bella said, at last. "And I know you're sorry for what you did. That's something else Bruno's persuaded me. He's a top guy, your cousin. You asked me if I'll ever forgive you, and the answer is probably. I probably will. But you have to give me some healing time. Can you understand that, Kitty? I just need some time to heal."

chapter nineteen

The nurse is walking along the corridor on silent rubber-shod feet, showing the way. She isn't wearing uniform but is dressed trendily in combats and a black T-shirt that shows just a hint of belly-button. She looks more like a member of a girl band than a nurse. Bella wonders whether this might actually be more confusing for the patients, but then dismisses the thought. The whole place is less like a hospital than a select hotel, all plush carpets and low-key lighting, and tasteful flower arrangements placed on small tables. The smell is the same as ever though, the institutional mix of disinfectant and stale cooking and despair that curdles Bella's stomach.

The nurse pushes open a door. "Here we are. She knows you're coming. She's been waiting for you. Hello," she calls out. A woman appears in the open doorway of the en-suite bathroom, holding a lipstick with the lid off. "Oh, hi. Your daughter's here. Would you like some tea?"

"That would be great." Sylvie smiles at the nurse, warmly, sanely, and Bella feels the relief spreading through her veins like warm honey. "We'll come down, shall we?"

"No, you're all right, love. I'll bring a tray up. Give you a treat." She beams at them, and hurries off.

"It's lovely to see you," Sylvie says to Bella, taking her hands and holding her at arm's length, inspecting her. "You're looking really well."

Bella looks at Sylvie. Her face is wrinkled like a woman's ten or even twenty years older, her hair almost entirely grey. But she has had it cut since the last time Bella saw her, a funky spiky style that suits her much better, and she is wearing bootcut jeans and kitten-heeled boots and make-up. Apart from the lipstick, that is, which she is still holding in her hand. She follows Bella's glance down to it. "Oops," she says. "Oh well. Never mind. It'll only come off on the cup, won't it?"

"You're looking well too," Bella tells her. And means it. "So. Things are on the up."

"Sure are. Moving back to the flat next month." She smiles proudly. "This latest chemical cocktail seems to be doing the trick, fingers crossed. Anyway. Enough of me. Who's this?" She peeps behind Bella at Bruno, who is hovering in the doorway.

"I've brought someone to see you."

"How exciting. Is this your man? How lovely

to meet you." She holds out a formal hand, her silver bangles sliding down her wrist with a faint jangle.

Bruno grins cheekily, enjoying being called Bella's man. He shakes her hand. "Hello, Mrs Jones."

"Oh, Sylvie, please. I haven't been Mrs Jones for more years than I care to remember. So does he have a name?" she asks Bella, smiling.

"This is Bruno. He's a friend of mine. A very good friend," Bella says. It is going to be OK. Not great, but OK. It is enough for now. She turns to Bruno. "And this is my mum."